SISSY

SISSY

by

LES SULLINS

J. Kenkade
PUBLISHING®

Bryant, Arkansas

J. Kenkade Publishing
5920 Highway 5 N. Ste. 7
Bryant, AR 72022
www.jkenkadepublishing.com
Social Media: @jkenkadepublishing

J. Kenkade Publishing is a registered trademark.

Printed in the United States of America
ISBN: 978-1-955186-37-7

CONTENTS

Love at First Sight

Clair and Carl Murphy met on a blind date and it was love at first sight, at least for Carl. Both Clair and Carl were in their final semester at the University of Memphis and neither had a clear plan for where they wanted to be in life following their graduation in just a few short months. Carl's family planned for him to return home to St. Louis, while Clair's family planned for her to return home to Smithville, TN. Mutual friends introduced the two, and immediately Carl knew he couldn't live without her. He didn't know how, but somehow, he knew he would marry her and spend the rest of his life with her. Clair wasn't immediately impressed with his rugged appearance and clumsiness. However, he was nice and a lot of fun to be around, so she continued to see him. It didn't take long for her to realize his awkwardness was pure nervousness because he was madly in love with her.

Their friendship quickly grew to love, and within the year they were engaged and married. The wedding was a small ceremony outside of her family home in Smithville with just a few friends and family present. While they both loved the small town life in Smithville, they both missed their time in Memphis and decided to move closer to the city for better job options. Carl immediately found a well-paying job at a large company in Memphis. They began trying to start their family. Days turned to weeks, weeks to months, and months into years. Just as Clair had given up hope of her dreams of being a mother, something miraculous happened. After many heartbreaks and setbacks, they finally conceived a baby girl. Everything was exactly how they planned and exactly how they hoped it would be. Carl had everything he could ever ask for, a beautiful wife that he adored and a baby girl on the way.

Zoey Grace's Grand Entrance

It was a clear night. Carl and Clair snuggling up on the couch to read their favorite children's books to their sweet baby girl when Clair sat up and cried out. "Carl! It's time! We've got to go now!"

Carl in a panic, jumped and up answered, "Wait, what? No, it's not time yet! We haven't even finished the nursery, picked out a name, cleaned out the car..."

"Carl honey, I don't think she cares about any of that. We have to go, NOW!"

As they race to the hospital, Clair, trying to remember her Lamaze breathing, was in more and more pain as the baby was clearly not waiting.

"Hold on baby, hold on! We're almost there! Please hold on! Get the hell out of the way!" Carl screamed at the other drivers as he blew the horn to get them to move. "Move over!"

"Carl! My water, my water! Oh my God, my water!"

"Hold on baby, I see the hospital. We are here Clair, we made it, baby, we made it!" Carl yelled as they skid sideways into the Emergency Room parking lot and come to a screeching halt in front of the Emergency Room doors. Barely waiting for the car to come to a stop, Carl jumped out of the car yelling towards the Emergency Room for help and ran to his wife's door. Just as she steps out of the car, Clair, terrified, collapsed into Carl's arms. Carl caught her and ran into the Emergency Room, crying out for someone, *anyone*, to help his wife and baby. Clair is rushed into the Labor and Delivery room while Carl is asked to wait outside in the waiting room. After three hours, Clair delivers a healthy baby girl with a head full of blonde hair and beautiful blue eyes; Zoey Grace Murphy. After what seemed like an eternity, a nurse finds Carl and brings him to see his wife and daughter.

"Carl, baby, come meet your daughter, Zoey Grace," Clair said as she smiled with tears running down her face.

"Oh baby, she is beautiful, she's perfect, she's absolutely amazing. I can't believe she's here. You did such a good job baby, I love you." As Carl took baby Zoey from her mother, he couldn't take his eyes off of his beautiful baby girl. With tears in his eyes and a heart filled with pride, he looked at his baby girl and said, "My sweet Sissy. I'm your daddy. Baby girl, I love you more than life itself. I will always be your daddy, and baby, you will always be my little Sissy."

Clair and Carl sat in amazement at the beauty that is their perfect baby girl, the nurse enters the room and tells them Zoey Grace needs to go to the nursery and be checked out by the Pediatrician. "Wait no, I can't let her go. Can't I just hold her for a little longer?" The nurse tells him he can carry Zoey to the nursery if he would like. Looking back at Clair, Carl asked if she would be okay if he left her and took Zoey to the nursery.

"I'll be fine baby, take care of Zoey Grace. I'll be here wait-ing for you both when you get back. I love you." As Carl turned to walk away, Clair called out to him stopping him before he walked out of the door and said, "Wait, I want to see her face one more time." Carl brought Zoey back to Clair for one more kiss before going to the nursery. Clair smiled and let them walk out of the room.

As Carl walked down the hallway to the nursery, he could barely take his eyes off his perfect baby girl. He never even heard one word the nurse or anyone else in the hallway said to him as he stared lovingly into the face of his baby girl. He was so mes-merized, in fact, he never heard the commotion of the alarms or nurses and doctors running past him in the hall towards his wife's room. Once he arrived at the nursery, letting Zoey Grace go into the hands of the nurses was the hardest thing he would ever have to do, or so he thought.

As Carl and Zoey walked down the hall to the nursery, Clair's heart stopped and they had to start CPR. After several rounds of defibrillation and epinephrine, Clair's heart was beat-ing but slowly.

Things Take a Turn for the Worse

hile the doctors and nurses worked to save Clair's life, Carl began to make his way back from the nursery to his wife's room. As he gets closer to the room, he hears the commotion and begins to run towards her room. He entered the room and he saw his wife surrounded by doctors and nurses. "Clair! What's wrong? Baby, what's wrong! Clair, say something, baby, please! What's wrong with my wife? Someone talk to me please!"

Carl felt someone place their hand on his shoulder. "Mr. Murphy, I need you to come with me." As Carl turned around, he sees an older nurse leading him to the waiting room.

After what seemed like an eternity, an older doctor with salt and pepper hair and thick, black-rimmed glasses approaches him. "Mr. Murphy?" Carl struggles to answer him but only manages to nod his head. "Mr. Murphy my name is Dr. Garrison. I am the Cardiologist on call."

"Wait, Cardiologist? Why does Clair need a Cardiologist? I don't understand. What happened to my wife? Can I go see her now?"

"Mr. Murphy, Clair's heart has stopped multiple times. She's stable now, but she is very weak. I'm still not exactly sure what caused her to crash on us, but we are running tests to find out."

"But she is going to be okay now though, right?" Carl asked with fear and trepidation.

"Clair has been moved to the CCU. My nurse will take you up there as soon as you can see her. Mr. Murphy, you need to be strong for your wife and daughter right now."

As Carl walked to the nursery to see his baby girl, he stopped in the hallway to call his parents. Carl's parents, Shirley, a retired schoolteacher, and Carl Murphy Sr., a retired Army Sargent, now live just outside of St. Louis, Missouri. As Carl waits for his mother to answer the phone, he tries his best to regain his composure.

"Hello?" Shirley answers sounding as if she's just been awakened from a deep sleep.

"Mom, it's me, Carl. Clair had the baby." Hearing his mother's voice is comforting but he knows deep down he is still struggling to hold it all together. "Mom, she's absolutely perfect. She has the most beautiful blue eyes and a head full of blonde hair. She weighed seven pounds two ounces and was twenty inches long. She seems so tiny. She looks so much like Clair, she's absolutely perfect!"

"Oh Carl, she sounds like an angel! I can't wait to see her. How's Clair?" Shirley is clearly wide-awake now and is shaking her husband to try and wake him up to share the news of their new grandbaby's arrival.

"Oh mom, I don't know what to do. Clair is not doing well at all. Her heart stopped after the delivery and they don't know what's going on. She's in the CCU now and I'm waiting to see her. Mom, I don't know what to do. I can't lose her, Mom. I can't do this without her." Carl said the words aloud and expressed his genuine fear that he may lose his wife. It was more than he could hold back. As he said the words, he began to sob and felt like he'd been hit with a ton of bricks. The realization that he may actually lose the love of his life and that his baby girl may grow up never knowing her mother was just more than he could take.

Shirley almost violently shook her husband out of his sleep. "Carl, we are on our way. We will be there as soon as we can. Baby it is going to be okay. Carl, dammit, get up now! We have to go! Carl and Clair need us! Get up *now!*" Carl Sr. sat up in the bed, clearly confused by what is going on. Carl answered his mother, pleading for them not to come until he knows more. Shirley had begun throwing clothes into an overnight bag, not willing to sit by and not do anything.

The next morning, exhausted, Carl ran back and forth between Clair's room in the CCU and the nursery to be with Zoey Grace. While Zoey is doing great, Clair is still in the CCU. Not willing to leave his wife and daughter, Carl's exhaustion is now very visible as he hasn't slept in over twenty-four hours. As Carl makes his way back to the CCU, he spots a familiar face; his parents have arrived. "Mom! Mom! Hey! I thought I told you guys not to worry about coming down until we knew something?" Carl was secretly relieved to have his parents there by his side.

As Shirley ran to her son she asks, "Carl, honey, how are you? How's Clair? Where's the baby? Have you eaten anything? Have you even slept?"

"Mom, we still don't know anything. No, I haven't slept.

How can I sleep? I have to be here for Clair and Zoey. And honestly... I don't remember the last thing I ate." As Carl answers his mother's questions, the three step into the elevator and head to the fourth floor where the nursery is located. "I'll take you guys up to the nursery so you can see Zoey Grace. We are still waiting on tests for Clair to see what's going on and what they are going to do." As they exit the elevator, Carl hears Clair's doctor calling his name.

"Mr. Murphy, I need a word with you." Carl turns to his parents for support then he turns to talk to the doctor, hoping and praying he is going to hear good news about Clair. "Mr. Murphy, your wife has a rare heart condition. It is hereditary, so she has had it her whole life, but the stress of the pregnancy and delivery was just too much for her heart to take. Unfortunately, the level of damage to her heart is irreversible. There's no surgery or medicines we can give her to repair the damage. Mr. Murphy do you understand what I'm telling you?"

As Carl listens to the doctor, he is still holding on to hope that his wife will pull through and be fine. "I think you are telling me Clair will be okay, she just will have to be careful?"

Dr. Garrison realizes that Carl, in fact, doesn't understand or doesn't want to believe what he is saying. He places his hand on Carl's shoulder and tells him, "I'm sorry, Mr. Murphy, that's just not the case. Clair is not going to pull through this. With the amount of damage to her heart, she has a few days at best. I'm so sorry"

As he hears the words come out of Dr. Garrison's mouth, Carl can't believe what he is hearing and begins to sob "What?

No! That can't be. There has to be something! You can't just give up on her! Do a transplant or something, *anything!*"

Shirley and Carl Sr. have now joined their son and are attempting to console him as Dr. Garrison says "I'm so sorry Mr. Murphy, I truly am. I wish there were something, but there's just nothing we can do for her now. I'm so sorry."

The next two days were the hardest days of Carl's life. All he could do was sit by his wife's side and watch her slowly fade away. Carl Sr. and Shirley stayed with Zoey so their son could spend every second with his wife while he had the chance. When the time came, Carl leaned down and gently kissed Clair's face, promising her that he would love her forever and that he would make sure Zoey always knew how much her mommy loved her. When the machines stopped, Carl felt like his whole world ended. Even though he had watched Clair slowly slipping away, minute by minute, hour after hour, he was still holding onto hope that he and Clair would wake up and this was all just a bad dream, but it wasn't. His best friend, the love of his life, the woman he planned to spend his life with and raise their children with, his Clair, was gone. Just when they were planning to start their life with their beautiful miracle, her life was over. As Carl stood by her side, he felt lost. How would he raise this beautiful baby girl without her mother? He tried to pull himself together to make the phone call to his parents, but the words wouldn't come out of his mouth. When his mother answered the phone and heard the silence on the other end, she immediately knew.

They both sat silently on the phone, crying and sobbing for Clair and for Zoey Grace who would never know her mother. After what seemed like an eternity of silence, Carl finally found the strength to speak and all he could say was, "Mom, I'm coming home."

When Carl arrived home, he went immediately to the nursery he and Clair had started to decorate. The crib and changing table lay in pieces on the floor next to the white rocking chair Clair found at a yard sale and refinished. After a few minutes of standing in the doorway, Carl went to work putting together the crib. He knew he had to finish what he and Clair started. He had to make Clair's vision for Zoey Grace's room complete. Carl Sr. joined his son with a few tools and the two finished the room, together, in silence. As they finished arranging the newly built furniture exactly where Clair had wanted it, they made the bed with the pink and grey bedding Clair had picked out and hung the lacy white curtains on the window. The last touch was hanging the framed photo of Carl and Clair taken only two weeks prior at the park where Carl proposed.

Just as they finished the room, Zoey began to wake up in the other room. Carl entered the living room where Zoey had been sleeping in her bassinet, Shirley gently lifted Zoey out of the bassinet and handed her to Carl. As he stood there looking at his beautiful baby girl, he couldn't keep back the tears. "Baby girl, it's you and me no matter what. That's how your mommy would have wanted it."

Three days later, Clair was laid to rest next to her parents and grandparents just thirty-three years after she was born. Carl and his father made the drive home. Carl asked his father, "Dad, what am I going to do? I don't know anything about raising a baby, much less a baby girl."

Carl Sr. shook his head and said to his son, "You aren't alone.

You know we will be there with you son. We have already talked about selling the house and moving to Memphis, or y'all can move in with us. Either way, you are not going to be raising her alone. You don't have to."

"Dad, why did she have to leave me? Why did she have to go? This wasn't the plan! She's supposed to be here with me! We are supposed to do this together! Why couldn't she just stay?" As Carl sobs, his father does his best to keep his eyes on the road while consoling his son.

Back in Memphis, Shirley stayed home with Zoey. As she walked around with Zoey, softly singing to her, she looked around at the pictures Clair had hung on the walls. Clair and Carl's baby pictures, wedding photos, and even the maternity photos they had taken just two weeks before Zoey was born. As Shirley stopped in front of a photo of Clair looking down at her pregnant belly, Shirley whispered softly, "Baby girl that's your mommy. She will always be looking down on you with love, just like she is in this picture. Don't worry Clair, we will take care of your baby girl."

Happy Birthday Zoey Grace

It's hard to believe it has already been a year since Zoey Grace made her way into the world. As Shirley works to finish a few last minute things before the party, Carl stands in the door of Zoey's bedroom thinking back over the last year and how much Clair missed. Zoey's first words, her first tooth, and her first steps. Zoey lays sleeping in her crib. Carl can't help but think back to that moment in the hospital room when he realized his baby girl would never know her mother.

Once the party starts, Carl does his best to look happy and not to show how much he truly missed Clair. While everyone sang Happy Birthday to Zoey, Carl stood in the back watching her, thinking about how much Clair would have loved to have been there; standing beside her, singing to her, and helping her blow out her candles. Encouraging her as she smashed her little chocolate cake with pink roses. How she would look up and smile at him while Zoey smeared icing all over herself and her mother. He couldn't help but think about how Clair would "ooh and ahh" over every present and toy as Zoey opened them. He smiles and pretends not to be hurting inside, but all he can think about is how much he loves and misses his Clair.

It didn't take long for Shirley to notice that Carl is distant and asks him "Carl, honey are you okay?"

It took a second for Carl to even realize his mother was talking to him. He had wondered in his mind back to the day at the park when he proposed to Clair and how happy she was when she turned and saw him on his knee holding a small blue ring box. "Oh yeah, mom, sorry. I was just thinking."

As he looked up, she came and put her arm around him, "I know son, we all miss her and wish she were here. She would have loved this and would be so happy with all you have done for Zoey Grace."

While Carl and Shirley talked in the corner, Zoey reached out and smeared some of her chocolate cake on her grandfather. Everyone erupted in laughter. Carl began to smile and decided to join his father in sharing Zoey's cake. Just as he leaned in, Zoey reached out to share her cake with her daddy, smearing it on his eyebrow. No matter how much he missed Clair or how sad he felt, Zoey could always put a smile on his face and make his heart happy.

Each year they would celebrate Zoey's birthday with a huge celebration surrounded by friends and family. It was hard for Carl to believe five years had passed since Zoey came into his life and since Clair passed. With Zoey's birthday being on a week day this year, they would wait until the weekend for the party, but Carl always made sure to make Zoey's birthday a day of celebration. As he walked into her bedroom he began to sing as off key and loudly as possible, "Happy birthday to you! Happy birthday to you! Happy birthday sweet Sissy. Happy birthday to you!"

Zoey covered her ears to avoid his terrible singing, but she smiled her biggest smile showing her beautiful little dimples in her cheeks. "Aw Daddy! I love you! Now stop that singing!"

They laughed and wrestled, Carl told her "I love you too baby girl, now it's time for your birthday spankings." The two laughed and wrestled until they both gave up and laid on the bed. "So what do we want to do for 'National Zoey Day' today my sweet princess? We can do anything you want"

Zoey sits up in the bed and asks her daddy "Can we really do anything I want Daddy?"

"Of course baby, today is your day." Carl replies as he sits up in the bed and puts his arm around Zoey.

"Can we even go see Mommy?"

Shocked by her request, Carl tells Zoey they can go see Mommy if that is what she wants to do for her birthday. It has been over three years since Carl made the drive to Clair's grave. He and Clair had agreed that they never wanted the other to be miserable if something happened to the other and had promised each other they would find happiness in life, even if the other had passed on. Even though Carl made that promise to Clair, he knew in his heart that there would never be another woman like Clair.

While Carl packed a picnic lunch, a blanket and some snacks for the drive, Zoey packed her own little pink backpack with her favorite books and stuffed animals. There was so much she wanted to show Mommy when she got there she could hardly fit it all in her backpack. Just before they headed out the door,

Zoey stopped and ran back to her room for one more thing, her favorite picture of her mommy. Now that she had everything she needed, they were ready to set out on the four hour drive.

It didn't take long for Zoey to fall asleep on the drive. As much as Carl loved hearing her sing along with her favorite sing-a-long songs, he did enjoy the quiet time to reflect on the last five years. He couldn't help but wonder how different things would be if Clair were there with him. Instead of a road trip to a cemetery, maybe they would be on a road trip to a theme park. Clair would be in the passenger seat and Zoey would be asleep in the stuffed animal filled back seat. He can't help but think of how much she would love Zoey and how happy she would be to be her mommy. Carl is so deep in thought, he nearly misses his exit. As he pulls into the cemetery he wakes Zoey and tells her they are there.

Waking up, Zoey can barely contain her excitement and is so eager to get out of the car she tries to take her seatbelt off before Carl has stopped the car. The car comes to a stop, Zoey begins squirming frantically for her daddy to come help her get out of her car seat. "Daddy, Daddy, hurry up Daddy! I got to get out and go see Mommy!"

Carl can't help but smile as he sees how excited being there has made his baby girl. As soon as he unbuckles Zoey, she takes off running towards her mother's grave and stops fast in her tracks, she's forgotten everything she brought to show her mommy. Running back to the car, she reaches for her backpack that her daddy is holding out to her. Once she has her things, she turns and runs back towards her mommy's grave eager to show her all of her favorite toys.

While Zoey plays and shows Mommy all of her toys, Carl spreads out the quilt he and Clair always used for their picnics in the park and sets out the lunch he's packed for the two of them. Zoey was so busy playing that Carl was barely able to get her to stop long enough to eat her lunch and blow out the candle on her little birthday cupcake. While Zoey played a little longer, Carl sat watching her and again his mind drifted away thinking about how much he missed Clair. He still didn't understand why she had to go and why she couldn't be there to play with their baby girl and experience these days with her.

A few hours had passed since they arrived and Zoey turned to her daddy and said, "Daddy, Mommy says it is time for us to go now. She doesn't want us to drive in the dark, and she said you shouldn't be so sad." Listening to his baby girl, it was all he could do to fight back tears.

They packed up their picnic and walked back over to Clair's headstone one more time. Zoey placed her favorite stuffed animal beside her mommy's headstone and leaned over and kissed her headstone. "I love you Mommy, I'll see you soon."

Zoey turns one more time to wave goodbye to her mommy and blows her a kiss. Leaving the cemetery, Carl fought back tears feeling the same way he did the day he left the cemetery for the first time when he laid Clair to rest there.

After buckling Zoey into her car seat, Carl walked slowly to his door taking just a little longer to compose himself before starting the drive home. They decide to stop and get dinner half way home. Sitting at the table, Zoey overheard the couple behind them talking.

She looked up from her coloring page and asked her daddy, "Daddy, what is an asshole?"

Shocked, Carl nearly spit his sweet tea out of his nose. Trying not to laugh, he asked her "Zoey Grace, where on earth did you hear that? We don't say things like that!"

Zoey, realizing she had said something bad, started to get upset. She got out of her seat and walked over to her daddy and hugged him. "I'm sorry Daddy. I didn't mean to, but really Daddy, what is an asshole? Why can't we say that?"

Again, trying his best not to laugh, Carl admonished Zoey telling her, "Baby that is not a nice thing to say at all. It is a bad word for someone who is very mean. It isn't nice to call someone that word."

Zoey looks up at her daddy with a puzzled look on her face and says "Does that mean Billy at daycare is an asshole because he is really mean to me all the time and I never did anything to him?" At this point Carl can't contain his laughter anymore.

"Yes baby, that is the right way to use that. But please, promise me you won't say things like that. You are too sweet to talk like that, baby girl."

After finishing their dinner, Carl and Zoey get back on the road heading home. It doesn't take long and once again Zoey is fast asleep in the back of the car. Carl, feeling very sleepy at this point himself, calls his mother to keep him awake. Shirley and Carl Sr. were watching television when the phone rang. "Carl, turn that down. It's Carl on the phone," Shirley says as she answers the phone.

"Hey Mom, how are you guys?"

Carl Sr. turns down the television, and Shirley puts the

phone on speaker so they can both talk to their son. "Hey Carl, how is Zoey's big birthday going? What did you guys do today?"

"Well mom, we actually went up to Smithville to see Clair today. That's what Zoey wanted to do so we came up here and had a picnic."

Surprised, Shirley asked how he was handling it since she knew he had struggled the last time he visited.

"Oh Mom, it was actually a really great day. You will never believe what happened at dinner. Zoey and I were sitting at the table, and out of nowhere, she asked me what an asshole was!"

As they all started to laugh, Carl Sr. asked, "Well, what did you tell her?"

"Well, once I stopped laughing, I tried to explain it to her." The three laughed hysterically for a few minutes. Shirley finally stopped laughing enough to ask where she had heard that from. "Mom, I don't know but it was so funny I damn near pissed my pants. Especially when she asked me if a boy from daycare was an asshole because he was mean to her." Shirley began laughing so hard she snorted.

As they pulled into the driveway, Carl told his parents, "Well we are home now, and it is getting late. I'm going to get Zoey in and get her a bath and put to bed. Thank you guys for keeping me awake on the ride home. And guys, thank you for always being there for me. I don't know what I would do without you guys."

As they got ready to hang up, Shirley stopped Carl and said, "We love you too son and give Zoey a big birthday kiss from us. We will see you guys at her party next weekend!"

A Very Bad Day

*A*fter church the Sunday following Zoey's fifth birthday party, Carl and Zoey were wrestling around in the living room, running and playing tag like they had done a million times before, when Zoey suddenly stopped and turned to her daddy with a look of fear in her eyes. "Daddy, I don't feel good, I feel funny." As she finished her sentence, Zoey collapsed to the floor, laying lifeless.

Carl ran to his daughter while pulling out his phone and dialing 911. "Zoey! Zoey, baby, wake up!" As the operator answered, Carl had now become hysterical, screaming, "Help me! Someone help me! My daughter has collapsed! She's not answering me. Zoey, baby, Zoey wake up!"

The operator attempted to calm him down as she called for emergency responders to Carl's address. After what seemed like an eternity, the first police officer arrived at the house and was immediately followed by a fire truck and ambulance. Zoey had a pulse, but it was weak. As the paramedics loaded Zoey into the ambulance, Carl was so out of it the police officers offered to drive him to the hospital and asked if there's anyone they could call to be with him. "It's just me and her," Carl responded. "I...I-I don't know who to call. My parents are four hours away."

When they arrived at the hospital Zoey, was immediately taken to the Cardiac Emergency Unit while Carl was escorted to the admissions desk to complete paperwork. While working on the paperwork he called his parents. "Mom...Mom it's Zoey. Something is wrong. We were running and playing, and then she collapsed. Mom, I don't know what to do. We are at the emergency room. Mom? Mom are you there?"

"Yes Carl, I'm here. We are on our way. We will be there as soon as we can. It's going to be okay. Zoey is strong she is going to be okay." Shirley hangs up the phone. She and Carl Sr., who had just returned home from an early dinner, immediately walk out the door and get into their car headed for Memphis.

The next three hours were the longest three hours of Carl's life. He paced the waiting room, waiting to hear anything about his daughter. He would stop pacing only long enough to ask at the desk if there was any news on his daughter's condition, only to be told they would let him know as soon as they heard something. Less than four hours after receiving the call, Shirley and Carl Sr. walked through the doors at the Emergency Room at the Children's hospital. "Carl! Honey, how's Zoey? Do we know what's going on yet?"

"Mom! Oh, thank God you are here. No, they still haven't told me anything. I haven't heard anything, and they just keep saying they will come find me when they know something."

"Carl, what happened?" Shirley is talking to her son as Carl Sr. walks to the nurses' station to see if he can find anything out.

"Mom, I don't know. We were playing like we always do,

and she said she didn't feel good. Then she collapsed. Mom what if she..."

"No Carl don't say that. Don't even think it. She is going to be okay. They are the best here and they will find out. Maybe she is just dehydrated or something. We have to think positive."

Carl, now sobbing, tells his mother, "Mom, I can't lose her too. I can't, I just can't!"

The two were so engrossed in their conversation, neither noticed Carl Sr. walking through the Emergency Room doors and returning with a young nurse. "Mr. Murphy? Are you Zoey Murphy's father?"

"Yes, yes that's me! How is Zoey? What happened? Can I see her?"

"Mr. Murphy, Zoey is stable for now. We are waiting for a specialist to come from another hospital to see if they can find out what's going on. I'll take you back to see her."

Carl and his parents follow the nurse to the ICU where Zoey is laying lifeless in the bed with machines beeping slowly behind her. Seeing her laying in that bed with IVs hooked up to her, Carl can only think about how much she looks like her mother and how Clair looked the very last time he saw her. Carl's heart sank as he collapsed to his knees beside Zoey's bed.

"Mom, what am I going to do? I can't lose my baby girl too, not my Zoey!" Carl sobbed as he held Zoey's hand.

"She's going to be okay son. You aren't going to lose her. We can't lose her. She has to be okay." Carl Sr., trying to comfort his son, joins Carl at Zoey's bedside.

After what seems like an eternity, a new nurse walks in to check Zoey's vitals. As she leans down to check Zoey's pulse,

Carl speaks up and asked, "Excuse me, can you tell me anything about what's going on with my daughter? No one has come in to see her and no one will tell us anything."

"I'm sorry, I just came on shift I'm really not sure what's going on. Let me check and I will come right back and let you know what I find out. My name is Anna, I'll be her nurse tonight. I'll be right back Mr. Murphy, I promise."

As Anna walks out of the room, Shirley, trying to lighten the mood in the room, nudges Carl with her elbow and said, "Hey, she's cute. I didn't see a ring on her hand." Embarrassed, Carl rolls his eyes as he walks out of the room to the nurses' station where Anna is reading Zoey's chart on the computer to see what she can find out for Carl.

Anna looked up and noticed Carl walking towards her and said, "Oh! I'm sorry Mr. Murphy, I was just catching up on Zoey's chart. I was going to come back to the room. You didn't have to come out here."

"Oh no, I just really had to get out of that room for a few minutes. It kills me to see her like that. I just really need to know something, *anything*. And please, call me Carl."

"Okay, Carl. It looks like they have ran several tests but they are waiting for the results and for the Pediatric Cardiologist to come over from the other hospital. He was called into an emergency surgery and was delayed. For right now, all we can do is wait. I'm really sorry I don't have anything else to tell you. From her chart, it looks like she was admitted early this afternoon. Have you eaten anything since you've been here?"

"Well no. I honestly don't even know what time it is," Carl answered as he looked at his watch.

"How about this; give me your cell number or your wife's cell number, and I'll call you as soon as we hear anything. The cafeteria is open for another two hours. You guys go grab something to eat, and I'll call you the very minute there's any news or if anything changes." Anna digs in her pocket, finds a small pink sticky notepad and a pen, and hands them to Carl. Carl takes the notepad and tries to write his name and phone number. By now, he has gotten so shaky he can barely write his own name.

"I'm so sorry. It's just...she's all I have. We lost her mother, and I just can't lose her too. I hope you can read my writing. If not, I'll be in the cafeteria just long enough to get something to eat and I'll be right back. Thank you so much for your help."

Anna smiled at him as she took the notepad and pen back and said, "You forget I read doctors' writing all day. This one is easy. Go grab some food, and I'll call you or come find you as soon as we hear anything. I'll take care of Zoey, and you take care of you so you can be there for her. She needs you too, you know."

Feeling comforted that Anna would be watching over Zoey, Carl took his parents down to the cafeteria to grab a bite to eat. After some coaxing, Shirley and Carl Sr. convinced Carl that they should take a few minutes and sit in the cafeteria to eat their food. "Carl, what exactly happened today before she collapsed, son?" Shirley asked as she took a bite of her hamburger.

"Mom, we were just running around the living room playing tag like we always do. I know, I know, 'we play too rough.' But honestly, Mom, we really weren't, and she really wasn't even doing *that* much running when she collapsed."

"Son, it wasn't your fault. You can't blame yourself. She's a kid. Remember all the wrestling and playing we did when you were a kid? Your mother swore you were going to get hurt too and look, you are just fine." Carl Sr. spoke up, cutting Shirley off before she could start her spiel on how dangerous rough housing in the house was.

"I know Dad, but I just don't know what I'm going to do. What if she's not okay? I promised Clair I would take care of her, and now she's laying in a bed hooked up to those machines and what if..."

"No, son, you can't think like that. You have taken the best care of Zoey. She's going to be okay. We just have to stay positive and—" Just then, Anna walked into the cafeteria and caught their attention. "Hey, isn't that the cute nurse taking care of Zoey?"

"Mom, stop, for real! Yes, that is Anna, Zoey's nurse."

Anna spots the trio sitting at the table from across the cafeteria she waves and approaches them. "Hi, Carl. Zoey is okay, I just wanted to come check on you and give you an update. The tests have come back, and the doctor is out of surgery. He should be here within the hour to read her results and talk to you."

"Thank you so much dear. Would you like to sit and join us?" Shirley replies to Anna before Carl has a chance to say anything to Anna. All Carl could do was smile and nod for Anna to join them. As Anna sits down, Shirley remembers something she needs to get from the car. She and Carl Sr. leave the two alone at the table to talk. As she gets to a place where she thinks Anna can't see her, Shirley mouths to Carl, "She's cute, talk to her."

Carl rolls his eyes motioning for his mother to stop. "Sorry, you'll have to ignore my mother. After my wife passed, she's always trying to play match maker."

"How long ago did you lose your wife?" Anna asks.

Carl takes a deep breath to compose himself and answers, "It was five years ago this week. She passed when Zoey was only three days old. It has been just me and Zoey from the very beginning. My parents help where they can, but they can only do so much."

"Oh no, I am so sorry. I can't imagine what you've been through. Especially trying to raise a baby girl all alone. Even after five years, I imagine you still miss her very much."

"Oh every day. The only thing that keeps me going is that baby girl. Do you mind if I ask you a personal question? You don't have to answer it if you don't feel comfortable."

Anna looks hesitant but answers, "Of course you can."

"How do you do it?"

She looks slightly puzzled "Do what?" Anna asks.

"How do you take care of these sick babies day in and day out knowing some will never get to leave?" Carl asks.

As Anna listened to his question, she reached out and touched Carl's hand. She answers, "Well Carl, three years ago I lost my baby girl. Her name was Sadie. She and my husband were on their way home from a ballgame one Sunday afternoon. A drunk driver crossed over into their lane and hit them head on. I was here at work when I got the call to the ER. They were killed instantly. I never got the chance to say goodbye to either of them. I didn't get the chance to hold my baby girl one last time or tell my husband I loved him one last time. They were just gone. I come to work every day trying to help these babies and help parents at least have the chance to hold their babies, even if it is one last time."

"Oh Anna, I am so sorry. I can't imagine what that was like for you, to not even get to say goodbye and to lose your baby girl. I don't know what I would do if I lost Zoey. I can't lose her, I just can't." As Carl finishes his sentence, he lays his head on the table and begins sobbing. Anna moves her chair over closer to Carl and puts her arm around him.

"Carl, no matter what, tell her you love her every day. Let her be silly and play, let her dance wildly like no one is watching. Play and be silly with her. But most of all, be there when she wakes up. Be there with a smile when she wakes up. She needs to see that you are positive and hopeful. Your smiling face needs to be the first thing she sees. She is going to be looking for you when she opens her eyes. You are her whole world." As Anna finished, Carl gently looked up and their eyes met. For the first time, Carl felt a connection with a woman that wasn't Clair, and to be honest, it scared him.

"I will be there, I'm going up there now and won't leave her side. Thank you, Anna. Thank you for telling me your story. It helps to have someone to talk to that understands. My parents try but they just can't understand."

"I have to get back upstairs my break is over, and Zoey's doctor should be back soon. I'll see you in just a little while, okay Carl?" As Anna walks away, Carl nods his head in agreement. Once she is out of sight, he puts his head back on the table sobbing for a few more minutes to regain his composure.

While sitting with his head on the table, Shirley and Carl Sr.

returned to the cafeteria and approached him, "Honey are you okay? Where did that cute nurse go?"

"I'm okay mom, I'm just really worried about Zoey. The nurse's name is Anna, Mom. Stop calling her 'that cute nurse.' I'm here with my sick baby, not to try and pick up a nurse." Carl replied clearly, trying not to get frustrated with his mother.

"I know Carl, I'm just saying it was nice of her to come down and sit with you for a little while. Besides, having a friend in the hospital can't be a bad thing, can it?" Shirley approached him and put her arm around him to console him.

"It was nice Mom. She had to go back to work. Her break time was over. It probably would have been a much better conversation if we had met under different circumstances." Carl started to clear the table so they could return to the room to be with Zoey. "We do need to get going. Zoey could wake up any minute and the doctor should be here soon to talk to us about the test results."

As they stepped off the elevator, Anna approaches them. "Hey Carl, I was just coming to find you guys again."

"What's wrong? Is Zoey okay? Did she wake up yet? Is the doctor here?" Carl starts walking fast towards Zoey's room.

Anna reaches out and stops him. "Wait, Carl, Zoey is okay. The doctor got called back into another emergency surgery and won't make it tonight. He will be here first thing in the morning."

Visibly frustrated Carl responds, "Are you freaking kidding me? *My* kid is sick too, isn't there someone else who can read her results and tell us *something*? What the hell man? We have been waiting hours, *hours*! No one can tell us a damn thing."

"I know Carl, I'm sorry. I know how upset you are, and I completely understand. The doctor is the best, though, and trust me you want to wait for him. Zoey is stable and is doing okay. How about you and I go see her? She should be waking up soon. The medication they gave her when she came in should be wearing off." Anna reaches out for Carl's hand and his countenance immediately changes. It is clear he has a soft spot for Anna.

"I know it isn't your fault and I'm really sorry I lost my temper with you. It's just that...Well that's my baby girl and she's my whole world. Thank you, Anna. Yes, let's go see her." Carl turns to his parents and asks, "Are you guys coming with us?"

Shirley takes a step towards Carl and Anna and Carl Sr. takes her hand pulling her slightly backwards, "No, son. You know, I think we should head over to your house and get some rest. We aren't as young as we used to be and staying up all night won't help us or Zoey. If anything changes, call and we will be right here. Otherwise, we'll be back in the morning." Shirley starts to protest leaving until she sees the look her husband is giving her and realizes that he is trying to give Carl and Anna some time to talk and get to know each other. Shirley hugs Carl and tells him to give Zoey a kiss. Shirley and Carl Sr. get back on the elevator to leave.

"And you get onto me for playing match maker. Look at you trying to hook those two up." Shirley jokes with Carl Sr. as she nudges him with her elbow and winks.

"What can I say? I haven't seen anyone calm him down like that since Clair. Maybe they will hit it off and he can be happy again."

Carl and Anna walk slowly through the hall towards Zoey's

room. The ICU floor brings back so many terrible memories and feelings for Carl, he is barely holding it together. As they walk into Zoey's room and he sees his baby girl laying there connected to all of the monitors, it proves too much for him to bear. As he breaks down crying. Anna reaches over and touches his shoulder, "Go talk to her. She can hear you. Let her know you are here."

Now softly crying, Carl whispers, "Clair, I'm so sorry. Please forgive me. I've tried to protect our baby girl, I promise I have."

Anna brings a small chair over to Zoey's bedside for Carl to sit in. He sits down, takes Zoey's hand, kisses it softly and tells her, "Daddy's here baby. I'm right here. I love you so much baby girl. Please stay with me Zoey. Please don't leave me."

Anna, standing behind him with tears streaming down her face, tells him, "Carl, she can hear you. Look at her eyes, she's trying to wake up. Keep talking to her."

Feeling a sense of relief at the first sign in hours that his baby girl might wake up, Carl keeps talking. "Zoey, baby, wake up for Daddy. When we get out of here, we will go do whatever you want baby girl. Please wake up for Daddy."

Slowly, Zoey's eyes begin to open and she squeezes her daddy's hand ever so slightly. With a small, trembling voice Zoey speaks for the first time in hours, "Daddy?"

"Yes baby, I'm here. Daddy's here baby girl."

"Daddy, where are we?" Zoey asks as she tries to look around and see where they are.

"Baby girl you are in the hospital. This is Anna, she's your nurse." Carl points to Anna who is now on the opposite side of Zoey's bed checking the IV bags and recording information from the monitors onto her notepad.

"Daddy, I had a dream. I dreamed that you and me and Mommy were at the beach. We were building a castle, and then Mommy said she loved me and she had to go. Daddy, where did mommy have to go?"

Trying to keep from bursting out in tears, Carl managed to say, "Baby girl, Mommy went to Heaven."

"Daddy, can we go see Mommy in Heaven?"

"Yes baby, one day we will all go to Heaven and we will see Mommy there."

"Nurse Anna, are you going to go to Heaven to see my Mommy?" Zoey asked as she turned her head and looked at Anna.

"Oh, I would love that Zoey. I bet your mommy is beautiful," Anna says with a sweet smile on her face.

"You could see your baby girl too. My mommy says she is beautiful like you."

Anna stops what she is doing and asks Zoey, "Your mommy told you I have a baby girl in Heaven?"

"Yes ma'am. She said she and Clair like to play ball and that was Clair's favorite thing to do."

"Oh no, honey. Clair is Mommy's name, not Anna's baby. You must be thinking about when Mommy was little; she liked to play ball." Carl replied as he looked at Anna hoping she wasn't getting upset.

"No daddy, Clair is mommy *and* Miss Anna's baby's name. Mommy told me so." Zoey yawns, "I'm really tired. Can I go back to sleep and see Mommy on the beach again? Maybe Clair will come with her and we can play this time." Hearing this, Anna quickly walked out of the door trying to contain her emotions.

"Sure baby, take a nap Daddy will be right here waiting when you wake up. I love you baby girl."

Zoey rolled over to go back to sleep and Carl followed Anna out into the hallway. "Hey, Anna, wait." Hesitantly, Anna stopped and turned back to Carl. "Hey, what's wrong? What's going on?"

"Carl, I don't know how Zoey knew that about my daughter." Anna replied with tears streaming down her cheeks.

"I'm confused, I thought you told me your daughter's name was Sadie? Why would Zoey say her name was Clair?" Carl asked Anna as he reached out and touched her arm.

"I'm so sorry Carl, I just didn't want to upset you anymore than I had to. My daughter's name was Sadie Clair but we called her Clair. I just don't understand how Zoey would know that. I'm sorry, I really have to go enter these notes. My shift is almost over and I have to give a turn over to the next nurse. I'm off at eleven. I promise I will be back in the morning when the doctor comes though. That is... if it is okay with you?"

"Oh, I thought you were here for the night with us?"

"No, I was only on-call from seven to eleven. The night nurse will be here from eleven to seven, I was only covering part of her shift."

"I would really like it if you would come back in the morning. I think it would help to have someone here with me that understands what's going on, especially if the doctor starts talking over my head. I'm sorry if Zoey upset you. I know she would like it if you came back too."

"She didn't upset me. No matter how long it has been, it never gets easier. I still miss my baby girl. I'll come in early tomorrow morning. Do you want me to bring you breakfast when I come in?"

"Oh no, I know my mom will be bringing food. She's always hounding me to eat something. You know how moms can be." Carl replied, trying to ease the tension.

Smiling, Anna replied, "Yeah, I can relate. I'll see you in the morning Carl." Anna walked away towards the nurses' station and Carl returned to Zoey's room. Upon arriving at the nurses' station, Anna was greeted by the night nurse Mallory. "I just have to enter the vitals for Zoey Murphy. She is awake and all of her IV's are good."

"I was just reading her chart. Was that her father you were talking to down there?" Mallory asked as she looked up from the computer.

"Yes, it was. He's a very nice man. I really feel bad for him. It's just him and his daughter. I couldn't bring myself to tell him her results. I guess I'm still hoping they were wrong and Dr. Conrad has a different take on the situation."

"So, he has no idea just how sick his baby girl really is?" Mallory asked, now standing so Anna can enter her information into the computer.

"No, Mallory, I just didn't have the heart to tell him."

"Well, it will probably be best coming from the doctor anyway. I'm going to go down and do my first check. I'll see you tomorrow. Thanks for covering for me so I could go to the kids' ball games. I owe you one for sure. Have a good night." Mallory walks down the hallway towards Zoey's room digging through her pockets to make sure she has her pen and notepad.

Anna finishes entering the information into the computer and clocks out for the evening. Walking towards the elevators, she stops and looks towards Zoey's room one more time, tempted to go back and sit with Carl and Zoey just a little longer, but decides to go ahead and go home for the night.

Just as Carl settled back into his seat beside a sleeping Zoey, there was a quiet knock on the door followed immediately by the door slowly opening. Carl immediately hoped it was Anna returning to sit with him a while and had to hide his disappointment when he turned and saw a new nurse walking through the door.

"Hi, I'm Mallory. I'll be Zoey's nurse for the rest of the night. You must be the dad?" Mallory spoke softly as to not wake up Zoey.

"Yes, I'm Carl."

"I'll be in and out throughout the night checking on Zoey. If there's anything she needs, I'll take care of her. Is there anything I can get you for now?" Mallory asked as she checked the IV bags and wrote down information from Zoey's monitors.

"No, well, actually. If you wouldn't mind, can I have a blanket?" Carl asked hesitantly.

"Well actually sir, family members aren't allowed to stay in the patient rooms overnight on this floor. There is a family waiting room just outside the unit. There are chairs that lay flat like beds and we will come get you if anything changes or if the doctor arrives."

"Wait, what? No, I can't leave her side. You don't understand, this is my baby. She's all I have. Please, please don't make me leave. I won't get in the way, you will hardly know I'm even here." Carl pleaded with Mallory.

"Okay. I won't make you leave, but if I come tell you that you have to go, don't question or make me tell you twice, just get up and go. Okay? You could get me in a lot of trouble letting you stay. It is against the hospital policy for this unit."

"Absolutely, I promise. I won't be any trouble and I won't get in your way. I just...I can't leave my baby girl. Thank you so much, thank you."

Throughout the night, Mallory was in and out of Zoey's room working quietly to check on Zoey and change out her IV bags. Carl stayed at Zoey's bed holding her hand with one hand and propping himself up on the side of her bed with the other. Around four, alarms and bells starting ringing on Zoey's monitors and Mallory came running into the room. Carl had accidentally knocked off one of the wires connected to the leads on Zoey's chest when he slumped over the side of the bed asleep.

"Mr. Murphy, you are going to have to sit back in your chair or go to the waiting room. You've pulled off one of her monitors and I can't keep running down here like this," Mallory said with a stern tone in her voice.

"Oh, I'm so sorry. I didn't mean to. I must have slipped when I was sleeping. I'm so sorry. Please, I'll move over and sit back." Carl pleaded with Mallory again to let him stay and not make him go to the waiting room. Mallory reluctantly agreed and replaced the wires silencing the alarms.

Another Day Without Answers

few hours later, even before sunrise, Carl was awakened by a gentle tap on his shoulder. "Carl? Carl, it's time to wake up." As Carl opened his eyes and turned, he saw Anna standing over him whispering to him while tapping his shoulder.

"Oh Anna, you came back. What time is it? Is the doctor here?" Carl whispered as he wiped the sleep from his eyes and tried to focus on Anna's face.

"Shhh, don't wake Zoey. Let's go get some coffee before the doctor gets here." Anna started walking towards the door motioning for Carl to join him.

As Carl stood to follow Anna, he gently placed Zoey's hand on her bed trying his best not to wake her. "Daddy? Where are you going?"

"Shhh Sissy, go back to sleep. I'm just going to go get a cup of coffee with Miss Anna. I'll be right back, okay?" Carl leaned down and kissed Zoey's head.

"Miss Anna came back to see us?" Zoey asked with a smile on her face.

"Yes, baby she did. She came back to see you, pretty girl. I'll be right back. I love you." Carl followed Anna down to the elevator. As they rode the elevator down to the basement where the cafeteria was, Carl began to think about how happy he was that Anna came back. It was nice to have someone to talk to, someone who seemed to care about his baby girl as much as he did. He wondered to himself if maybe Clair sent Anna to him to help him through this.

Carl and Anna were the only two in the cafeteria other than the employees working to get everything ready for the breakfast rush. They sat talking quietly at a table in the corner of the room. They talked about their baby girls and how much Zoey reminded Anna of her daughter. It was obvious to both of them there was a connection between the two of them. Neither had felt anything like it in years since they lost their spouses. Anna had poured herself into her work taking on any extra shifts she could, while Carl poured himself into being Zoey's whole world.

Anna was just about to ask Carl if he had considered dating when her phone started to buzz in her pocket. As she looked down and read the message she immediately stood up and told him, "Carl we've got to go now. Mallory just paged me. The doctor is here. We've got to go now."

Carl immediately jumped up and the two rushed to the elevator. Even though it only took a few minutes, that elevator ride seemed to take an eternity to Carl. He just wanted to get back to his daughter and hear from the doctor what was going on with her.

As they walked into the room, Dr. Conrad, a Pediatric

Cardiothoracic Surgeon, stood beside Zoey's bed. "Mr. Murphy, I presume?"

"Yes, I'm Carl Murphy. I'm Zoey's father. Is she going to be okay? When can I take her home?" Carl asked as he reached out to shake the doctor's hand. As Carl reached out his hand, he noticed the doctor was actually holding Zoey's wrist and watching the clock on the wall.

"I'll be with you in just a moment. I need to finish my initial exam before I can tell you anything," Dr. Conrad replied, now removing his blue stethoscope with little furry animals hanging from it off his neck and placing it into his ears. "I need to listen to your heart Miss Zoey. I'm sorry if this is a little cold." As he places the stethoscope end on Zoey's chest, she wiggles and laughs that it tickles.

"Doctor, what's wrong with my baby girl?" Carl asks as he steps towards Zoey's bed.

Anna reaches out and takes his hand, stopping him from moving any closer. "Carl, he has to check her vitals and read her chart. Let's go in the hallway so he can hear what's going on." Anna motions for the door and starts to walk out with Carl.

"Wait, Anna, are you on shift yet? Have you been working on this case?" Dr. Conrad asks.

"I am just about to go clock in now. I was here last night with them for a little while. Yes sir, I am familiar with the case," Anna replied.

"Okay, go clock in and come back. I'm having you assigned to my service to work with me on this one," Dr. Conrad responded as he turned back to listen to Zoey's heart again.

"I'll be right back Carl. Here, you can wait right here by the door. Just make sure you are quiet so he can hear, okay?" Anna pointed towards a small hallway inside of the door where Carl would be out of the way but still in the room. Anna walked down the hallway as quickly as she could, clocked in for her shift, and then returned walking so fast she was almost running.

Upon her return to the room, Dr. Conrad motioned for her to join him beside the bed while he reviewed her chart. They spoke in hushed tones so quietly Carl couldn't make out what they were saying, even though he was leaning and straining to try and hear them. Finally, after what seemed like an eternity, they closed the computer and turned to Carl. "Mr. Murphy, let's go out in the hall and talk." Dr. Conrad motioned for the door.

The trio walked into the hallway closing Zoey's door behind them. "Good morning Mr. Murphy. I'm Dr. Conrad. I am the Pediatric Cardiothoracic Surgeon. I apologize for not getting here last night. I had several emergencies, but they assured me your daughter was stable."

"I understand. How's my daughter? What happened? When can I take her—"

"Carl, slow down. Just take a deep breath and let Dr. Conrad talk to you," Anna interrupted as Carl was clearly starting to get upset, talking faster and faster.

"Sorry, I'm just, I'm exhausted and I'm worried about Zoey." Carl took a deep breath and tried to calm his nerves.

"It's okay, I completely understand. I've reviewed her chart and the tests they ran last night were inconclusive. They showed that there's something going on with Zoey's heart, but right now there's just not enough information for me to make a diagnosis. I've ordered several more tests to find out exactly what is going on. I will be in and out throughout the day as I have several surgeries today."

"Wait, what? You still don't know?" Carl asked, clearly getting frustrated.

"Carl, it's okay. Zoey is going to have more tests to help us know what is going on and what we can do to help her. We don't want to rush and make a mistake." Anna reached out and placed her hand on Carl's arm to comfort him. "I'll be with Zoey every step of the way through all of her tests. I promise I will let you know everything and I am going to let Dr. Conrad know as soon as every test has been completed."

"I mean, how long are we talking?" Carl asked looking at Anna.

"I put in the orders before we left the room. As soon as they can start they will come get her. Everything should be completed today unless there's an emergency with another patient. I know you are anxious to know something Mr. Murphy but just remember, Zoey is stable right now. Anna is going to get some more background information from you. We need a more detailed family history. Do you have any history of heart problems, Mr. Murphy? Or does your wife?"

"I don't, but her mother..." Carl has to stop and take a breath to calm his emotions. "Her mother passed when Zoey was three days old. She had Cardio... Cardio... I think it was called Cardiomyopathy or something like that. Do you think it is the same thing?"

"Well Mr. Murphy, to be honest, I just want to make sure I cover all angles. I may even have you do some bloodwork just to make sure we aren't missing anything. Would you be open to that, sir?"

"Of course, anything for my daughter." Carl answered as he looked at Anna.

"Let's check for Cardiomyopathy and Brugada Syndrome. Let's go ahead and do a blood panel on him as well. Get that history updated with as much as we can. I'd like to see the mother's records if we can get them." As Dr. Conrad talks, Anna writes down all of the items he is asking her for and nods her head that she understands.

While Dr. Conrad talks to Anna, Carl is clearly confused. He asks Anna, "What is he talking about? Why does he need Clair's records?" Anna motions for Carl to wait as she finishes writing everything the doctor has asked for.

"Mr. Murphy, I will be in touch." As Dr. Conrad walks away, he pats Carl on the shoulder and nods his head to Anna.

"Okay, what in the hell was all that? I have no idea what he just said." Carl waits until the doctor is out of earshot to ask Anna.

"Give me one second to enter this in the computer and I promise I will explain everything he just said." Anna walks over to a workstation just outside of Zoey's room and begins typing in the orders Dr. Conrad has just given her. "Okay, I'm sorry I had to get all of that in the computer so we could get everything started. I need to run down to the desk and get some paperwork for you to sign. I know this is going to be hard, but we need you to sign a release so we can get Clair's medical records sent over." As Anna starts to walk to the desk, Carl grabs her hand.

"Wait, Anna, I don't understand. Why do you need Clair's

records? Is my daughter going to be okay? Please just tell me. I need to know," Carl pleaded with Anna.

"Carl, honestly, I don't know. From what I can tell, it looks like he believes Zoey has the same heart condition Clair had. That's why he wants to get her records and wants you to be tested. I know this is hard. Go ahead and go back in with Zoey. I've got to get some paperwork for you to sign and I'll go ahead and do the blood draw for your tests." Anna was trying to be reassuring but knew in her heart the news was not good and Carl had good reason to be worried.

"I'll sign whatever, I'll do whatever. Please, I need my baby girl to be okay. I can't make it without her Anna. I can't do it, I won't." Carl turned and walked back to Zoey's room wiping the tears from his cheeks before going into Zoey's room. He had to do everything he could to be strong for Zoey. No matter what, he couldn't let her know how worried he was.

A few minutes passed and Anna returned to Zoey's room with a clip board and a small pink caddy with needles and tubes for drawing blood. "I've got the forms for you to sign. The top form is a release to allow them to run the tests Dr. Conrad ordered. The other form is the release for Clair's records. Are you okay with me drawing your blood or would you rather someone else did it?"

"No, I would much rather you do it. I trust you, Anna." Carl reached out and took the clipboard and signed all of the forms without hesitation.

Pulling up a stool beside Carl's chair, Anna took the signed documents and placed them on a nearby table. "Do you care which arm I draw the blood from?"

"Whichever is easiest for you." Carl replies as he turns to Anna so she can look at the veins on his arms.

"I promise I'll make this as painless as possible." Anna has now reached into her tool caddy and taken out several tubes a needle and a blue tourniquet.

"Oh, it's fine, with all the pain I've been through a little needle stick isn't going to bother me." Carl replied as he looked into Anna's eyes, he couldn't help but smile. Anna kept her word and got the blood needed on the first stick. Carl was so mesmerized by Anna that he never even felt the needle.

"I'm going to turn in these forms and take this blood down to the lab myself. I'll be back as soon as I can. Are you okay Carl? Do you need me to bring you any juice or anything when I come back?" Anna asked as she placed her hand on Carl's arm.

"Thank you, I'm fine. You did good, I never even felt the needle," Carl replied, now looking at his sleeping baby girl.

Just a few short minutes after Anna left the room, a different nurse and what appeared to be a student doctor entered the room and started preparing to take Zoey out of the room. "Wait, who are you? What are you doing?"

"Oh, sorry sir, we are taking Zoey down for her tests. It will take a little while. You can wait here in her room. We will bring her back here as soon as everything is finished." The young medical student replied as they started the take Zoey out of the room.

Just after the two left with Zoey, Anna returned to the room out of breath. "I'm sorry Carl I was trying to get back up here before they came to take her, but there was a line at the lab."

"It's okay. I just didn't expect them to come for her so soon. How long will this take?"

"It will probably take several hours. It could be tomorrow before we have all of the results back and know exactly what's going on with her heart," Anna replied.

"Tomorrow? All of this makes me feel so helpless. I just want my baby girl back and healthy. How long before we have any answers from my blood work? What was he looking for anyway? I've never had any heart problems," Carl is now pacing the room.

Anna walks over to Carl and stops him from pacing. "I know. We— I mean, you just have to be patient. Dr. Conrad has ordered tests that will show him exactly what is going on with Zoey's heart and how we can start to fix it or treat it at least. He is looking for any hereditary heart conditions that you may be a carrier for. Even if you don't have the condition, you can still pass on the trait and Clair's records will tell him what condition caused her death. I know how hard this is Carl, but you have to stay strong for Zoey. She needs you right now."

"I'm trying. I just need to know. I need her to be okay." Carl walks over to the chair in the corner.

Anna turns to walk out of the room. "I've got some charting to do and other patients to check on. As soon as I hear something I'll come find you, okay?"

"Anna, please, will you check on her and make sure she's okay?" Carl asks, stopping Anna as she exits the door.

Smiling sweetly, Anna replies, "Of course. I'll check on her throughout all of her tests. Maybe try and take a nap Carl. It is going to be a long day."

Carl tries his best to take Anna's advice, but he can't sit still. He can't just sit by and wait. He paces back and forth in the room for a while before going to the nurses' station to see if there's any news. Minutes drag on feeling like hours. After his fifth or sixth trip to the nurses' station, Anna stops him before he gets there. "I just talked to the lab. She's finished her first two tests and is heading into the third one. Do you think you could do me a huge favor?"

"Sure, why not? I'm not doing anything right now anyway. Besides, you've helped me and Zoey out so much already. What can I do?" Carl responded.

"I could really use a cup of coffee and the coffee maker on this floor is messed up again. Do you think you could go down to the cafeteria and get me medium coffee and a muffin? They are swapping over from breakfast to lunch, but they should still have some muffins out."

"Of course, do you want cream or sugar? Oh, and what flavor muffin?" Carl asked feeling somewhat relieved that he had something to do to take his mind off of everything for a few minutes.

"Any flavor they have out is fine. We have creamers up here, just no coffee. Thank you so much. Hold on one second, so I can go grab you some money to get it." Anna replied as she started to walk towards the break room where her purse was locked in her locker.

"Oh, no need. I've got it. You've done so much for us, buying you a coffee and a muffin is the very least I can do. I'll be back in a few minutes," Carl started walking towards the elevator.

Upon his arrival in the cafeteria, Carl noticed there was only one employee in the room and no customers. He didn't immediately see any muffins, so he approached the employee who was stocking the chip rack in preparation for the lunch rush. "Excuse me? One of the nurses asked me to come get her a muffin and some coffee. Do you still have any muffins or am I too late?"

The employee, an older gentleman with white hair turned and looked at him and smiled, "Let me guess, Anna sent you down?"

"Um, yes?" Carl replied slightly confused.

"She always waits until after breakfast. We have some over here. Follow me." The man replied with a slight chuckle. "The name's Frank."

"Carl. Nice to meet you," Carl replied as she shook Frank's hand.

"So, if Anna is your nurse, that means your child has something going on with their heart?" Frank asked.

"Yes, my daughter. They are running tests. Anna has been so sweet and helpful through all of this so when she asked me to come get her something I knew I had to come do anything to help her."

"You know what, I don't have any fresh muffins out. I do have some in the oven. You mind hanging out for a little while to wait on it?" Frank asked as he pointed towards a nearby table.

"Sure, I don't have anything else to do. I'm waiting on them to finish running tests on my Zoey. I was actually a little relieved when Anna asked me to come get her something."

Frank walked over to the coffee machine and poured two cups of coffee. He brought them back to the table and sat down with Carl and handed him one of the cups. "Oh sorry, you want cream or sugar? I never remember to ask. Since the military, I only drink my coffee black."

"Oh, no, this is fine thank you," Carl replied as he took the coffee from him.

Frank and Carl sat talking about their daughters. Frank had a daughter that just left for college. The two pulled out their phones and showed off pictures of their daughters like the proud fathers they were. After what seemed like only a few minutes, Frank looked at Carl and said, "Carl, do you believe in Guardian Angels?"

Thinking to himself that was a strange question he answered, "Um, well, actually I do. I like to believe my Clair is watching over Zoey and I."

"Well, I believe that some people are Guardian Angels. People who God puts in our lives to protect us or lead us through something that could potentially break us. I had a guy in Desert Storm that I am sure was my Guardian Angel. God used him to step in and save my life. I was on my third tour and was shot four times. He pulled me out of the line of fire and got me to safety. On our way back, there was an explosion in the road. Just before our truck reached the explosive device, he swerved, and the worst of the blast missed us. I know I wouldn't be here if it weren't for God sending him into that building. My partner was gone and I was alone, until Ryan walked in and found me." Frank stopped and took a sip of his coffee. "Anna is an incredible nurse and an even better person."

"I've only known her a couple days, but I definitely can see that she is an incredible person. She has been so sweet to my Zoey. She's definitely helped me through this so far. She's like no other person I've ever met. She has been genuinely nice to both of us, going out of her way to come in early to be with us," Carl replied with a thoughtful smile.

"Well, I tell you Carl, I have to admit, Anna called me this morning and told me she had a patient that she felt really needed prayer and that she was going to send the patient's father down to see me before lunch to help calm his nerves. In a way, I think Anna just may be your guardian angel. She seems to really care for you and for your daughter. If you don't mind, I'd like to pray with you for your baby girl and I'd like to put her on my church's prayer list." Frank moved closer to Carl so they could speak quietly as others were walking into the cafeteria.

Surprised and touched, Carl replied, "Really? She called and told you about me and my daughter?"

"She didn't give any names, she's not allowed to. She just told me that she had a very sweet little girl and her father that needed prayer. She said I would know when I saw him and, no offense, you definitely looked like you could use some distraction and a lot of prayer."

"Thank you, Frank. Please do add my Zoey to your prayer list and I would really appreciate you praying for us. You are so right, I needed this distraction, and I can use all the prayers I can get," Carl replied in appreciation.

Frank reached out and put his hand on Carl's shoulder and begins to pray with him. As they were praying, several people noticed the two and joined around them forming a prayer circle around the two. It wasn't until they finished praying that Carl became aware of the circle of men that has formed a around them praying. Not knowing who they were, Carl was just appreciative of all the care and love he was feeling from strangers.

While Carl thanks the strangers for taking the time to pray with him, Frank notices a message on his phone and taps Carl on his shoulder. "Carl, sorry to interrupt. Anna just texted me. They are bringing Zoey back to the room now. The doctor should be up within the hour to talk to you. You should head back upstairs.'

"Thank you, thank you so much for everything." Carl starts to walk away quickly and stops in his tracks and turns around almost in a panic, "I forgot Anna's coffee and muffin."

Frank starts to laugh, "Oh yeah, about that. Anna doesn't eat muffins. Here, she does drink coffee and will appreciate this." Frank hands Carl a medium cup of coffee with the lid on it.

"Wait if she doesn't like muffins, why did she send me down here for one?" Carl is now clearly confused. Frank smiled and Carl immediately understood that Anna had planned the whole thing for him to talk to Frank and get a break from pacing the floor in Zoey's room.

"Go on up and see your baby. I'm here all day if you need to come back down and talk or just to 'get Anna a muffin,'" Frank smiled as Carl walked out of the door, running for the stairs instead of waiting for the elevator.

Bad News

Carl arrives on the CCU floor. He has spilt quite a bit of coffee on his arm and is severely out of breath when he sees Anna walking down the hallway towards him. "Carl, Lord did you run all the way here? I told Frank you had an hour before the doctor would be here."

"I know, but I wanted to be here when Zoey got back. Sorry that I spilled a little." Carl hands Anna the cup, trying not to drip any of it on her.

Anna smiles, "Thanks for the coffee, Carl. How much do I owe you?'

"Oh, you don't owe me anything. In fact, I kind of feel like I owe you. Thank you for introducing me to Frank. It was really nice talking to him and getting a lot of stuff off my chest. I forgot your muffin." Carl replied with a smirk and a wink to Anna.

"Frank is great. I just love going down and hearing his stories. Did he tell you about his 'angel'?" Anna asked.

"Yeah, some guy named Ryan?" Carl shrugged.

"He's not just 'some guy,' he's the founder of Halo for Humanity. He's kind of a big deal. He comes to the hospital once or twice a month to visit the kids and gives a *huge* check every time he comes." Anna replied.

"Oh wow, he didn't tell me *that* was who he was talking about. That is crazy. What a small world that he ended up working in the same hospital the man that saved his life gives major contributions to."

The elevator opens and Carl sees Zoey being returned to her room. Zoey is sitting up and smiling while hugging a pink teddy bear that is nearly as big as she is. "Hey, bright eyes! Where have you been? I've been standing around waiting on you all morning." Carl says with a smile on his face as he walks towards his baby girl.

"Look what I got for doing good on my tests daddy! I named him Frankie Bear. Feel him! He's *so* soft and squishy!" Zoey smiled as she pushed her teddy bear towards her daddy so he could see him better.

"Oh he's soft. Did you get him just for me? Why, thank you!" Carl joked as he pretended to hug Zoey's bear.

"No Daddy, he's mine! You can go get your own if you let them test you." Zoey smiled as she took her bear back from her daddy.

Soon after they settled into her room, Anna walked into the room. "Hey Zoey, how are you feeling? Looks like someone visited the Teddy Bear room; you must have done really well in your tests this morning. That's a really pretty bear. Does it have a name yet?"

"Yes ma'am, his name is Frankie. Do you want to hug him? He's really soft and squishy!" Zoey smiled and handed her bear to Anna.

"Oh wow, he is really soft and squishy! I have a friend named Frank too! He's not really soft or squishy, though." Anna laughed as she handed Zoey her bear back and turned to Carl. "Dr. Conrad is reading Zoey's results now. He should be here any minute. I just wanted to let you know."

"Thank you, Anna," Carl replied now feeling even more anxious to find out what was going on with his baby girl. Anna smiles and leaves the room.

A few minutes later, there is a soft knock on the door and Dr. Conrad enters the room. "Hi Zoey, how are you feeling today?" Dr. Conrad smiles as he walks over to Zoey's bedside.

"I feel better. I got a new bear today. He is really soft and squishy, see!" Zoey smiles and holds her bear up for the doctor to see.

"Oh, I see, someone must have been to the Teddy Bear room. Miss Zoey, do you mind if I borrow your daddy for just a minute? I need to talk to him for just a few minutes, if that's okay?" Dr. Conrad motions for Carl to join him in the hallway.

"I guess so. I'll be okay Daddy, you can go with him. Can Miss Anna come sit with me?" Zoey asked her daddy.

"Sweetie, Nurse Anna is actually finishing her paperwork to go home. I can see if one of the other nurses can come sit with you if you want," Dr. Conrad answered Zoey.

"Oh no, I will be fine. I just wanted to see Miss Anna again. It is okay." Zoey looked disappointed.

"I'll only have your daddy for just a few minutes, I promise." Dr. Conrad and Carl walk outside of Zoey's room to a small waiting area a few feet away. "Have a seat Mr. Murphy."

"Do you know what's wrong with Zoey? When can she go home?" Carl asked as he took a seat next to Dr. Conrad.

"Well Mr. Murphy, I'm not going candy-coat it. It's not good. My suspicions were right: Zoey has Cardiomyopathy. Looking at your wife's medical records, that was the cause of her death. Untreated, Zoey's heart will fail like her mother's did."

"Wait, what? So, what are we going to do? We have to do something. I can't just sit by and watch my baby die. I've already had to sit by and watch her mother die!" Carl is now in tears as his worst nightmare is becoming reality.

"Well, we have caught this early. We have a couple options and I'm not going to lie, you aren't exactly going to like either one." Dr. Conrad is now thumbing through the file in his hand to get information to show to Carl.

"Look, stop dicking around and just tell me! I will do whatever needs to be done to save my daughter." Carl's fear is now turning to anger. He doesn't feel the doctor is being open and honest with him.

"Mr. Murphy, I'm sorry. I'm trying to make sure you understand the dangers we are going to dealing with. One option is to try a more conservative route and use medication. I can't lie, there is a lot of risk involved with this option. The medicine itself could potentially kill her or cause more damage." Dr. Conrad has given up searching for the information papers and is now just talking to Carl.

"Wait, that's the so called conservative treatment? It could kill her? What the hell?" Carl is back to being filled with fear again.

"The other option is more aggressive but is, I feel, the better option. It too comes with a risk of Zoey not making it. We could do a heart transplant. She is young, so the chances are really good that her body will accept the heart and she will do just fine."

"So, you're telling me if we don't do the transplant and go with the medicine she may die, and if we do the transplant there's a risk that she could reject the heart and die? Is that seriously what you are telling me right now?"

"Honestly, it is slightly worse than that. First, we have to put her on the transplant list and get her a heart. Until we get the heart, she is going to need to be monitored and kept calm." Dr. Conrad is trying his best to keep Carl calm.

"Wow, so medicate and possibly kill her, or put her on a list and she could die waiting... Are those really my only options here?" As Carl sits trying to fight back tears, Anna walks over and sits beside him. "Anna, what should I do? I don't know what to do?"

"Carl, I can't tell you what you should do. You have to trust your gut. You should know, Dr. Conrad is the best at what he does." Anna reaches over and takes Carl's hand in her hands.

"Mr. Murphy, I don't mean to rush you or push you, but we don't exactly have a lot of time here. I need you to make a decision quickly so we can either get the medicine started or get her on the transplant list."

"Dr. Conrad, do you mind if I talk to Carl alone? I will get his decision and get it to you as soon as he makes his choice," Anna asked.

"Yes, that's fine. Here are the documents. Just don't take too long, the sooner we get her started on the medication or on the transplant list the better. Time is of the essence." Dr. Conrad handed release forms to Anna and leaves the two sitting together.

"Anna, I don't know what to do. What would you do if it was your daughter?" Carl asked Anna as he turned to her with tears in his eyes. "I just need someone to tell me what to do, Clair would have known what to do."

"Carl, I'm sorry but I can't tell you what to do here. I just can't," Anna replied.

"I need a few minutes to call and talk to my parents." Carl reached into his pocket and pulled out his phone.

"Go ahead. I'll go sit with Zoey so she doesn't have to wait alone." Anna stood and walked to Zoey's room.

"Thank you, she was actually asking for you earlier." Carl smiled at Anna as she walked into Zoey's room. Carl takes a deep breath before dialing the phone. Looking down he sees a picture of himself and Zoey taken by his mother at one of her birthday parties. They both have cake and icing smeared all over their faces. Looking at Zoey and her huge smile, his heart hurts. He doesn't know what to do and he doesn't know what he will do without her. Finally, he works up the nerve and taps on his mother's contact icon to make the call.

"Carl? Hey, how's Zoey? Have you heard anything yet?" Shirley answers almost in a panic.

"Hey, Mom. Zoey is awake and talking. They got the test results back. Mom..." Carl hesitates.

"Carl are you there? Carl? Carl? I think I lost you. Carl?" Shirley is moving around the room thinking she has lost the connection.

"I'm here, Mom. I just don't know what to do. They know what's wrong and the options to help her are both horrible. I can medicate her and possibly kill her, or they can put her on a list for a transplant. She could possibly never get the transplant and die, or she could get the transplant, reject the heart and still die." Carl is now crying. "Mom, I just don't know what to do."

"Okay, Carl let's think this through." Shirley responds after a few seconds.

"Mom, I have to give them an answer like now. Zoey doesn't have time."

"Well, can you ask for a second opinion? Maybe they got it wrong?" Carl Sr. responded.

"Dad there's no time for that. Besides, I've been told by multiple people that this doctor is the best. Dad, if it were me, what would you do?" Carl pleaded with his parents to just tell him what to do.

"Son, we are on our way back there now. Just pray about it and let God lead you. You have to follow what He puts in your heart. You know that's what Clair would tell you." Shirley answered. Carl Sr. has already started putting his shoes back on and Shirley is standing near the door waiting for him so they can return to the hospital. "We will see you in just a little bit. Son, we love you. Zoey is going to be okay."

"Okay, I'll see you soon. Love you guys." Carl hangs up the phone and stands to go back into Zoey's room. Before Carl can walk across the hallway and into Zoey's room, Anna walks out of the room with a concerned look on her face. "Anna, what's wrong? Is Zoey okay?"

"Carl, she's getting worse. I've got to go call Dr. Conrad to come back. We have less time than we thought. You really do have to make a choice," Anna replied.

Carl could see the fear in her eyes. "Anna, as a friend, I need you to tell me: if this was your daughter, would you do the transplant? As a mother, if this was Clair, would you do the transplant?" Anna, hesitant to answer looks at Carl with tears in her eyes and simply nods as she walks to the nurses' station to call the doctor. Carl stops her. "Anna"

"Carl I can't, I have to call the doctor, he needs to get back here now." Anna keeps walking.

"Anna, get me the papers. We're going to do the transplant."

Hearing his words Anna stops and walks back to him, "Carl this has to be your decision. You can't base it off what anyone else has said. I can't tell you what to do so please, it has to be *your* decision," Anna pleads with him.

"I know Anna. I feel it in my gut this is what I have to do for my baby girl." Carl signed the papers and handed them back to Anna. She took them and rushed to the desk. Once at the desk she talked to a younger nurse that Carl had never seen before. The look on their face told him there was something more going on and he rushed into Zoey's room. As soon as he walked in, he could tell Zoey had gotten worse. Her skin was pale and she was no longer awake and laughing. She lay in the bed lethargic and lifeless. The beeps on the monitor were much slower than they were when he was in the room before. He couldn't take it, it was more than he could bear. His baby girl was laying there dying, just like her mother had. He fell to his knees crying and begging God to spare his baby girl.

The door burst open, Dr. Conrad, the young nurse and

another doctor came rushing in with Anna trailing not far behind them. "Mr. Murphy, Mr. Murphy we need you to step out. Mr. Murphy." The young nurse was pulling on his arm as the two doctors and more nurses pushed past him to get to Zoey's bed.

"Carl, Carl come with me so they can work." A familiar voice in the crowd, it was Anna. Anna took Carl by the hand and led him out of the room. Everything happened so fast he barely had time to realize what was going on.

"Anna, what's wrong? She was fine earlier. What happened? Did I take too long? Is this my fault?" Carl is frantic and in tears as Anna tries to console him. Before Anna can answer, Shirley and Carl Sr. step off the elevator and see Carl and Anna standing in the hallway.

"Carl, son what's wrong? Why are you out here and not in Zoey's room?" Shirley asks as she approaches and sees Carl is crying.

"Mom, I-I don't know what's going on. She was awake one minute and talking and now— Oh mom she looks...She looks like Clair did," Carl sobbed to his mother almost collapsing as he said it.

"Zoey's heart isn't pushing enough blood through her system. She's going into heart failure. I'm not sure what they are going to do just yet. The doctors will come out and speak to you. Right now, they just have to keep Zoey alive until we can get her a new heart," Anna responded.

"Well shouldn't you be in there helping them?" Shirley responded, sounding somewhat annoyed that Anna was in the hallway and not in the room helping save Zoey.

"Well Mrs. Murphy, I'm actually off now. My shift ended

two hours ago. I stuck around to see if I could help Carl and to sit with Zoey a little to give him a break. Now that you guys are here, I'll let you have your family time. I'm sorry," Anna replied as she began to walk away.

"Mom, really? She's been so good to us, and you talk to her that way. Anna, wait! Anna, please stay. I'm sorry," Carl replied giving his mother a somewhat dirty look.

"I'm so sorry Anna, I didn't mean to snap at you like that. I'm just so worried about Zoey. Please don't leave." Shirley knew she was wrong and did feel bad for how she snapped at Anna. "You have helped so much we really do appreciate you."

"I don't want to intrude."

"No please, Zoey would love for you to stay, I think Carl would too honestly," Shirley replied as she reached her hand out for Anna and nodded over towards Carl.

"Yes, we would both really like it if you would stay Anna. Unless you just need to go, I understand. It has been a very long day for you, and I don't know if you have to be back later tonight or early in the morning." Carl smiled at Anna.

"No, I am it's okay. If you don't mind, I would like to stay and at least hear what the doctor says." Anna smiled at Carl and looked over at Shirley for her approval. Shirley smiled and nodded.

While the four stood in the hallway, more nurses came down the hallway and into Zoey's room. An older doctor followed them into Zoey's room. "Who is that?" Carl asked Anna.

"That's Dr. Kate. She is the respiratory specialist. Carl, I can't lie, it isn't a good sign that they are calling her in on Zoey's case." Anna couldn't hide the concern in her facial expression any longer. "They usually only call her in on the worst cases. She is the best though." Anna realized she needed to try to give Carl hope and not let him know just how bad things were.

"Anna, I need to know what is going on with my baby. I *need* to know, Anna," Carl pleaded with her.

"Carl, we need to wait for the doctors to come out and tell us something." Carl Sr. stepped closer and put his arm around his son.

Twenty minutes pass as Carl paces the hall in front of Zoey's room waiting for someone to walk out and tell him what is going on with his daughter. Finally, Dr. Conrad and Dr. Kate walk out of the room followed by nearly all of the nurses. "Mr. Murphy, this is Dr. Kate, our Respiratory Specialist." Dr. Conrad introduced Dr. Kate. "Mr. Murphy I'm going to get straight to the point; Zoey's condition is significantly worse than we previously thought. We no longer have the option to try the medication first. Zoey will need a transplant if she has any chance of seeing her next birthday. We will need you to sign the papers so we can get her on the transplant list right now."

"I think I already signed them, Anna is that what I signed?" Carl turned to Anna with tears in his eyes.

"Yes sir. Dr. Conrad, the release forms are at the desk. He signed them just before Zoey's condition turned," Anna replied.

"Good, that's a start. Her condition being what it is will get her moved up on the list. Unfortunately, the damage is to the point now that her body isn't getting enough oxygen. She is on a ventilator right now that is helping her breathe, but we are going to need to take more drastic steps to get the blood pumping to her organs," Dr. Kate replied looking at Dr. Conrad.

"Wait what do you mean more drastic steps? A ventilator? Like life support? Are you saying my baby girl is on life support?" Hearing these words seemed to hit Carl like a ton of bricks.

"Yes. Mr. Murphy, your daughter's heart isn't pumping blood to her organs. She is starting to have organ failure. The vent is helping relieve some of the strain on her heart and lungs, but she is going to need to be put on a bypass machine. This machine will actually pump the blood for her allowing her heart to rest." Dr. Conrad explained.

"Bypass? Organ failure? What do you mean? She was just fine not an hour ago she was sitting up in her bed playing with her bear and now her organs are failing? I just don't understand. Please, do whatever you need to do just save my baby!" Carl was confused, angry, and scared all at the same time.

"She is being prepped to go to the OR right now as we speak. We are going to do everything we can for your daughter. We will come find you as soon as she is out of surgery," Dr. Conrad replied as he and Dr. Kate walked away.

Before the two doctors could make it to the elevator, Zoey's door opened up. Two surgical residents were pushing Zoey's bed out of the room. "Wait, can I please just give her one last kiss before she goes to surgery?" Carl asked.

"Yes, but please, we have to get her into the OR as quickly as possible." One of the residents replied.

Carl leaned down and kissed Zoey's forehead and whispered to her, "Sissy, Daddy is here. I will be right here when you get back. I love you baby, come back to me." As they wheeled her bed down the hallway, Carl, Anna and Carl's parents stood in the hallway with tears streaming down their cheeks.

"I'll be right back. There's someone I have to talk to." Carl started walking towards the stairs. Anna, Shirley, and Carl Sr. looked at each other with confusion. Anna then realized where Carl was going and told his parents he was going to get Frank to pray with him. Carl rushed down the stairs not waiting for the elevator and was almost running when he walked into the cafeteria. "Excuse me, I'm looking for Frank." He asked one of the ladies behind the cash register.

"Oh, I'm so sorry, but you just missed him. He left maybe fifteen or twenty minutes ago. Is there something I can help you with?" The lady replied.

"Are you freaking kidding me?" Carl rolled his eyes and sighed.

"I'm sorry sir, he will be back in the morning. Are you sure there's nothing I can help you with?" The cashier replied.

"No, no I'm fine," Carl replied as he walked over to an empty table and sat down. Feeling hopeless Carl put his head in his hands and began to quietly cry and pray. "God, You know how much I need her. I would do anything to trade places with her. I need her. God You've got to heal my baby." Carl cried.

A few minutes later Carl felt a gentle touch on his shoulder, it was Anna. "Carl? Are you okay?" Anna asked as she pulled a chair close to him and sat down.

Startled, Carl jumped up, "What is everything okay, did they come back already?"

"No, not yet. They did call and said they have gotten started and everything was going well. I just wanted to come check on you." Anna took Carl by his hand.

Carl sat back down, moving his chair closer to Anna. "I came down here to see if Frank was here. I really just needed to talk to someone, and I thought it might make me feel better to pray with him."

"I figured that's where you were headed. You know you can talk to me. I'd also be more than happy to pray with you Carl," Anna replied.

"I know, it's just that you have done so much for me and Zoey. I hate to be any more of a burden on you. I appreciate all you have done, I really do. I can't thank you enough, Anna." Carl looked over at Anna and smiled. Anna smiled back and the two sat in silence for a few minutes before Carl's parents walked into the cafeteria.

"Carl, the doctors called the nurses' station. They are bringing Zoey back in just a few minutes and want to speak to us when they bring her back. We need to go back up now." Shirley motioned for him to come with her towards the elevators.

Carl stood, took a few steps and stopped, "Anna are you coming with us?"

"Oh no Carl, I really need to go get some sleep. I have to be in early in the morning and I haven't had any sleep at all. Not to mention I really need to get a shower. I will be back early in the morning before my shift. Dr. Conrad has already said I'll be assigned to Zoey when I come in, so I know I will see you guys. Do you need me to bring you anything when I come back?" Anna replied as she stood up and pushed in her chair.

"I understand. Thank you again for staying with us all day.

You have done more than you will ever know," Carl replied as he walked over and hugged Anna. He hugged her tightly and she hugged him back. Feeling her arms around him made him feel something he hadn't felt since he lost Clair, like the hole in his heart created when he lost Clair wasn't quite as big as it once was. Like there could actually be someone else that he could love and that could love him and his daughter the way he knew Clair loved them.

"Get up and talk to the doctors. I will see you all in the morning," Anna said as they walked towards the elevator. She stopped at the door and watched them as the got on the elevator. As the doors closed, she raised her hand to waive goodbye to Carl and his parents.

Doctors Conrad and Kate were just stepping out of Zoey's room when the elevator doors opened and the Murphys stepped out. "Mr. Murphy, perfect timing" Dr. Conrad spotted them and began walking to them. "We just got Zoey settled back into her room. Everything went as planned."

"Oh good. Can I go see her? Is she awake already?" Carl smiled and started walking towards Zoey's room.

"Mr. Murphy, we need to talk before you go see your daughter. Please come have a seat." Dr. Conrad motioned towards the small area of chairs to their left.

"Okay?" Carl was slightly confused and concerned that they didn't want him to immediately go see his daughter.

"Mr. Murphy, Zoey's heart is severely damaged. We placed her on the bypass machine. This will keep her organs going until we can get her a heart. However, because of her age and other factors, she is going to need to remain in a medically induced coma until we can get her a heart," Dr. Conrad explained.

"Wait, what?" Carl looked to his mother and then back at the doctors.

"Mr. Murphy, we are going to keep Zoey asleep to protect her heart and keep her comfortable until we can get her a heart," Dr. Kate explained.

"We just want you to be prepared. She is connected to a machine to help her breathe and another that is pumping her blood for her. It seems overwhelming, I know, but just know this is the best way to keep your daughter alive so we can get her a new heart. Dr. Kate and I will monitor her and keep a close eye on everything. She has been added to the transplant list with the highest priority."

"So, she is going to be in a coma until she can get another heart? How long will that take? Will she wake up once she gets a new heart?" Shirley asked.

"Well, honestly we don't know how long it will take. Thankfully we caught everything early enough there shouldn't be any deficits. For now, we wait. I'm sorry we don't have any other information right now," Dr. Conrad replied

Waiting Is the Hardest Part

After the doctors walked away, Carl and his parents sat in silence for what seemed like an eternity before Carl Sr. finally spoke up, "Let's take a minute to pray before we go in there. When we go in to see her, we have to be strong, united, and positive." Carl Sr. reached out his hands for both Shirley and Carl. The three joined hands and Carl Sr. began to pray. "God, we need you right now. We need your strength. Most of all, we need your healing for our baby girl. God, you made her heart and I know you've made another one that will save her. God, we know you can take care of her, we know that you will! God, please, give strength to the other family that we know will suffer a loss for Zoey to be saved. We thank you now for her healing and we worship you the Almighty God for all you are doing and for all you've done. Amen!" As they all raised their heads and opened their eyes, they were all three crying. They embraced each other and wiped their faces before turning and walking into Zoey's room.

The air in Zoey's room felt heavy. Seeing her laying in the bed, seemingly sleeping peacefully hooked up to machines with tubes and wires all over her, it was all Carl could do not to collapse at the sight. He stopped and composed himself, reminding himself that he had to be strong for Zoey. She needed his strength right now because she had none of her own. He walked over and sat in the chair next to the foot of her bed. He placed his hand on her little foot and told her, "Sissy, Daddy is here. Everything is going to be okay baby girl. Daddy is here."

"Carl, we are going to go back to your house. We will be back in the morning. Do you want us to bring you anything? Maybe a change of clothes?" Shirley asked as she placed her hand on Carl's.

"That would be nice Mom. Thank you, guys, thank you for everything." Carl looked up and placed his hand on top of his mother's hand on his shoulder. After his parents left for the night, Carl laid his head at Zoey's feet and cried, praying again for God to touch his baby girl. At some point he dozed off and slept there with his head leaned down by his baby's feet. In the early hours of the morning, Mallory came in the room to check on Zoey. Seeing Carl bent over the foot of her bed sleeping touched her heart. After finishing her required tasks, she left the room and returned with a pillow and blanket for Carl.

"Oh, sorry, did I knock something loose again? I'm sorry, I'll sit up" Carl asks half asleep as Mallory touched his shoulder to wake him.

"No, you are okay. I found you a pillow and a blanket. Sorry it isn't more; this is the best I could find." Mallory smiled as she gave him the pillow and laid the blanket over him. "She's stable, you should sleep a little."

"Thank you," Carl replied as he put the pillow on the edge of Zoey's bed and laid his head down.

Just before dawn, Anna came into Zoey's room. Seeing Carl asleep leaned on the edge of the bed, she turned to walk away trying not to wake Carl. The sound of the door opening had already awakened him, so when she left the room Carl stood up and followed her. "Hey Anna," Carl whispered as he walked into the hallway.

"Oh, I'm so sorry. I didn't mean to wake you. You looked so peaceful sleeping, I figured I would just wait and talk to you later when I came on shift." Anna turned and walked back to him.

"No, no it's okay, I'm glad you woke me up. You have time to go get some coffee before your shift?" Carl asked.

"Actually, I don't, I overslept this morning and didn't get here as early as I hoped to. I was just coming to check on you and make sure you were doing okay before I clocked in. How about lunch later?" Anna responded with a somewhat disappointed look on her face.

"Sure, that sounds good. I think I am going to go down and get some coffee. Need me to bring you a muffin?" Carl smiled.

Laughing, Anna replied, "Nah, I'm good."

Carl decided he was going to go ahead and go get some coffee. He needed to be awake when the doctors came back to talk to him this morning. He was also hoping he would find Frank down in the cafeteria. He could really use someone to talk to right about now. As he walked into the cafeteria he immediately noticed Frank was there cleaning the counters and setting out the freshly baked muffins. "Good morning, Frank."

"Oh, hey Carl, here for another muffin for Anna?" Frank chuckled. "Seriously though, how is your baby girl doing? Zoey, right?"

Carl walked over and poured a cup of coffee from the freshly brewed pot. "Frank, she's not good, not good at all. We found out late last night she needs a heart. They put her on a machine to pump blood for her and another one to breathe for her. It's bad Frank, it's so bad."

Frank picked out a couple muffins and motioned for Carl to come sit down at a nearby table. "Here some sit down. Let's have some breakfast and talk. Blueberry or Banana Nut?" Frank asked as he held out two muffins.

"Um, blueberry, I guess." Carl reached for the muffin. "Thanks, I don't remember the last thing I ate. This has been the hardest thing. I just want my baby girl to be healthy and back to her happy self. It's killing me to see her laying in that bed lifeless." Carl looked down and picked at the muffin finally taking a small bite.

"Look, I don't know what it is like to have a baby sick like that, but I know God can heal her. She will get a heart and those doctors will have her back to her happy self in no time," Frank replied as he took a bite of his muffin.

"Frank, I sure hope you are right. I know God can take care of her, I just need Him to do it now. I feel so bad knowing that in order for my baby girl to live, she will need some other little girl's heart, but I *need* my baby to be okay. I can't stand the thought of losing her. I just can't take it." Carl set his muffin on the table and pulled a napkin from the dispenser to wipe the tears from his eyes.

"Carl, God has this in His hands. They will find her a heart and she will be okay. I've been praying all night for that baby. God's never let me down and I don't suspect He will this time. We've just got to have faith. You know the Bible says we only need faith the size of a little ole mustard seed. We just have to hold onto that little mustard seed of faith. I know it is hard, but Zoey needs you to hold onto that faith Carl." Frank reached out and placed his hand on Carl's shoulder.

"Thank you, Frank, I really needed to hear that today. I guess I better get back up there. My parents should be coming back here soon, and the doctors said they would come talk to us first thing this morning." Frank and Carl both stood up. "Oh, I don't see a cashier to pay for my coffee and muffin. Can you ring me up?"

"It's on me." Frank smiled and waived him on.

"Are you sure? Thank you again for everything Frank. Really, thank you." Carl hugged him and walked towards the elevators. Carl returned to Zoey's room and sat there in silence listening to the machines beep, hoping and praying he would soon see his baby girl's beautiful blue eyes open again.

Around eight there was a soft knock on the door. Carl Sr. and Shirley walked in carrying coffee and a bag full of biscuits. "Hey son, how's she doing today?" Carl Sr. asked.

"So far, no change. Other than the nurses checking up on her no one has been in," Carl replied.

"Here, we figured you could use some food." Shirley handed Carl the bag of food and a cup of coffee.

"Thanks, mom. Did you happen to remember my clothes?

I'm starting to feel pretty grungy in these jeans." Carl took the biscuits and a sip of the coffee.

"Oh yeah, I did, here. I hope I grabbed the right stuff. Your closet wasn't very organized." Shirley handed Carl a small duffle bag.

"She stayed up last night 'organizing' your closet. Sorry I couldn't get her to stop." Carl Sr. rolled his eyes and nodded towards Shirley.

Laughing, Carl responded, "Thanks Mom. I guess I should have known you would organize for me." Smiling, he started towards the door. Just as he reached for the door, there was a soft knock and then Anna opened the door.

"Good morning." Anna smiled as she entered the room. "Something sure smells good in here." Anna walked over to Zoey's monitors and began writing down information from them.

"Oh yeah, they brought some biscuits, want one, or two or three? I don't know why she thought I needed so many." Carl laughed as he offered Anna a biscuit from the bag.

Laughing, Anna replied, "Thanks, I may take you up on that."

"Hey, do you by chance have a place where he can shower? He's starting to smell," Carl Sr. joked as he held his nose and pointed towards Carl.

"Actually, there is a shower in the Resident's break room. None of them are here yet you could probably sneak in there and get a quick shower," Anna replied. "Give me just a minute to get these readings and I'll take you down there." Finishing the last

71

of her tasks, Anna took a biscuit from the bag. "Thank you, Mrs. Murphy. Carl, I'll show you to the break room if you are ready."

The two walked out of the room leaving Carl's parents to sit with Zoey. "Hey, thanks for this. I really appreciate it. You'll have to excuse my parents, they are just trying to cheer me up and keep my mind off of things." Carl smiled.

"It is no problem. Now you will need to be pretty quick, I'm not supposed to let anyone in here and they usually come in around eight thirty." Anna scanned her badge and opened the door marked 'Resident's Lounge.'

Stepping in, Carl replied, "I promise I'll be right out thank you again." A few minutes later Carl emerges from the lounge with wet hair and fresh clothes on. Anna was still standing next to the door keeping watch. "Oh, my goodness, thank you so much. I feel like a new man. It is amazing how much better you feel after a hot shower."

"Wow that was fast! You do smell better," Anna laughed.

As the two walked back down the hallway towards Zoey's room, Carl tried to make small talk for an excuse to talk to Anna. "Did you have a good evening? Get some rest at least?"

Smiling Anna replied, "It was okay. I did get some sleep, but I did stay up a while worrying about how you were handling all of this. I almost called you a couple times but didn't because I was hoping you were sleeping."

"Oh. you could have called. I don't know when exactly I fell asleep. I just remember leaning down at the foot of Zoey's bed and then Emily woke me up giving me a blanket." Carl smiled. It made him feel good that Anna cared enough to worry about him.

"Emily? You mean Mallory?" Anna stopped and turned to him.

"Oh yeah, sorry I'm not really good with names. The night nurse that we had the other night too," Carl was embarrassed.

Laughing, Anna replied, "That's okay Carl. You remember the important names, right? Like mine." Anna smiled and the two laughed. "This is where I leave you. I've got some charting I need to get done. I'll be down here in a little while to check on our girl. See you later." Anna stopped at the nurses' station and Carl continued on to Zoey's room.

"You look like you feel a little better after a shower," Shirley commented as Carl walked into Zoey's room.

"Man, I do feel better. It's crazy how much better a shower can make you feel." Carl replied.

"Especially when you get escorted to and from by a pretty girl huh?" Carl Sr. smirked while ducking his wife's swat.

"Oh, Carl you hush." Shirley smiled at her son while swatting at her husband for his comment.

"Yeah, yeah, yeah. Whatever, Dad. How's Zoey? Any change?" Carl rolled his eyes and walked over to Zoey's side.

"Still holding in there. Hopefully we will hear something soon. We are all ready to see those beautiful blue eyes again." Shirley stood and walked over beside Carl and looked down and Zoey's face.

At eleven thirty there was a soft knock on the door, it was Anna. "Carl, can I talk to you for a minute?" She nodded out towards the hallway.

"Um sure." Carl stood and walked out of the door. "Is it your lunchtime already?"

"No, not quite. Carl... We thought we had a heart for Zoey. Turned out it wasn't a good enough match, so the doctors decided to send it to a different hospital for another patient."

"What? How do they know that wasn't the right heart, you mean they gave up what could have been Zoey's heart?" Carl was getting very upset.

"Carl, I didn't want to tell you, but I just felt like you should know. They ran the blood types, and it just wasn't a good enough match. They were worried Zoey would reject the heart and that would put her in worse condition and move her down on the list for a transplant. Please, Carl, I'm sorry I didn't want to tell you, but I just feel like you need to know *everything* that is going on. I hope you aren't upset with me." Anna felt terrible telling him that they had to continue to wait.

"No, I'm not upset with you Anna. I just... I want my baby girl back. I know y'all are doing everything you can for Zoey, and I appreciate it. I really do." Carl's countenance changed as he realized he was getting angry with the wrong person.

"I've got another thirty minutes before lunch. Do you still feel up to having lunch in the cafeteria?" Anna asked.

"Of course, I'll meet you down there," Carl replied as the two went their separate ways. Before walking back into the room, Carl stopped at the door and took a deep breath to regain his composure. He only had seconds to decide whether or not to share this information with his parents. What good would come from them knowing that they were so close to having a heart for Zoey only to find out it was not a match? It was in that moment he decided not to say anything. There was no need in upsetting his parents any more than they already were.

"Is everything okay?" Shirley asked as she stood up and turned to Carl.

"Oh yeah, she was just asking me if I still felt up to having lunch. Do you guys mind sitting with Zoey while I go down and have lunch? I'll bring you guys something back up with me," Carl replied.

"Of course, we aren't going anywhere." Shirley replied.

Carl Sr. had dozed off in a chair in the corner, hearing there was food coming he woke up and said, "I'll take a cheeseburger with extra bacon and some fries."

"Yeah right, with your cholesterol, you'll have a salad with *no* bacon," Shirley snapped at him.

"Whatever, I'm dealing with a lot. I need *real* food not rabbit food. Boy, if you bring me a salad I'll whoop you." Carl Sr. laughed.

"Okay Dad, I'll bring you a burger as long as you keep Mom from getting me." Carl laughed as he dodged his mother's swats at the two of them. Carl turned and left the room and headed for the stairs. He knew he had thirty minutes before Anna would be down for lunch, but he really needed to take a walk to clear his head.

He decided to take a different route to the cafeteria, this time he walked past the hospital gift shop. As he passed by the window, something caught his eye and made him stop and turn around. There in the window of the gift shop was this delicate, little, white angel. It didn't seem like anything particularly strange or special, but something about it caught his eye and made him think of Anna. He didn't know why, but he just felt he had to buy it for her. While purchasing the angel, he also saw a small teddy bear dressed in an angel costume that he knew Zoey would love so he purchased it as well.

Walking towards the cafeteria, Carl suddenly had this nervous energy come over him that he hadn't felt in many years. It was the same nervous energy he felt the night he went on his first date with Clair. Even though this was only a lunch with a friend, for some reason it felt like a date. Could it be that he really did have feelings for Anna the way he had for Clair? Did she feel the same way about him? His mind raced as he walked towards the cafeteria. He was so lost in thought he almost walked into the wall past the cafeteria doors.

"Carl, are you okay?" Anna asked. She saw him nearly walk into the wall and was concerned maybe the exhaustion was beginning to take its toll on him.

"Oh yeah, sorry. I got so lost in my mind I wasn't even paying attention to where I was going." Carl chuckled and played it off.

"Oh man, I thought I was the only one that did that. I walked into a parked car one time because I was just so lost in thought. At least no one saw you, there was a street full of people laughing at me," Anna laughed.

"Well, it is bad enough that you saw me." Carl's face was red from embarrassment. "Ready for lunch? I promise I won't walk into any more walls, at least until after lunch," Carl laughed.

"Yes, I'm starving. That biscuit your mother gave me wore off a long time ago. Shall we?" Anna stepped towards the door.

Carl stepped up and said, "No, please, let me get the door. After you." When the two walked in the door, Carl immediately spotted Frank who smiled and winked at him when he saw Anna walk in with Carl. "So, what's actually good here?" Carl asked Anna.

"Well, I usually get the salad bar, but I hear the burgers are pretty good. Oh, and the muffins of course," Anna laughed and winked at Frank. Walking over to the salad bar Anna and Carl both began making themselves salads.

Frank walked over, "Hey you two. How's it going today? Long time no see Anna, how you been?"

"Hey Frank-O! I've been great! How have you been?" Anna walked around and hugged Frank.

"Been good, you never come down and see me anymore. You forget to bring your lunch today?" Frank asked with a smirk.

"Nah, I just decided I would rather eat something different today. A girl can't live on potpies alone," Anna smiled.

"Hey Carl! How's Zoey doing? Any news yet?" Frank turned to Carl who was somewhat fumbling through making his salad.

"She's still the same, no news yet. Hey, can I ask you a strange question?" Carl replied.

"Of course man, what's up?" Frank stepped over closer to him.

"What is this?" Carl pointed at pickled beets and laughed.

"Ha, ha, those are pickled beets. Yes, I know they are weird, but some people really like them. Me? My salad ends up as two pieces of lettuce, a pile of cheese, and bacon," Frank laughed.

"Now that's my kind of salad. Thanks Frank!" Carl finished piling his salad with croutons and bacon. He stepped to the side to wait for Anna to finish adding all of the vegetables to her salad. Once finished, the two walked and got their drinks and then to the cash register. "I've got both of these," Carl motioned to Anna's tray and handed the cashier his credit card.

"Oh no Carl you don't have to do that," Anna replied.

"It is absolutely my pleasure. I've got them both, ma'am." As he scooted Anna's tray over towards his. After paying for their food, Carl and Anna found a seat in a quiet corner away from everyone else.

As soon as they sat down, Anna reached for Carl's hands to pray over their food. After a few seconds he heard her say, "In Jesus's name, Amen." She lifted her head and smiled at him. The two continued to hold hands for just a little while longer after the prayer. Carl didn't want to let her hands go but felt awkward and didn't want to show her just how nervous he really was, so he let go first.

"Oh, Anna, I have something for you. It's not much but I thought of you when I saw it and I just had to get it for you." Carl was reaching into the bag from the gift shop.

"Carl you really didn't need to get me anything. It's enough that your mother gave me breakfast and now you've bought me lunch. You've done too much already, really," Anna replied as she reached out and touched his arm.

"Well, I guess if you don't like it you can take it back. I just saw it and thought of you and had to get it." Carl pulled out the angel and sat it on the table in front of Anna.

Anna reached down, picked it up and brought it closer to her face so she could see it better. "Oh, Carl, it is beautiful! I absolutely love it! Did Frank tell you I collected angels?" Anna lowered it and looked at Carl and then over at Frank.

"Actually, no he didn't. I was on a walk and saw it and it just made me think of you. I don't know if it was the blue eyes or if it was the fact that you have been an angel to me and Zoey." Carl was blushing with nervous energy.

"Well, I love it. Thank you so much," Anna smiled. She could tell he was nervous, and she was nervous herself. She was doing her best to hide her nervous energy but felt like she was talking ninety miles an hour. She kept telling herself to calm down, that he's just a friend, but she definitely felt more than just friendship for him. She felt something she hadn't felt since she lost her husband and daughter three years ago. She was worried she was falling for him and that it might seem inappropriate considering she was his daughter's nurse. Nonetheless, she couldn't help but feel like there was a connection between the two of them.

"Anna, can I ask you something? You can absolutely tell me no and it won't hurt my feelings at all I promise," Carl asked.

"Of course, Carl, you can ask me anything." Anna was slightly worried he could tell what she was thinking.

"Do you think you would be interested in going to dinner with me? Either tonight or maybe tomorrow?" Carl looked down at the table to try to hide his nervous expression.

"You want to go out to dinner? Like, a date?" Anna asked while trying to hold in her excitement.

"Well, yes, I guess that's what I mean. I just...I want to take you somewhere other than the cafeteria. Anywhere you want to go, really. I'll even go home and take a real shower and shave. I'll come pick you up from your house, or if you don't want me to know where you live, I can meet you there or here. Whatever you want, really."

"Carl, I would love that. Tonight or tomorrow either one

works for me. I get off at seven both days, so it would have to be a late dinner if that's okay with you? I mean I might be able to see if Mallory will cover me to leave a little early if you can't wait that late." Anna was smiling ear to ear.

"Oh no, that is perfectly fine. That is actually perfect, that way my parents can go eat dinner and then come back and sit with Zoey." Carl was leaping for joy inside that Anna had accepted his offer.

"Okay, well I'll text you my address. I get off at seven and it takes me about thirty minutes to get home. I can be ready to go by eight. Does that sound okay?" Anna asked.

"Yes of course. I'll pick you up at eight. Do you know where you would want to go? I don't really know the Downtown area all that well. We can go anywhere you want, anywhere." Carl was having a hard time keeping back his excitement.

"Tonight or tomorrow?" Anna asked.

"Hell, we can go out to dinner both nights if you want," Carl laughed.

"Well how about we start with tonight and we'll see where it goes from there?" Anna smiled. "Unfortunately, for now I have to go back to work. I only get thirty minutes for lunch. I will see you on the floor and for sure tonight." Anna smiled and stood up. "Oh and thank you so much for my angel. I love it."

As Anna walked away Carl sat in his chair smiling from ear to ear like a love-struck fool. After a few minutes, Frank walked over. "Hey Carl, you okay over here? You've just been sitting here for a little while man."

"I asked Anna on a date, and she said yes!" Carl was so excited to tell Frank. "Oh wait, I haven't been on a first date in over ten years. I have no idea what I'm doing. Frank, you've got to help me man. Do I take her flowers? What kind of flowers? Do I get her another gift? What do I wear?" Carl was talking extremely fast, not letting Frank have a chance to answer even the first question.

"Whoa, man, slow down. Take a breath." Frank sat down next to Carl and put his hand on his shoulder. "Just breathe man, breathe." Carl stopped talking and took a deep breath. "Now, isn't that better?" Carl nodded as Frank continued. "Okay, let's start from the beginning. Do you know where you are taking her yet?" Carl shook his head no. "Okay, then just wear some nice pants and a button down. Flowers. I know she likes pink roses. Maybe stop on your way to her house and get her a couple pink roses. Don't get the ones from the gift shop, they look terrible. You still with me?" Carl nodded his head as he took out his phone and started taking notes. "What are you doing, man?"

"I'm taking notes. I'm telling you, I feel lost." Carl showed Frank his phone where he was putting the information Frank was giving him into a note.

Laughing, Frank responded, "Man, you don't need to take notes! You need to just be yourself. Anna likes you man, can't you see that? She wouldn't have come down here for lunch or accepted your dinner invitation if she didn't. She never comes down here for lunch and I've never heard of her going anywhere but home after work."

"Wait, really?" Carl was starting to feel less nervous.

"Yes really. Just calm down and be yourself. Oh, and don't forget the pink roses. Her husband always sent her white roses, and she never had the heart to tell him pink were her favorite."

Frank smiled and stood up from the table. "For the love of God, make sure you comb your hair before you go pick her up." Frank laughed and pointed at Carl's disheveled hair.

As Frank walked away, Carl took his fingers and tried to smooth down his hair. He hadn't even thought to look in a mirror before coming down to lunch. "Thanks, Frank!" Carl called out to Frank across the cafeteria as Carl cleared away his and Anna's trash from their lunch table. Leaving the cafeteria, Carl felt like he was floating, like his feet never touched the ground the whole way back to Zoey's room. When he walked into Zoey's room, reality came crashing back in on him. He began to feel guilty for being happy while his baby girl lay in the bed connected to machines keeping her alive.

"Hey sweetheart, how was lunch? What's in the bag?" Shirley turned and asked.

"Oh, I found the cutest little bear in the gift shop. I just had to get it for Sissy. She will love it. Look, it's in a little angel costume. Isn't it adorable?" Carl pulled the teddy bear out of the bag and showed it to his mother.

"Aw, how cute! Zoey is going to love it. Her Frankie Bear will have a new friend." Shirley smiled.

"Hey, do you guys think you would mind coming back later this evening and sitting with Zoey? I um, well... I asked Anna to go to dinner tonight. If you don't feel up to it, I understand and can cancel with Anna," Carl asked

"Of course, we will! If that girl accepted your offer, you better not cancel on her son. You don't get too many opportunities to go out with a beautiful woman like that, so you better not cancel," Carl Sr. insisted.

Rolling her eyes at her husband, Shirley responded to Carl, "Of course, sweetheart. We are going to go to your house for a little while and get something to eat. What time do you need us back here so you can go get cleaned up for your dinner?"

"Um, well she gets off at seven and I desperately need to shave and get a real shower. Six thirty sound okay for you guys?" Carl asked as he walked over to Zoey's bed.

"Will that give you enough time? We can be back earlier if you need us to," Shirley replied as she started to gather her things so they could leave.

"I think six thirty will give me time. I don't have to pick her up until eight," Carl responded.

"Okay, see you at six thirty then. I'll lay you some clothes out," Shirley leaned over and kissed Zoey on her forehead and Carl on his cheek. Shirley and Carl Sr. left the room headed to Carl's house. Carl shook his head rolling his eyes at his mother.

Carl leaned over and kissed Zoey on her forehead. "Sissy, Daddy's here. I got Freddie Bear a new friend. She has an angel costume on. It looks like the one you wore last year at Halloween." He placed the new bear under her left arm. Freddie bear was tucked in under her right arm. Leaning down close to her again he decided to talk to her about his date with Anna. "Sissy, I hope it is okay with you, but I am going to take Anna to dinner, like on a date. I know you like her, and I hope you know that no one will ever replace your mommy. I really like her, and I think she likes me too. I know she really likes you. I wish you could wake up so I could ask you if it is okay that I take Anna on a date." Sitting up slightly he said to himself aloud, "Wow, how many grown men ask their daughter's permission to go on a date."

Just then there was a soft knock on the door, it was Anna. "Carl?"

"Yes ma'am," Carl replied.

"Um, you were leaned against the intercom," Anna said with an embarrassed look on her face.

Carl turned red with embarrassment immediately. "Oh my God, please tell me you couldn't hear everything I just said to Zoey?"

Anna walked over and kissed him on his forehead. "I did, and I do like you. And I am smitten with Zoey." She walked over to the wall, pushed the button to clear the call light, and checked Zoey's monitors. "You know she can hear you right?"

"I have heard people in a coma can hear what people say. I just...I don't know what to say. I don't know if I should tell her what's going on. I just don't know." Carl looked down at his beautiful baby's face and fought back tears.

"Carl, just talk to her. She's still your Zoey, or what did you call her? Sissy?" Anna walked back over and stood behind him with her hand on his shoulder.

Smiling, Carl replied, "Yeah, that's my Sissy. I've called her that since the first time I saw her the day she was born. My sweet Sissy. The first time I saw her, I told her she would always be my sweet Sissy and that I would love and protect her no matter what. I feel like I let her down. Like I didn't do my job or she wouldn't be in this bed right now."

Anna stepped closer and turned Carl's face towards her, "Carl, you haven't let her down. There's nothing you could have done differently to prevent what happened. It is one of those things that just happens. You are here for her now, loving her, and protecting her. Fighting for her. There is nothing more a father could do for his daughter than all you've done for her. She is beyond blessed to have you as her daddy." Anna looks into Carl's eyes and the two smile.

Carl places his hand on Anna's hand on his face, smiles and says, "Thank you. That honestly means more than you will ever know."

The two stand there staring into each other's eyes for what seems like an eternity until Anna's phone buzzes. "I'm so sorry I've got another patient I have to go check on. Eight o'clock, right?" Anna starts walking to the door.

"Oh yeah but you haven't sent me your address yet. I don't know where to pick you up or where we are going." Carl turned towards the door.

"I'll text you my address now." Anna smiled and walked away typing into her phone. A few minutes later Carl received a text from Anna with her address and a note; *Looking forward to dinner. XOXO ~Anna.* Carl smiled as he looked down at his phone.

He read the text aloud to Zoey and said, "You hear that, Sissy? She's looking forward to dinner. Even put in 'hugs and kisses.'" As he sat beside Zoey with only the sound of the machines in the room, he decided he would pull up some of her favorite sing-along songs on his phone and play them. If she really could hear what was going on in the room, he knew hearing her favorite songs would make her happy.

At six fifteen, Carl's parents walked into Zoey's room. Carl was leaned back in the chair asleep while children's songs played on his phone. Shirley looked at her husband and whispered, "I honestly hate to wake him up. Maybe we should just let him sleep?"

"Um, no. He is not going to stand that girl up. Carl! Wake up son," Carl Sr. replied speaking loud enough to wake Carl up.

"I'm up! What happened?" Carl, startled, jumped up. "Is Zoey okay, what happened? What time is it? Am I late?"

"No, no you aren't late. Everything is fine. Zoey is the same. It is six fifteen. You still have plenty of time." Shirley tried to reassure Carl while rolling her eyes at Carl Sr. for being so abrupt. "Go ahead and go though, traffic was pretty heavy on the way here."

Carl searched for his keys and realized his car was not there. He had ridden in a police car there and hadn't left the hospital. "Um, dad? I feel like I'm sixteen again. Can I borrow your car for my date?" The two of them laughed.

"Sure son, do you need some money too?" Carl Sr. laughed and handed Carl the car keys.

"Well since you're offering..." Carl laughed and put his hand out like he wanted some money. Carl Sr. laughed and smacked his hand. "Thanks again for hanging with Zoey. I really appreciate it. I'll be back as quickly as I can." Carl turned to go.

"Son don't rush. Take your time and enjoy your date," Carl Sr. winked at his son.

"Whatever dad, I'll see you guys in just a little while." Carl rolled his eyes and walked out of the room. Once he got to the parking garage, he realized he forgot to ask his parents where they parked and he had no reception on his phone. He had no choice but to walk around the parking lot hitting the alarm button on his parents' car until he found it. By the time he found the car he was in a panic feeling like he would be late to pick Anna up. He rushed home and took a shower making sure he shaved and combed his hair like Frank said. When he walked into his bedroom his mother had laid out some clothes. In an effort to save time, he just went with what she laid out and got dressed as quickly as possible.

Carl rushed out to the car only to find he had grabbed the wrong car keys and had the keys to his own car. He quickly swapped vehicles and put the address into his GPS. On the way to her house, he noticed a grocery store and remembered he needed to get flowers. Running into the door he found the first employee he saw and asked where the Floral Department was. Upon arriving at the Floral Department, he stood there trying to remember what color roses Frank had told him Anna liked. "Red? White? Pink? Orange? Why the hell are there so many freaking colors of roses?"

An employee overhears Carl talking to himself and walks over. "Can I help you with something, sir?"

Turning around with a clear look of panic on his face Carl replies, "Yes, I need help. I'm running late for a first date, and I really want to take her some flowers but I can't remember what color my friend said she likes. It's either white or pink but I honestly can't remember, and I don't have his number to call. I *really* want to impress this girl. What would you do?"

"Well, if it is either white or pink, why don't you go with those over there?" The employee pointed to a bouquet of roses in the back of the case that were white with only the tips of them pink. "Those are white *and* pink. Best of both worlds. That's what I would do, to be honest."

Carl nodded in agreement while grabbing the bouquet out of the case. "Thank you! You are a lifesaver!"

"Here, I can even ring you up right here so you don't have to wait in line. Do you want a card to go with them?" The employee stepped over behind the counter and signed into the cash register.

"No, I don't think so. Thank you again so much. You just have no idea how nervous I am" Carl replied as he dug his wallet out of his pants pocket.

"You know it is late, those were going bad anyway. Let me see if I can't even get you a discount on those," the employee said as he started punching in numbers on the register. "Yep here you go; half off. That should help set the tone for your date. Hope it goes well!"

"Oh my, thank you so much. Man, you just don't know how much I appreciate that!" Carl swiped his card and took the roses.

"Good luck!" The employee shouted as Carl ran out of the door.

Back on the road Carl looked at the clock in his car and realized his watch was fifteen minutes fast. It wasn't seven fifty-five, it was only seven forty. He wasn't running late at all. In fact, he was going to be ten minutes early. Maybe he did have a guardian angel all along.

Starting Over

Carl arrived a few minutes before eight. When he pulled into the driveway, a wave of nervous energy rushed over him like it did the first time he saw Clair sitting across from him in that restaurant. Before he got out of the car to walk up to the door, Carl closed his eyes and said, "Clair, baby, I love you. I will always love you. If you sent Anna to me, please, let this go well."

Carl slowly exited his car and walked up the stone path to Anna's door. Standing there in front of a big red door with a huge fall wreath, Carl took a deep breath and summoned up the nerve to reach out and knock. Just as his hand touched the door, the door opened and Anna was standing there smiling. "I wondered if you were ever going to actually get out of your car." Anna laughed.

"Wait, how did you know I was here?" Carl was confused.

"I have a camera on my doorbell that lets me know when there is motion in my driveway. I saw you pull in. Are those for me?" Anna pointed at the roses.

"Oh yeah, sorry. Here these are for you." Carl handed her the roses.

"They are beautiful. I've never seen any that were half pink and half white! Pink is my favorite, but I think I may like these even more. Thank you, Carl. Here, come on in and have a seat. Would you like something to drink? I need a couple more minutes to finish getting ready, I'm sorry. I left work a little late." Anna opened the door and motioned for Carl to come in.

"Oh, no, I'm fine, thanks. Take your time. I did get here a little early. I was afraid I was going to be late." Carl walked in and sat down on the couch.

Anna disappeared into the hallway and came back out a few minutes later. "Sorry about that; I'm all ready. You ready to go?"

"Sure, you look beautiful." Carl smiled as he stood up.

"Thanks! I thought we could go to this little local place. They stay open late and have the best food. Sound okay with you?" Anna smiled.

"I'm game for whatever you want. Just tell me how to get there." They walked out of the door and Carl rushed over to Anna's side of the car to open the door for her.

"Aw, thank you. It's been a long time since a man opened a car door for me." Anna smiled.

"So, where we going?" Carl asked as he got into the car.

"You are going to go out of the neighborhood and take a left. It is a little steakhouse my husband and I found by accident years and years ago. Wait, that doesn't bother you, does it? If it does, we can go somewhere else," Anna realized after she mentioned her husband that it might make Carl uncomfortable.

"Oh, no, not at all. I hope it doesn't bother you if I mention

Clair sometimes. She was such a big part of my life that I know it will happen at some point." Carl stopped at the end of the street waiting for directions from Anna.

"Oh, honey no. That isn't going to bother me at all. In fact, it would almost bother me if you didn't mention her. Oh, sorry, you are waiting for me, right? Take a left here and get in the right lane." Anna felt relieved that she didn't upset him. As they drove down the road, Carl leaned slightly to his right side resting his hand just beside Anna's left hand. Slowly Anna scooted her hand closer to Carl's until they were holding hands. When Anna reached over and held his hand, Carl thought his heart would jump right out of his chest.

"Just up here on the other side of that brick building there is a little alley. You are going to take a right there." Anna pointed with her right hand, still holding Carl's hand with her other hand.

"That dark alley right there? Are you taking me to get robbed?" Carl joked.

"I know it looks shady, but I promise it is a great place. Just a little hole in the wall, but they have the best steaks you will ever put in your mouth. I promise," Anna laughed.

"I trust you. Turn here?" Carl asked.

"Yep, and you can park right down there to the left." Anna pointed to a small parking lot at the end of the alley. Carl parked the car and quickly got out and ran around the car to open Anna's door. "Thank you, Carl."

Anna stepped out of the car and the two walked in to the small restaurant. As they walked into the restaurant the hostess immediately recognized Anna. "Hey Anna, how have you been? Your usual table?"

Anna smiled and looked over at Carl, "Yeah, I come in here a lot." Turning to the hostess, "My usual table will do. I do have company tonight though. This is my friend, Carl." Anna steps aside to introduce Carl.

"Hi Carl! Welcome! Please, follow me." The hostess turned and led the two to a table in the back corner. "Here you go. Alexis will be over in a minute to get your order. Can I go ahead and get your drink orders for you?"

"They have the best lemonade. I don't know what they do to it, but it is phenomenal." Anna looked at Carl and then back at the hostess.

"Okay that sounds good to me," Carl replied.

A few minutes later their waitress Alexis emerged from the kitchen with their lemonades. "Hey Anna. I see you brought a friend, finally." The two laughed. "You going with the Chef's special tonight or did you want to actually look at the menu?"

"Um, well... I am good with the Chef's Choice, but I don't know if Carl would be up for that. He may need a menu." Anna looked at Carl and explained, "Chef Jeremy likes to send out new foods for the regulars. Nothing he sends is ever on the menu but is *always* worth trusting him to choose."

"Sounds good to me. I'll go with the Chef's choice. Anna hasn't steered me wrong yet." Carl smiles at the waitress and then at Anna.

The two talk for what feels like only minutes while enjoying the appetizers, salads and steaks the chef sent out to the table. Before they knew it, four hours had passed and the restaurant staff were cleaning up to close. "Wow, it has been a long time since I shut down a place," Carl laughed. Carl paid the check and as they were walking out the chef had walked out of the kitchen. Carl stopped and thanked him for a wonderful meal.

Once in the car, Anna reached over and held Carl's hand again as the drove back to her house. The two continued to make small talk on the ride home. Once back to Anna's house, Carl again rushed around the car to open Anna's door. "I'm really going to have to get used to that. I'm really not used to someone opening my door for me. Thank you, Carl."

At the door, Anna reached in her purse and took her keys out of her purse. Rather than immediately unlocking the door she turned to him and said, "I had a really good time tonight, Carl. This has been the best night I've had in as long as I can remember."

After a few minutes of standing at her door talking, Anna took a slight step back. "Look Carl, I've got to tell you something. I really want to invite you in but..."

"It's okay, Anna. We have plenty of time for that," Carl replied, cutting her off.

"No Carl, really, let me finish. I want to invite you in but here's the thing. This is really awkward. It's just that... Well, I've only ever been with one man. I don't want you to think I'm not interested in you or don't have feelings for you. It's just that I don't want to rush into anything." Anna struggled to get the words out afraid she would scare Carl away.

"Anna, honestly, I'm relieved to hear you say that. I've never been with anyone other than Clair. I was truly scared that I am not ready to take that step and that you would think I wasn't interested in you," Carl replied with a sigh of relief.

"I'm so glad we are both on the same page. It has been so long since I was in any kind of relationship, I honestly don't even know what I am supposed to say or do," Anna replied with a smile.

Carl leaned in and kissed her on the cheek. "How about we leave it at that for tonight? Thank you for going to dinner. I really enjoyed it. Do you work tomorrow?" Carl asked.

"I do, I have to be in at seven in the morning. I better go in and get some sleep or I am going to be worthless tomorrow. I will see you in the morning. Goodnight Carl." Anna leaned over and kissed him on the cheek.

"Sweet dreams Anna." Carl smiled and waited for Anna to get inside before turning and walking to his car. Carl pulled out of Anna's driveway and started down the street. Once he got to the stop sign, he sat there for a little longer and took a few deep breaths. He felt relieved that Anna felt the same way but conflicted at the same time because he knew he had feelings for Anna that he hadn't felt for anyone other than Clair. He didn't want anyone, including Zoey to think he was trying to replace Clair.

While Carl sat in his car at the stop sign, Anna stood with her back to her door. She too felt a sense of relief that Carl was okay not rushing into things, but also knew she had stronger feelings for Carl than she had ever had for anyone other than her husband. She honestly didn't even know how to handle her feelings knowing what he was going through with his daughter and the fact that his daughter was one of her patients. She couldn't stay up worrying about that, she did have to be at work early in the morning, so she decided to call it a night and go to bed.

Carl returned to the hospital. When he walked into Zoey's room, only his mother was still awake. She sat at the side of Zoey's bed, reading Zoey her favorite bedtime stories while Carl Sr. slept in the other chair. "Hey how's our girl?" Carl whispered as he leaned down and kissed his mother on the cheek.

"Oh, hey sweetie. She's doing good. We were just reading some bedtime stories. These were your favorite ones when you were little. I found them when I was cleaning up at the house earlier." Shirley lifted a stack of books and showed Carl. "So how was the date?"

"Oh Mom, it was great. I never thought I would feel this way about anyone after Clair, until I met Anna. She is so kind, and loving, and oh Mom, she is so much like Clair. She's just so much fun to be around. Thank you for sitting with Zoey for us to go to dinner." Carl sat down at the foot of Zoey's bed.

"I'm so glad Carl. We have really been praying for God to send you and Zoey someone. Are you going to go out with her again? Soon I hope?" Shirley asked.

"I thought about asking her out tomorrow if you guys don't mind hanging out with Zoey again. That is, if she wants to go out again and if nothing changes with Zoey." Carl reached down and rubbed Zoey's feet.

"Oh, I'm sure she will say yes. I think she really likes you, Carl." Shirley stood and walked over to him. "Of course, we will sit with our baby girl any time."

"Mom there's something else. She lost her husband and daughter three years ago, so she's in a weird place right now too.

I don't want to rush her or push her away. But I...Mom, I think I'm falling in love with her." Carl looked up to his mother for support.

"Carl sweetie, things will happen when they happen. She knows your history and you knowing her history will make it easier for you two to talk and empathize with each other. You will know when things are moving too fast, you both will. Just take your time and let things happen." Shirley hugged Carl and walked over to wake her snoring husband. "Carl honey it is time to wake up. Come on let's go sleep in a real bed babe."

Slightly startled, Carl Sr. opened his eyes and sat up. "Oh, hey Carl, how did it go? You get any?" Carl Sr. laughed

"Really dad?" Carl rolled his eyes as Shirley popped Carl Sr. in the back of the head, telling him not to be disgusting.

"Woman quit hitting me. I'm just trying to ask my son how his date went," Carl Sr. chuckled.

"Yeah, yeah. Come on you dirty old man let's go get some sleep. Carl, we will be back in the morning. Love you son. Love you Zoey Grace! We will be back to see you in the morning." Shirley grabbed her husband by the arm and walked out of the room with him.

"Thank you, guys, again. See you in the morning!" Carl laughed and waived to his parents as they walked out of the room. Sometime during the evening while Carl was gone, Mallory replaced the arm chair in the room with a reclining chair. Happily, Carl stretched out in the recliner and drifted off to sleep.

Early the next morning Carl was woken by Anna. "Good morning sunshine," Anna smiled as she handed Carl a cup of coffee and a cup of watermelon cubes. "I figured you might need a 'wake me up' this morning and maybe a little breakfast. The doctors are just down the hall doing their rounds. They should be in here in just a little bit."

"Oh, thank you, I definitely need some coffee. Someone kept me out all night on the town." Carl laughed as he took a sip of the coffee. "So has there been any change with Zoey? Any news on a heart?" Carl asked.

"Nothing that I have heard of. They will tell you more when they come in." Anna checked the monitors and wrote down the readings. "I'll be back in after they leave," Anna turned to go.

Carl wondered to himself if he had upset Anna since she really didn't say anything about their dinner the night before. Before he could walk out of the room to go talk to her, the two doctors along with several medical students walked into the room. Carl stood at the back while they talked amongst themselves using jargon he really didn't understand. Once they finished, the students left the room and the two doctors turned to talk to Carl. "Good morning, Mr. Murphy," Dr. Conrad said as he turned to Carl.

"Good morning. Has there been any change? Have you heard anything about a heart for her or how long it could take?" Carl asked.

"The good news is Zoey is stable and seems to be holding on just fine. Unfortunately, we have no way of knowing when we will get a heart for her. I know it isn't really what you want to hear, but this could take a while. I've had patients wait weeks, even months for a heart." Dr. Conrad looked at Zoey's chart and then turned to Dr. Kate. "Anything to add?"

Dr. Kate shook her and simply said, "Her respiratory seems to be tolerating the life support well. We are just in a holding pattern."

"So, you're telling me that you have no news and that we just have to sit here and wait? That's it? Seriously? *That* is it?" Carl is clearly getting frustrated.

"Mr. Murphy, you need to know that this is a marathon, not a sprint. Zoey could be here for a very long time. You may need to consider going home and sleeping in your bed. I don't know what your work situation is, but you may need to even consider going to work. If anything changes, we will let you know." Dr. Conrad was trying to be empathetic, but with Carl's emotions running understandably high he felt like the doctors were both being dismissive.

"Really? Is that what you suggest? Leaving my daughter here alone and going home? Really?" Carl went from being frustrated to being angry. "Thanks, maybe work a little harder on finding my daughter a heart and leave the parenting to me."

Sensing his anger, the two doctors apologized that they didn't have more answers and left the room. Carl sat back down beside Zoey and picked up his phone. He knew he needed to call his work since he hadn't updated them in a couple days. He had vacation, but not enough to cover months of waiting. He let his manager know what was going on with Zoey and what the doctors had just told him. Immediately his manager offered him the opportunity to take as much time as he needed, and when he was ready, he could work remotely from the hospital. He even offered to bring Carl his laptop so he didn't have to drive to work. Relieved, Carl thanked him and told him he would let him know when he was up to working.

Shortly after Carl hung up the phone, there was that familiar soft knock on the door. Before the door ever opened, Carl knew it was Anna. Seeing her face immediately softened Carl's anger. "Hey Carl, I saw the doctors left. I just read her file. Are you okay?" Anna walked over and pulled a stool up beside Carl's chair.

"Anna, I just don't know what to do. They think I can just leave and go sleep at home and leave her here alone. I just want my baby girl back." Carl turned towards Anna but kept his head down to hide the tears streaming down his face.

"Carl, you know she won't ever be alone." Anna reached over and touched Carl's face slightly lifting his chin so he is looking at her. "Though I completely understand. I would feel the same way if it were my baby girl laying in that bed. You are going to have to take care of yourself if you are going to be strong for Zoey. That means you are going to need to get some real sleep. Sleep you can't get in that recliner or sitting in a chair."

Knowing Anna was right, Carl took a deep breath and said, "I know, but how can I go home and sleep knowing she is laying in a hospital bed?"

"Would it make you feel better if you knew someone was here with her? Maybe your parents can take turns with you staying with her? I'd even be willing to stay with her on my days off if that would help you." Anna was trying anything she could think of to help Carl.

"I really appreciate that Anna, but I can't ask you to do that. You already do so much for her and take care of her all day. I know I have to take care of myself. This is the hardest thing I've ever been through. I don't know how I'm going to make it through this. I need her to be okay. I need her to be better." Carl tried to cover his face in his hands, but Anna leaned forward and hugged him. As he rested his head on her shoulder crying, she did her best to comfort him.

"Carl I am here for you. I will be here whatever you need." Anna was trying her best to fight back tears. Seeing Carl in so much pain broke her heart and brought back all of the memories of losing her baby girl.

Around eight thirty, Carl's parents walked into the room. Seeing Carl crying on Anna's shoulder, Shirley was startled and started running towards the bed. "Carl, what's wrong? Carl what happened?"

"Mom, the doctors came in this morning. They said it could be months before she gets a heart. *months*, Mom." Carl turned and looked at his mother.

"Carl we just have to have faith that God is going to send her the right heart. This is not something we want to rush. We have to wait for the perfect heart for our perfect baby girl." Shirley leaned down and hugged her son.

Anna stood up and quietly started walking towards the door. "Wait, Anna. If we sit with Zoey tonight, do you think you can get Carl out of this room again tonight? He definitely needs to get out of here again even if it is just for dinner," Carl Sr. whispered to Anna hoping Carl didn't hear him. Anna smiled and nodded winking as she walked out of the door.

"Son, we will do everything we can to help relieve you. One of us can stay here with her to give you the opportunity to go home and sleep in a real bed. Sweetheart Zoey needs you. She needs you to take care of you so you can be there when she does get her heart." Shirley sat down on the stool next to Carl. "Have you called your work and talked to them yet?"

"Yeah, I called and talked to Joe earlier. He said I could take as long as I needed and when I was up to it, he would bring me my laptop so I could work remotely." Carl knew his mother and Anna were right, but he was still struggling with the idea of leaving Zoey overnight. She had never even spent a night away from home. He felt guilty for even leaving the hospital for dinner the night before. It hit him hard; how could he be happy and going on dates when his baby was laying in the bed lifeless?

"Carl, Zoey would not want you to sit here moping around all day and every night. You know we're right Carl." Carl Sr. walked over and put his hand on Carl's shoulder. "That baby is the happiest little girl on the planet, and you know she hates it when you get sad. We will be here with her when you aren't. Can you imagine how happy she would be to wake up to you being happy, and maybe even having a 'friend?' Plus, she loves Anna so..."

Carl looked up at his dad and smiled, "She is a happy little girl, and she does love Anna. I just don't know guys. Isn't it kind of wrong for me to be going on dates and being happy while my baby is lying here in this bed?"

"Not at all," Carl Sr. and Shirley said in sync.

"In fact, I'll stay the night with Zoey, and you and your father can go home. You can go to dinner and then go get some sleep. Just get him out of my hair." Shirley smiled and nudged Carl Sr. with her elbow and winked at him.

"No offense, Dad, but I think I'll see if Anna can go to dinner first." Carl smiled at his dad who smiled and winked back at him.

"Yeah, yeah, yeah. I see how you are. You'd rather have dinner with a pretty girl than hanging with your pops for the night. Honestly, if you don't ask her to dinner, I will." Carl Sr. laughed and Shirley rolled her eyes. The three sat in silence for a while listening to the machines beep when finally Carl Sr. spoke up, "Hey I am going to run down and get some lunch. You guys want anything?"

"Seriously? Carl we just ate. How are you hungry?" Shirley shook her head.

"Darlin', it is nearly one o'clock. We ate at seven thirty this morning. I'm starving. Besides, I'm grown. I'll eat when I want... if that's okay with you dear." Carl Sr. smiled and winked at his wife.

"Actually, Mom, if you don't mind sitting with Zoey I kind of need to take a walk and stretch my legs a little. I'll walk down with you, Dad." Carl stood up and started to walk towards the door with his father.

"Oh, I guess you are right. It is getting late. Of course, I will sit with Zoey. I guess bring me back a sandwich or something. Oh, and an unsweet tea. Thank you." Shirley smiled as they walked out of the room. Once alone, Shirley scooted closer to Zoey and brushed her hand through Zoey's soft blonde hair. "Baby girl, Grandma's right here. Everything is going to be okay. They are going to get you all better. When you get better, Grandpa made new flowerbeds just for me and you to plant whatever we want. I love you baby girl."

As Carl and his father walked down the hallway, they spotted Anna leaving another patient's room. "Hey, there's Anna. Here's your chance boy. Go ask her if she is busy for dinner tonight. Otherwise, you're stuck with me and I'm ordering pizza and hot wings." Carl Sr. motioned over towards Anna.

Carl looked at his dad and laughed, "Does *Mom* know you are having pizza and hot wings?"

"No, and what she doesn't know won't hurt her. Now get over there and ask that girl to dinner." Carl Sr. nudged Carl towards Anna and turned towards the elevators. "And make it quick, I'm hungry dammit."

Carl walked down the hall to where Anna was standing at a computer. "Hey Anna, you real busy?" For some reason he felt awkward asking her out, even though they had dinner the night before.

"Never too busy for you Carl," Anna smiled as she looked up from the computer. "What's up?"

"Well, I was wondering if you might be up for dinner again tonight? My mom is going to stay the night with Zoey." Carl started fidgeting with the button on the bottom of his shirt like a nervous teenager.

"Sure, that sounds great! I get off at seven again. Is that too late?" Anna closed the computer and the two of them started walking down the hall back towards the elevators where Carl Sr. was impatiently waiting for Carl.

"No, that is perfectly fine. Should I pick you up at eight again? Does that work for you?" Carl was starting to feel less nervous.

"Yes, and I promise I will actually be ready this time." Anna smiled and waved at Carl Sr.

"Okay good it's settled. You guys are having dinner and now I finally get to go get lunch. Hurry up before your mother changes her mind and decides to come with us. I *really* want that bacon cheeseburger I didn't get yesterday." Carl Sr. waives for Carl to get on the elevator and starts pushing buttons.

"I guess I better go. He's taking full advantage of being unsupervised in the cafeteria." Carl and Anna laughed as Carl got on the elevator and Anna returned to the nurses' station. Carl and his father ordered their food and found a seat in the cafeteria. Just as they got their food and started to eat, Shirley came walking in the door.

"How did I know you would be eating a greasy cheeseburger. Enjoy it now because when we get home you are going right back on your diet sir." Shirley pulled up a chair. While her husband had his hands full with his cheeseburger, she reached over and stole a few of his fries.

"Is everything with Zoey okay?" Carl was concerned that she was alone.

"Oh yeah, she is fine. Anna and another nurse were in the room changing the sheets and what not. Anna said they would be in there long enough I could come down and get something to eat." Shirley responded as she stole another fry from Carl's plate this time.

"Woman, if you want fries I'll go order you some fries. Here's your sandwich." Carl Sr. swatted towards her hand.

"Oh whatever, like either one of y'all *need* all those fries." She laughed as she took her sandwich and stole another one from

Carl Sr. just because she could. "Hey by the way Carl, did you get around to talking to Anna or did you decide to stay in with your dad tonight?"

"Oh yeah, I did. I am going to pick her up at eight again. Guys, I really feel guilty going out on dates when Zoey is laying in the hospital. I don't know if this is really the right time. Don't get me wrong I really like Anna, I mean I *really* like her but..."

Shirley cut him off, "Carl, did you think maybe you and Anna met for a reason? Maybe this *is* the right time? Don't over think it."

Carl sighed and took a bite of his burger. "I guess you are right."

"Of course I am. I'm your mother. I'm always right don't you know?" Shirley laughed.

"I took her flowers last night, should I stop and get flowers again tonight? She doesn't really eat candy or sweets, so I don't know if I should show up empty handed or what." Carl looked to his mother. Never in a million years did he think he would be sitting around a table in a hospital asking his mother for dating advice.

The three finished eating and returned upstairs to Zoey's room. At five thirty, Carl and his father left and headed home. Even though he knew Zoey wouldn't be alone, he still felt so guilty for leaving for the night. "Where are you taking Anna tonight?" Carl Sr. asked but Carl was so deep in thought he never even heard his father and didn't respond. "Hey, anybody home?" Carl Sr. snapped his fingers in front of Carl's face.

"Oh, yeah, sorry. What?" Carl shook his head and turned to his father.

"Boy, where are you at? You okay?"

"Yeah, sorry. I was just thinking that's all. Dad, do you really think it's a good idea for me to be going out and leaving Zoey at the hospital all night? I mean, what if something happens and they get her a heart or God forbid..." Carl's voice started to crack as he tried to keep his emotions in check.

"Don't even think like that. If they get her a heart, they will call you. Your mother will call me. Hell, Mallory will call Anna. We all have cell phones. There's nowhere in this town you can go that you can't get a phone call. Your mother will be right there with her. You need to get out of that room and sleep in a bed. Now, it doesn't have to be *your* bed per say," Carl Sr. smiled.

"Dad, seriously you've got to stop that. Anna and I have been on one date. It isn't even like that." Carl was turning red from embarrassment.

"Look, you are both adults. Plus, you have spent the last week together non-stop. That's all I'm saying'. I'll leave it alone but just in case..."

Carl interrupted him, "Dad, I get it. Just please *stop*, man." The two finished the ride home listening to the radio and not saying anything. After they arrived, Carl unlocked the door and turned to his father, "I'm going to grab a quick shower."

"Okay. I'm going to go run down and get my pizza and wings. You want me to bring you anything back? A beer to calm your nerves maybe?" Carl Sr. asked as he walked back to the car.

"Thanks Dad, but I haven't had a beer in so long it might not be a good idea for me to start tonight, especially since I'm going to pick her up in just a little while." Carl smiled and chuckled.

"Okay, well if your mother asks, the beer, pizza, and wings

were yours." Carl Sr. called out as he got in the car and left the driveway.

Carl went upstairs and started his shower. After the water warmed up, he stood there letting the water run over his head until the hot water was nearly gone. As he realized the water was getting cold, he quickly washed up and got out of the shower before it got too cold. After grabbing his towel, he picked up the phone and saw that he had a missed call from Anna. "Crap!" Carl rushed to dry off his face so he could call her. In his rush, he accidentally hit the video call button instead of the audio call.

"Um hello?" Anna was slightly confused when she answered the video and could only see the side of Carl's face.

Thinking he had hit the speaker phone button Carl pulled the phone away from his face and quickly noticed Anna could see him, standing in his bathroom, with only a towel on. "Oh my God I did not mean to video call you Anna. I am so sorry."

While Carl fumbled to disable the video call and return the call to audio only, Anna began to laugh. "Nice unicorn towel Carl."

"Oh my God I am so embarrassed. I am so sorry I did *not* know I was on video. Naturally I pick up one of Zoey's beach towels and that's when I video call you. I can't believe I did that." Carl was beyond embarrassed that he had not only video called Anna wearing nothing but a towel, but that towel also happened to be one of Zoey's cartoon towels with unicorns and rainbows.

Anna was laughing hard by this point. "That's okay. It's nice to know you like unicorns and rainbows." By now, Anna was laughing so hard she had tears running down her face. Carl couldn't help but smile and laugh with her. He had not heard anyone laugh that hard in a long time.

"Yeah, yeah, yeah. You're just jealous of my awesome towel. I saw that you called. Sorry, I was in the shower, as you probably guessed by my dripping hair and inappropriate attire." Carl was laughing pretty hard himself by now.

"I was just calling to tell you that I got off a little early if you wanted to come over early. I mean, you *might* want to get dressed first though. My neighbors might look at you sort of funny if you get out of your car wearing only that towel."

"Oh, they would be so lucky to see my unicorn towel," Carl laughed. "I'm getting dressed now. I'll go ahead and head over there. Any ideas where you want to go eat tonight?"

"Well, actually, if it is okay with you, I thought about ordering in. Maybe, Chinese food and a movie? I mean, if not, we can go wherever you want. I just thought maybe a night in without any hustle and bustle might be a nice change from all of the craziness you've been dealing with this last week." Anna was starting to second-guess her idea now that she was actually saying it aloud. She didn't want to seem forward or like she was trying to move things along too fast and worried she might actually scare Carl off.

"That actually sounds like a great idea. Do I need to stop and pick it up on my way?" Carl felt a wave of nervousness come over him, he didn't want to sound too eager and make her think he was reading too much into a quiet evening at home with her.

"No, I figured we can order when you get here and have it delivered. There are some good movies on satellite, or we can rent one if we don't see anything we want to watch. If you want something other than water or sweet tea, you might want to stop and get it though." She felt relieved that he was open to the idea of just staying in a relaxing on the couch.

"It has been so long since I watched anything other than a cartoon movie, I'm pretty much open to anything that isn't animated." Carl and Anna laughed. "See you soon, I'm almost dressed now."

"I guess it is a good thing you turned off the video then huh." Anna laughed and they got off the phone.

Carl was feeling very nervous as he finished getting ready to leave to go to Anna's. He hadn't been to a woman's house on a date, ever. When he and Clair dated, she lived in the dorms and no men were allowed. He started to call his dad for advice but knew that would be the worst person to ask. His dad had already made it clear what he thought they should be doing on their date. Instead, he put his phone in his pocket and checked his hair one more time. "Well, that's as good as it gets, I suppose. Here goes nothing," Carl said to himself as he walked out the door to head to Anna's house.

As he pulled out of the driveway, his father was returning from getting his own dinner. "You headed out already? I thought you didn't have to pick her up until eight?"

"Oh, yeah, she called. She got off early, so I'm going to head over. You've got your key right?" Carl yelled out of the window over to his dad.

"Yeah, I'm good. Have fun and be careful!" Carl Sr. yelled back as Carl pulled out of the driveway.

Driving to Anna's house, Carl was getting more and more nervous the closer her got to her house. All of that nervousness melted away as soon as he pulled in the driveway and saw her standing at the mailbox. It was crazy how simply seeing her face seemed to calm his nerves and make his heart feel happy. The last person that made him feel that way was Clair. The more time he spent with Anna, the more he convinced himself Clair had put them together.

"Hey!" Anna smiled and waved as she walked towards the house with her mail in her hand. Carl smiled and parked the car. He was so eager to get out of the car and see her he nearly tried to get out before unbuckling his seatbelt. He had just seen her that afternoon, but it felt like it had been days since he last saw her. As he exited the car, she approached him and gave him a hug. "Glad you decided to go with something other than the unicorn towel."

As they walked to the door the two laughed about the video call incident. Carl's embarrassment and nervousness was completely gone. He felt at home and comfortable with Anna. Why wouldn't he? After all, she's seen him in nothing but a towel at this point.

"What do you feel like having for dinner? I was thinking Chinese, but we can get damn near anything delivered," Anna asked as they walked into the house. "Come on in make yourself comfortable." Anna threw the mail onto a table near the front door.

"Actually, Chinese sounds good to me. Zoey isn't a fan, so I never really get to have it." Carl walked over and sat down on the couch.

"Okay, that sounds good to me. There's this awesome place that delivers so I'll go grab the menu." Anna walks into the kitchen and Carl gets up and follows her. Reaching down to open a drawer, Anna stops, smiles, and says, "Okay Carl, please don't judge me." She opens the drawer that is stuffed full of takeout menus. "I hate cooking, especially for just me."

Carl laughs and puts his hands up shaking his head, "Hey no judgements here. Nothing wrong with being the Queen of Take-Out."

Anna laughed as she dug through the stack of menus. "Ah, here it is. This place has the best noodle bowls. What do you usually get when you order Chinese?" Anna hands him the menu.

Carl doesn't even look at the menu. He hands it back to Anna and says, "Just order me whatever it is you get. I learned last night to trust you when it comes to ordering food."

"That is so much pressure! Do you like spicy or not spicy?" Anna asked.

Carl hesitated for a second then answered, "Hm, let's go with not spicy."

"Okay, gotcha." Anna picks up her cell phone and calls in the order. "They said it will be thirty to forty-five minutes. They always say that, and they are always here in less than twenty."

Carl reaches into his pocket and pulls out his wallet to hand Anna the money for dinner. "How much is it? I might need to run down to the ATM."

"Nope, not this time. This one is on me. I insist. My house, my rules. Put your wallet up." Anna smiles and puts the menu back into the drawer with the other menus.

"No that's not right. I should buy dinner." Carl insisted.

"That's okay, I'll just answer the door when they get here and pay the driver." Carl smiled as the two started walking back towards the living room.

Laughing, Anna replied, "Yeah good luck with that. They've already charged my card. They have it on file." Anna turned and looked over her shoulder at Carl and winked at him.

"Okay, there was no judgement on the stack of menus, but having your card on file? That's a whole different level." Carl laughed and Anna turned and nudged him.

"Yeah, whatever. Okay so movies. What kind of movies do you like? Scary? Comedy? Romantic?" Anna plopped down on the couch and patted the seat beside her for Carl to sit down beside her.

As Anna grabbed the remote and started to search through the list Carl replied laughing, "Hm let's see. It's only the second date, so I don't think I should have to suffer through a chick-flick just yet, how about a comedy?"

"Wait, I thought second dates were the chick flick dates?" Anna laughed as she searched the list for a comedy movie. "No worries, I honestly can't stand those movies. As long as you don't want to watch something really scary, I'm good with pretty much anything."

"If we watch a scary movie, are you saying I'll have to snuggle up close and protect you?" Carl smiled and winked at her. "Just kidding. I'd rather watch a comedy, but for you I would sit through pretty much anything other than a singing dinosaur movie."

Anna started laughing, "Oh my God, I know exactly which movie you are talking about. There's no way in *hell* I would turn that on."

After a few minutes of searching, they decided on a movie and settled in close on the couch to start watching it. No sooner than the movie got started, the doorbell rang. The food was already there. They paused the movie and Carl went to the door while Anna went into a nearby closet and took out two TV trays. As Carl walked back into the room with the food Anna asked, "Hey, did you want to eat in here or in the kitchen? I guess I just assumed we would eat in here while we watched the movie."

"It's your house, your rules remember?" Carl smiled and winked. "We will eat wherever you want to." Carl walked over and sat the bag down on the tray in front of Anna. "Do I remember you saying something about some sweet tea earlier?"

"Oh yes, sorry. I'm such a terrible hostess. I never even offered you anything." Anna stood up and walked into the kitchen. "I'll grab the tea. I ordered us the same thing. You want a real fork or are you going to use chopsticks?"

"Definitely a fork. I'd hate for you to see how clumsy I am with chopsticks." Carl laughed as he opened the bag and set the containers on each table.

After dinner, Carl cleared the trash from the tables and Anna cleaned and put them away. The two snuggled back up on the couch. When the first movie ended, they decided to watch a second movie. About half way through the second movie, Anna realized Carl wasn't watching the movie but was looking over at her. When she looked back at him, she couldn't resist leaning up and kissing him. It was the first time either of them had truly kissed anyone other than their deceased spouses.

After a few minutes of kissing, the two went back to watching the movie. At some point before the end of the movie, both

Anna and Carl fell asleep on the couch snuggled up together, wrapped up in each other's arms. It wasn't until daylight that they woke up.

Carl was the first one awake. Trying not to move too much and wake Anna up, Carl slowly reached into his pocket to get his phone and check the time. It was six thirty. He had spent the entire night sleeping on her couch. He knew he needed to get up, mainly because he needed to go to the bathroom, but he just couldn't bring himself to wake Anna. She was so peaceful and beautiful. As he moved to put his phone back down, Anna woke up.

Sitting up and rubbing her eyes, "Oh hey. Good morning." Anna smiled. "Do you know what time it is?" Anna started looking for her phone to check the time.

"It's um, six thirty. What time do you have to be at work?" Carl stood up and stretched. "And where is the restroom?"

"Oh sorry, it's the second door on the right down that hallway." Anna pointed to the left of the stairs. "I'm off today." As Carl walked down the hallway Anna went into the kitchen. "Hey, do you want some coffee?"

"Oh, that would be awesome!" Carl yelled back as he walked into the bathroom.

Anna started a pot of coffee and went into her own bathroom. Seeing herself in the mirror she was horrified. Her hair was a mess and her makeup definitely looked slept in. She brushed her hair back into a ponytail, quickly brushed her teeth and cleaned off her make up as best she could. As she walked back into the kitchen Carl was standing in front of the coffee pot. "I have a weird question for you."

Anna stopped and looked at him strangely, "Um, okay?"

Carl took a deep breath and asked, "Do you have an extra toothbrush by any chance? I feel like I could melt paint off the walls with my breath right now."

Anna laughed. "Actually, I do. One second." She disappeared back into her bathroom and emerged with a new toothbrush and a tube of toothpaste. Carl took the toothbrush and tooth paste and went back into the hall bathroom. After brushing his teeth and washing his face, he returned to the kitchen where Anna was standing at the counter and sipping on a cup of coffee.

"Thanks, that's much better." Carl walked over and Anna handed him a cup of coffee. "Thank you so much for dinner last night. I'm sorry I fell asleep on your couch, but I have to say that really was the best sleep I've had in what feels like forever."

Anna smiled, "No need to be sorry. I am pretty sure I drooled on your shoulder while I was snoring right beside you." The two laughed. "Would you like some breakfast?" Anna walked over to the refrigerator to see what she had to make for breakfast.

"Actually, I need to get back to the hospital. I'm sure my mother is ready to go home and get a shower and probably some sleep. I don't want you to think I'm rushing off. I just know my mom and I'm sure she sat up all night." Carl didn't want to leave Anna, but he also wanted to be at Zoey's side.

"Hey, no problem at all. I don't blame you. I'm really glad you came over Carl." Anna walked over, kissed Carl on the cheek and gave him a hug.

"Me too, Anna, I hope this doesn't seem out of place or like I'm jumping the gun, but I really feel like I need to say this." Carl hesitated.

"What is it, Carl?" Anna took a small step back.

"Anna, I'm falling for you. I've not felt this way about anyone since Clair. I know we haven't known each other that long but..."

Anna interrupted him, "Carl, I feel the same way about you. I never thought I would feel this way about another man after I lost my husband, but I knew the very first time we talked that you were special. I've known for a few days now that this wasn't just a friendship."

Hearing that Anna felt the same way made it even harder for Carl to walk out of the door. He knew he needed to be back by Zoey's side, but he also knew he wanted to be there with Anna too. Carl leaned in and kissed Anna one more time before he left. "Maybe I'll see you later?" Carl knew Anna was off but really hoped they could see each other again that day.

"Maybe." Anna smiled.

When Carl arrived back at the hospital, he stopped by the cafeteria to grab his mother a cup of coffee before going up to Zoey's room. As soon as he walked in, he heard a familiar voice from across the room. "Mornin' Carl." It was Frank.

"Hey Frank, how's it going?" Carl walked over to Frank who was cleaning near the coffee machine.

"Oh, it's going great. How's Miss Zoey doing? Any news?" Frank stepped aside so Carl could grab a cup.

"Still the same. We are still just waiting. They said yesterday we could be here for months. This is just so hard." Carl filled the cup and searched for the lids.

"Here you go." Frank handed him a lid. "Look, they can say what they want but I tell you, we both know God has a heart for that baby and it will be here in His time."

"Thanks Frank. I'm still holding on to that mustard seed."

Frank smiled and said, "Hey, that's all we need. Just a mustard seed of faith and God will move the mountains for us. Tell Anna I said hello when you see her." Frank walked away. Carl paid for the coffee and headed up stairs.

He opened the door of Zoey's room and sure enough, his mother was sitting wide awake but clearly exhausted from not sleeping all night. "Mom did you sleep at all?"

"Um, I think so. Maybe? What time is it?" Shirley started rubbing her eyes.

"It's a quarter passed eight. Here, I got you a coffee. You need to go to the house and get some sleep. Are you okay to drive or should I call dad to come get you?" Carl handed her the coffee and walked to Zoey's side.

"Oh no I'm good. I need your keys and where did you park the car?" Shirley took the coffee and reached her hand out for the keys as she stood up. Carl handed her the keys and described where he had parked so she wouldn't have to wonder around lost like he did. Shirley kissed Zoey's forehead and then Carl's and walked out of the door.

About forty five minutes after Shirley left, Madison, the nurse that filled in for Anna on her days off entered the room. "Mr. Murphy?"

Carl turned, "Yes ma'am."

"Mr. Murphy, I don't mean to alarm you but the ER just called up and said they have a car wreck victim in the ER by the name of Mrs. Murphy. They didn't give a first name. You might want to go down and check and make sure that isn't your wife."

Without saying a word, Carl ran to the stairs and ran down

the four flights of stairs and into the ER. In a panic, he ran to the desk and asked where Mrs. Murphy had been taken. The receptionist pointed him to the curtain. Peaking in, he quickly realized it was not his mother. Relieved he walked away and sat in the chairs near the elevator. The adrenaline wore off and the fear washed over him. He pulled out his phone and called his mother just to make sure she made it home safely.

On a Wing and a Prayer

ays turned to weeks, and weeks into a month. Carl and Anna continued their relationship and developed a bond like neither thought they would ever experience. Zoey had now been in the hospital thirty-nine days. On the fortieth day, Carl and Anna were having lunch in the cafeteria when Anna's phone began to buzz on the table. Before she could reach to get it, Carl's phone began to buzz. They were both being paged to the CCU floor.

Neither took the time to clear their trash, they simply ran out of the room and up the stairs. By the time they reached the fourth floor they were both winded. "What's wrong? What's going on? We both got paged." Carl managed to speak between gasping for air.

"Mr. Murphy, we've found a heart. It is a perfect match." Dr. Conrad didn't seem as happy and excited as he should be, considering all they had been through over the last month trying to find Zoey a heart.

"Oh, that's awesome! So, when is the surgery?" Carl was so excited he felt like he would jump out of his skin.

"Wait, Mr. Murphy we have a new problem," Dr. Conrad tried to calm Carl down and explain the situation.

"Problem? What? It is a match, do the surgery. *No* problems." Carl was starting to get annoyed.

"No, we do have a problem. The heart is in Chicago."

Carl interrupted, "Okay so send a helicopter, a plane, or hell, a taxi for all I care. Get it here and get my baby out of that damn bed."

"It isn't that simple. There's a problem in Chicago. There is an early snowstorm, and all commercial traffic is grounded into and out of the main airports. There are a couple smaller private airports open, but we don't have a plane. Our team flies out on a commercial jet and returns on a commercial jet. We can't just drive up there. There's not time for all of that." Dr. Conrad was genuinely worried they wouldn't be able to get the heart to Zoey in time. "There's a time limit. We only have twenty-four hours to get the heart from the donor and into Zoey before it isn't viable."

"Okay, it's like a six hour drive. Hell, I'll leave right now. I don't get what the problem is." Carl went from annoyed to angry.

"The roads are shut down. I don't think you understand sir. This isn't just a small snowstorm, it is literally a blizzard." Dr. Conrad was trying to be empathetic to Carl and his frustrations.

"What the hell. We finally get a heart and now this? Look, I don't give a damn what you have to do get my baby's heart here and get it here now. This is garbage and we all know it." Carl walked away and into Zoey's room. He couldn't stand there any longer listening to excuses about why they couldn't get his baby her heart.

"Anna, I don't know what we are going to do. The transplant

team is standing by to go to Chicago, but we don't have a way to get them there. Please, he listens to you. Let him know we are trying everything we can right now." Dr. Conrad turns and walks away leaving Anna standing alone in the middle of the hallway.

Anna doesn't know whether she should give Carl time alone with Zoey or go in and try to reason with him. She decides she really needs to go talk to her friend and find out what he thinks. Anna walks to the elevators and returns to the cafeteria where she quickly finds Frank. After explaining the situation and the problem, Frank tells Anna, "Don't worry about it. God has got this. I may know someone who can help." Anna looked at Frank slightly confused and before she could ask him who he was talking about. He said, "Hey, don't worry about it. You will know in due time. Let me make some calls and see what we can do okay? Trust me?"

"Of course, I do Frank. You've never steered me wrong." Anna smiled and turned to leave. "Hey, so should I go in and talk to him or let him be?"

"Girl, that boy is in love with you, he needs you. Go be with him even if you don't say anything and just sit and hold his hand." Frank motioned for her to get upstairs. As soon as Anna left, Frank pulled out his cellphone and scrolled through his contacts. Once he finally found the number he was looking for, he hit the button to dial the number. "Hey Ryan, this is Frank, from Desert Storm. You told me to give you a call if there was every anything you could do to help me. Well, I need a favor. Give me a call when you get this message, please, sir." Frank hung up the phone and said a quiet prayer to himself while he finished cleaning around the coffee area.

Ryan Sullins, CEO and Founder of Halos for Humanity was just leaving a board meeting when he noticed he had a missed call and a voicemail on his phone. He stopped and told the others he was walking with to go ahead, he needed to make a phone call. He stopped and listened to the voicemail. As soon as he finished the voicemail, he walked over to a nearby window so he would have better reception and called Frank back. "Hey Frank, this is Ryan. How's it going man? I haven't heard from you in a while. Is everything okay? What's this favor you need?"

Frank paused a second to try and think of the best way to ask for a plane. "Well Ryan, here's the thing. There's a little girl here in the hospital that is in desperate need of a heart transplant. She's been waiting something like forty days and they finally found her a heart."

"Oh, that poor thing. What can I do man?" Ryan was curious.

"Well, here's the thing. The heart is in Chicago and all commercial jets are grounded. There are only a couple private airports open. We need someone to fly a small team up into one of those smaller airports so they can get the heart and then get her back," Frank hesitated, "and it has to be within the next 23 hours or so."

"Hm, so you need a plane to fly into a snowstorm and you need it today? How many people on that transport team?" Ryan started thumbing through his contacts while he listened to Frank on speaker phone.

"Yes, that's right. It is a lot to ask I know. It's just, if you meet this girl's father you would see why I want to help them so bad.

She's all he has. Her mother passed away just after she was born. He is completely devastated watching his baby girl lay lifeless in this hospital." Frank had to stop before he started to tear up just thinking about what Carl was going through.

"I gotcha Frank. How many are on the team? I've got to know what size plane I'm getting and how many pilots I'm calling in. I'm going to make this happen. Just have to get some more information." Having children of his own, Ryan felt he had to do anything he could to help this little girl and her father.

"I'm not sure, usually there's only two or three, maybe four since it is a heart?" Frank had seen the transplant teams before but wasn't sure if they were different based on what organs they were going after.

"Okay Frank, I know what I need to get. Give the surgeon my number so he can get me the rest of the information for the logistics of everything. I've got a pilot crew that will take care of this. They have flown in much worse conditions than that we are seeing in Chicago right now, so they won't hesitate. Now when I come next week for the Board of Directors meeting, you know I expect you to buy me a cup of coffee right?" Ryan laughed.

"Hell for all of this I'll even buy you a muffin. Thanks again, Ryan. I'm going up to tell the doctor now." Frank hung up the phone and ran up the stairs. As soon as he reached the fourth floor, Frank found Anna. Out of breath Frank tapped Anna on the shoulder and through heavy breath, "Anna, Anna! Hey, I've got something to tell you."

"Oh my God, Frank are you okay? Take a breath. Slow down and breathe. Are you okay?" Anna was worried that Frank was going to make himself sick.

"Anna, there's no time for that. Listen I've got news. I made a call and I've got a friend that has a plane. He is getting a flight crew together and will fly the transplant team into Chicago. We've got to get Dr. Conrad on the phone with this guy right now!" Frank was slowly catching his breath.

Hearing this news Anna got excited and hugged Frank. "Oh my God, Frank, you truly are an angel. Come on, we've got to go page Dr. Conrad!" The two of them rushed over to the nurses' station and paged Dr. Conrad with a 9-1-1 page.

It didn't take long and Dr. Conrad came rushing around the corner. "Someone paged? What's wrong?"

"Dr. Conrad this is Frank. He has found us a plane to carry the transplant team to get Zoey's heart!" Anna pushed Frank forward in front of Dr. Conrad.

"Frank, don't you work in the cafeteria? You know someone with a plane?" Dr. Conrad raised his eyebrows and looked at Anna.

"Yes sir, I was in Desert Storm with Ryan Sullins."

Dr. Conrad interrupted, "Ryan Sullins, like Halos for Humanity, Ryan Sullins?"

"Yes sir, that's him. So, I talked to him and he can get us a plane to go into the Chicago area. He is getting the flight crew together. He needs you to call him with the information." Frank handed Dr. Conrad his phone so he could take down the number. After taking down the number Dr. Conrad thanks Frank and Anna and steps away to make the phone call.

"Come on Frank, I want you to come with me to tell Carl." Anna started walking towards Zoey's room.

"Oh no, I couldn't. I didn't do anything special, I just made a phone call. You go tell him." Frank tried to walk back towards the elevators.

"Oh no, you don't." Anna reached out and put her arm inside of Frank's arm and lead him to Zoey's room. "You did this. You made this miracle happen for him. Besides, you haven't gotten to see Zoey yet." Anna knocked softly on the door and the two entered the room.

Carl looked up and saw Frank and Anna. "Hey guys, what's going on?"

"Carl, Frank has something to tell you. Go ahead Frank." Anna nudged Frank forward.

"Hey, Carl. So, you remember me telling you about my friend Ryan from Halos for Humanity?" Frank timidly asked Carl who nodded his head with confusion. "Well, I called him, and he is getting a flight crew and a plane ready to fly to Chicago to get Zoey's heart."

"Wait what? Seriously? Oh my God, Frank that is the best news! Zoey, baby, do you hear that? Mr. Frank has found a way to get you your heart." Carl was so happy he had tears in his eyes as he stood and hugged Frank and then Anna. "Frank, I can never thank you enough for saving my baby."

"Carl sweetheart, I don't want to be a downer, but we still have to get the heart, get it here, and get Zoey through the surgery. This is a step in the right direction, but by no means is she out of the woods yet." Anna put her hand on Carl's cheek.

"I know but we are that much closer to Zoey being out of that bed." Carl put his hand on Anna's and smiled. "Okay so what's next? What do we do?"

Anna smiled at Carl as Frank snuck out of the door quietly.

"Well, sweetheart, for now we wait. Dr. Conrad is reaching out to Mr. Sullins and getting him the details for the transplant team. As soon as we hear anything I will let you know I promise."

Carl stood and hugged Anna, "Thank you so much. I don't think I could make it through this without you. I love you so much, Anna."

"I love you too." Anna kissed him on the cheek. "I've got to get back to the desk and make sure I'm caught up with all of my patients. I'll be back as soon as I can." As she turned to walk away, she stopped and walked back over and kissed Carl then walked out of the door. Now alone, Carl called and filled his parents in on the newest developments.

Across town, Ryan Sullins is making phone calls to get a flight crew and an aircraft arranged for the transplant after getting the details from the hospital. "Jacob, hey man, I need to ask you to do something I normally wouldn't ask you to do but this is life and death for a little girl."

"Hey, Dad, what's up? Whatcha got?" Jacob didn't normally get calls from his father directly for a flight.

"There's a girl in a local hospital in need of a heart. They've found her a heart, but it is in Chicago. They have a very short window to get the heart and get it into this little girl. They need a flight crew to fly their team there and back." Ryan explained.

"Wait Chicago? Today? Man, have you seen the news? There's a record snowstorm up there right now. Can we even get clearance to land or much less take off when we get there?" Jacob knew he could make the flight but was worried about air traffic control when they got there.

"I've already made some calls and have gotten clearance. We

can get in and out with the little jet. You will need a co-pilot on this one. You think you can get Owen to go with you?" Ryan started typing on his computer trying to get the flight plan started.

"Hey, you know us, we're all about helping the kids. Whatever we can do, I know he will be all over it. Send me the flight plan and the information and I'll get Owen on the phone and get him headed to the airport. Do you have a plane lined up already for us?" Jacob started packing a bag to get ready for the flight.

"Oh yeah, I have the Challenger getting fueled up and ready for you now. The transplant team should meet you guys at the plane. There's two of them that will be riding with you. I've already called and have the car service planned out and ready for them in Chicago. Thank you so much for being willing to make this flight at the last minute." Ryan finished the flight plan and hit send on the email. "Flight plan has been emailed to you and Owen."

"Man, you know I'll do anything for the kids. I can't imagine if that was one of mine that needed a heart. I would hope some other stranger would do the same for my baby." Jacob stopped packing and looked over at the picture of his three children on the nightstand. "I haven't looked at the flight plan yet. Which airport are we flying into? O'Hare, Midway?"

"Well actually, the closest I can get you guys is Rockford. It will be about an hour and a half drive each way for them. It is the closest we can get clearance to land and hopefully the storm doesn't move that way so you can take off." Ryan knew this was going to be a stretch to get the transplant team to and from the hospital, but it was the best he could do under the circumstances. "I did put in a call up to PWK. If by some miracle the storm clears, we will try to get into there. It is much closer to the hospital, about half the distance."

"Well just let me know if the flight plan changes. I'm headed to pick up Owen and get our pre-flight done. I'll keep my cell on." Jacob hung up the phone and headed out the door to pick up his brother and get the plane ready to go.

Back at the hospital, Anna rushed into Zoey's room, "Carl, they have a plane and the transplant team is leaving for the airport now!"

Carl was so happy he couldn't hold back his tears, "Do you hear that, Sissy? They are leaving to go get your heart! It won't be too much longer baby girl, just hold on." Carl stood and hugged Anna.

A few minutes later Dr. Conrad walked into the room. "Mr. Murphy. I'm sure you've already heard but the transplant team has left for the airport. A benefactor has found a plane and a flight crew. You've clearly made some good friends that are looking out for you and Zoey. A lot of things had to fall into place just right for this to be happening today."

"I do have some great friends, whether I deserve them or not." Carl smiled and looked over at Anna who was checking the monitors behind Zoey.

"Here's what's going to happen now. Once the transplant team arrives at the hospital in Chicago, we will come get Zoey and get her prepped for surgery. There is a helicopter that will be waiting at the airport here in Memphis and will airlift the heart strait here once they land in Memphis. Everything will go fast once that heart touches down. Until then, we wait. The flight crew can only get as close as an hour and a half away from the hospital in Chicago. So, there will still be a good bit of waiting we have to do." Dr. Conrad walked over and looked at Zoey. "We aren't out of the woods yet. Even after we get her the heart. There is still a chance she could reject it and we won't be able to put her back on bypass. If she rejects the heart, Mr. Murphy, there's nothing more we can do for her. In the event she rejects the heart, you might want to consider donating—"

Carl cuts him off, "Wait are you seriously about to ask me to donate her organs? Have you lost your damn mind! That is my baby we are talking about. You are supposed to be trying to save her and you are standing here asking me to give away her organs?" Carl was very visibly angry.

"Carl, wait, just listen to what he is saying." Anna walked over and held Carl's hand.

"Mr. Murphy, all I am saying is in the event we can't save Zoey, she may be able to save other children. I know this isn't something any parent wants to hear, much less think about. I just need to give you all of your options." Dr. Conrad tried to be as gentle as possible with the information knowing it would upset Carl.

"Well, your only option is to save Zoey. Let's not even think about the other crap right now." Carl turned and looked at Zoey.

"Anna, I'm going to leave the forms with you. They will need to be signed before she goes into surgery if this is something he will consider." Dr. Conrad handed Anna the donation forms and left the room.

"Anna, I just don't know what to do. I can't live without her. I was so happy thinking this was finally it and now that asshole is talking about her dying and taking her organs. Anna, if she rejects that heart, would it be possible to give her mine? There's no one that could possibly be a better match for her than me? We wouldn't have to wait on a donor." Carl turned to Anna with tears streaming down his face.

Anna tried but couldn't hold back her own tears, "Carl, sweetheart that wouldn't solve anything. Think about it darling; you have the heart of a grown man, she's just a baby. Besides, there are people who need you around too. Your parents need you. Hell, I need you. I finally find someone I can open up my heart to, I can't lose you too. Carl, I love you. We will get through this. If for some reason Zoey rejects the heart, she could save so many other little girls just like herself with parents sitting in hospitals hoping and praying for something or someone to save their babies. Just like we have been doing for Zoey."

Carl reached over and brushed Zoey's hair from the side of her face. "Sissy, I need you baby girl. Daddy needs you to be okay. I love you baby." Carl turned and looked at Anna, "You're right. If something happens and she rejects the heart, I will let them take her organs. But I want time with her. I don't want them giving up on her. She will have the opportunity to fight. If they can't promise me that then I'm not signing a damn thing."

"Carl, I promise, I will fight tooth and nail for that baby. I would fight tooth and nail for you." Anna hugged him and walked out of the room leaving the donation papers on the table, unsigned.

At the airport, Jacob and Owen have finished their pre-flight checks and have programmed their flight plans into their navigation systems. As soon as the transplant team arrives, they will be ready for take-off. "Okay guys, just so you know, it is going to be a little bumpy once we get close to Chicago. Be prepared."

Just as they were getting ready to taxi out, Jacob's phone rang; it was Ryan. "Hey Jacob, change of plans bud, you guys are going to PWK. I just emailed the flight plans."

"Man, you cut it close. We were just getting ready to taxi. Owen, pull up your email we have a change in flight plans. We're going to PWK." As Jacob read out the information Ryan was giving to him, Owen made the changes in the systems. "Okay, we got it. I'll give you a yell when we land and let you know how everything is going. Is the car service going to be at the airport waiting for these guys to get to the hospital?"

"Yes, I'm making that call as soon as I hang up with you. Fly safe guys. I'll talk to you in a few." Ryan hangs up and makes a few more calls to make sure he has all of the logistics in place before the transplant team arrives in Chicago. While on the last of his calls to get everything arranged, his assistant walks in to let him know he has a meeting with the Board of Directors over at the hospital. On his way out of the office he tells his assistant, "Go ahead and cancel everything after the Director's meeting. I've got some personal things I need to take care of." His assistant nods and starts making phone calls.

Ryan arrives at the hospital and sits through yet another boring meeting distracted by the thoughts of everything he's been arranging all day. Finally, the meeting is over and he can head downstairs to the cafeteria and see his old friend. He walks in and immediately sees Frank. "Hey Frank, how have you been? It's been too long."

Frank walks around the corner and hugs Ryan, "Man you ain't lying. Here, have a seat. Want some coffee? I think I owe you at least that."

"No, no I'm good. You do owe me, but not today." The two laughed as they sat down at a nearby table. "Have you heard how that little girl is doing? The flight crew should be getting pretty close to landing here soon."

"Zoey? Oh man, I can't thank you enough for all you've done for her. You've got to go up and meet her dad while you are here. I know he wants to meet you."

"I wouldn't want to intrude. I know this is a stressful time for him. It was honestly the least I could do. I can't imagine if that was one of my daughters or granddaughters laying in that bed needing a heart. I'd move mountains to help them." Frank nodded as he listened to Ryan talk.

Ryan's phone rang; it was Jacob. "Hey, Dad, just wanted to let you know we landed and the team has left for the hospital."

"Great, man that's great news! How was the flight? How's the weather? Still clear?" Ryan gave a thumbs up to Frank to let him know the flight had landed safely.

"It's holding out for now. You can tell they have been getting slammed here though. I just hope they get back quick. It looks like there's another storm cell coming through that is going to bury this place." As Ryan listened to Jacob, he tried not to show the concern on his face. He didn't want Frank to know there was a chance the heart could still get snowed in at Chicago. Not to mention the concern that he had sent his own two sons into a snowstorm to save a stranger's daughter.

Ryan finished the phone call with Jacob. "Come on, let's go

upstairs. You really should meet Carl and Zoey." Frank stands up and motions for Ryan to come with him not taking no for an answer.

"Man, I don't remember you being quite this pushy when I was dragging your ass out of that Humvee." The two laughed as they walked towards the elevator. On the elevator the two caught up on old times. It had been a while since they had seen each other but they picked right up where they left off.

As they approached Zoey's room, Anna spotted the two and walked down the hall to them. "Hey Frank, what's going on?"

"Hey Anna, this is Ryan. He's the one that arranged for the flight to bring Miss Zoey's special delivery." Frank stepped aside to introduce the two.

Anna was so excited as Ryan reached his hand out to shake her hand, she reached over and hugged him. "Oh my God, thank you so much! You just don't know how much you have done for this little girl." Anna realized she had probably over stepped and took a step back. "I'm sorry, it's just that this little girl and her father have made such an impact on me, on everyone, really."

Ryan smiled, "I can tell. Frank has never called in a favor for anyone else. Clearly, she is a very special little girl."

"I'm so glad you are here. Carl is going to be so happy to meet you. You just have no idea how much this means to us, I mean him." Anna knocked softly on the door and the three walked in.

Carl was leaned back in the recliner beside Zoey and was sleeping. "Oh no, I don't want to wake him. I can meet him another time." Ryan whispered as he started to walk back out of the room.

"No, he would be so upset if he missed you. I promise he

would want to be woken up for you." Anna walked over to Carl and touched him gently on his shoulder. "Carl, Carl sweetheart, there is someone here to see you and Zoey."

Carl looked up at Anna and smiled. "Hey, sorry, I guess I fell asleep. Is it time already?"

"No, sweetie there's someone here to meet you." Anna turned and motioned for Ryan and Frank to come closer to where Carl was sitting. "Carl this is Ryan Sullins. He made the..."

Carl jumped up and ran over to Ryan and hugged him. "You are the one that got my baby her heart! I know exactly who you are."

Ryan smiled and hugged Carl back. "I didn't get the heart, just the transportation. It was the least I could do."

"Man, I can't thank you enough. There are no words to come close to how grateful I am for all you've done for my baby. She's sleeping, but please come meet her." Carl and Anna stepped aside so Ryan could step over to the side of Zoey's bed.

"Why, hello Miss Zoey. I hope you get better soon sweetheart." Looking down at Zoey, Ryan couldn't help but to think of his own granddaughter, Emma. They were about the same age. As Ryan turned back towards Carl, Anna, and Frank, he had to pause to wipe the tears from his face. "If there is anything she needs you let me know." Ryan reaches in his pocket and pulls out a business card. "This has my personal cell on it. If you need me, please call."

Carl took the card and hugged him again. "Man, you have done so much already. I seriously can't thank you enough." The four talked for a while longer before Frank and Ryan left the room. Anna stayed and sat with Carl a little longer after the others left until she got a page to come to the nurses' station.

As Anna approached the desk, her phone rang; it was Danielle from the transplant team. "Anna? Hey, this is Danielle. They have retrieved the heart and are transporting to the airport now. We will be up in just a few minutes to get Zoey prepped for surgery. Will you update the family?"

"Oh, that's great. Yes, I will update the family. Thank you Danielle." Anna hung up the phone and rushed back to Zoey's room to give Carl the good news. "Carl, the transplant team called. They have retrieved Zoey's heart in Chicago and are on their way to the airport. They will be coming to get Zoey here in just a few minutes. Once they get the heart here and get the surgery started, it will be a long surgery."

"My parents should be here in just a few minutes. Can we wait so they can see her? If they aren't here before they come to get her?" Carl turned and looked at this phone to try and see where his parents were.

"If they aren't here, I don't see why a few minutes would hurt. I'll see what I can do." Anna left the room and almost ran right into Danielle. "Hey Danielle, are you going to get Zoey Murphy now?"

Danielle looked at the chart in her hand and replied, "Yes ma'am that's where I'm headed now. Why?"

"Can we give them a few more minutes. Her grandparents are on their way back up here. They want to give her a kiss and pray before you take her to pre-op." Anna frowned.

"Well, I guess it wouldn't hurt to wait a few minutes. The heart is still actually in Chicago, so we do have a little time.

How long are we talking for them to get here?" Danielle looked at her watch.

"They are close, maybe twenty minutes at the most." Anna was hopeful the Murphy's would get there quickly.

"I think I can find something to do for twenty minutes." Danielle smiled and walked over towards the break room.

A few minutes later, Carl Sr. and Shirley stepped out of the elevator. "Oh man, am I glad to see you guys. I didn't think I would be able to stall the transplant team too much longer. Hurry and go see Zoey before they take her to get her prepped for surgery."

Anna started to walk away and Shirley grabbed her and hugged her tight. "Thank you so much! We were hurrying as fast as we could, but you know how traffic is this time of day on the interstate—"

"Oh woman, come on, she just said hurry up." Carl Sr. pulled Shirley away from Anna and rushed her towards Zoey's room. "Anna, thank you for stalling for us. Are you coming with us?"

"Oh no, I don't want to intrude, this is a family thing." Anna politely tried to decline but Carl Sr. wasn't hearing it.

"No ma'am, you get your tail in that room with us. That is, unless you are busy. I guess I can let you have a pass if you are busy, since you are at work and all." The three laughed as they all walked into Zoey's room. Carl was clearly relieved to see his parents and Anna walk in the room. The four of them prayed together holding hands and had barely finished their prayer when Danielle walked into the room.

"Okay, I can't delay anymore or Dr. Conrad is going to get mad. We have to get her prepped." Danielle unhooked machines and transferred them over to temporary power so she could take Zoey down the hall. "I'll call up and let you guys know when they actually start the surgery. Anna, when do you leave? Do I need to call your cell or the desk?"

"Oh, I get off at seven but I will be here. If you call my cell, I'll let them know what's going on. Thanks, Dani! I really appreciate it and I know they do." Danielle and Zoey left the room and left Anna and the Murphy's standing in the room.

"I'm not really sure what I should be doing right now. I feel lost without her being right here with us." Carl turned to Anna for guidance.

"Well, honey right now all we can do is wait. We can wait in here, or we can go down to the cafeteria, or we can sit in the waiting area. I'll be right back. I have to go clock out and give turnover from the day." Anna kissed Carl on the cheek and walked out.

Meanwhile in Chicago, Jacob and Owen have completed their pre-flight checks and ensured the plane is ready to go as soon as the transplant team arrives. The phone rings; it is the transplant team. "Mr. Sullins? This is Reese from the hospital. We have a slight problem."

Rolling his eyes and looking over at Owen, Jacob puts the phone on speaker so they can both hear the call. "This is Jacob, what's the issue Reese?"

"The snowstorm has moved in again and we are stuck in traffic. We haven't moved in over thirty minutes." Reese was clearly frustrated and concerned.

"Hold on, we need to check the weather and see where that is headed. If it has hit you guys it may be headed here. We really don't have time for this. Aren't you in an ambulance? Can't they hit the sirens or something?" Owen spoke up from the First Officer's seat.

"We have the lights and sirens on but there's just no where for us to go. The cars have nowhere to move and you can barely see three feet in front of the ambulance."

"Oh, shit, that storm is headed right for us. We only have a short window to get the hell out of here. I need you guys here as soon as humanly possible or we are going to be stuck. Maybe for freaking days looking at this storm." Jacob hung up the phone and turned to Owen. "Seriously look at this, who's bright idea was it to bring us here? Rockford is clear, we should have stayed with the original flight plan dammit."

"Hey, you know who sent us the flight plan. Dad had no way of knowing they would get stuck in traffic. Just calm down, no sense in getting all pissed off. It is what it is. Remember we are trying to save a little girl." Owen tried to calm his brother down but knew Jacob was right.

"Yeah, that's easy to say, but now I've got to call and tell these people their little girl may not get the heart in time. You know what, I'm just going to call Dad and let him know he can call and tell them. We've got to be ready. As soon as they are close, we are starting the engines. Man, I hope we don't get grounded." Jacob picked up his phone and dialed his father letting him know what was going on there.

"Dammit, I was really hoping the weather would hold out. I'll call and talk to the doctor and let him know what is going on." Ryan paused, "Son, you guys be careful. I know we are trying to save a little girl, but you two are my sons and I need you guys to come home safe. If you don't feel comfortable taking off, get a hotel room. They have my account on file at the hotel just off that airport property." Ryan hung up the phone and called Dr. Conrad breaking the news to him that there were issues in Chicago.

Dr. Conrad explained the situation to Danielle. Danielle knew she had to break the news to Zoey's family and just couldn't bring herself to do it over the phone. With the delay in Chicago, she knew she had time to walk up to the CCU and talk to the family. Danielle sent a text to Anna to make sure where they were. Anna replied that they were down in the cafeteria. Upon her arrival in the cafeteria, she spotted Anna and Carl immediately.

"Hey guys, I wanted to come down and give you and update." Danielle startled Carl.

"Is everything okay? Have they started yet? I thought you said you would be with her through the surgery?"

"Mr. Murphy, they haven't started the surgery yet. There's a problem with the transport in Chicago. It seems the weather moved in on them and they are stuck on the highway trying to get back to the airport right now." Danielle explained.

"Stuck on the highway? What are they going to do? They will still get here sometime tonight, right?" Carl looked at Anna with a look of confusion on his face that broke her heart.

"Honestly Mr. Murphy, we won't know how long the delay is until they get to the airport. It is a bad storm." Danielle felt terrible having to break the news to him. "I will let you guys know as soon as we hear anything else. I've got to get back up to Zoey."

"Thank you for coming down and letting us know." Anna

smiled at Danielle even though her heart was aching for Carl and Zoey.

After Danielle had walked away, Carl, feeling defeated turned to his mother, "Seriously? It is one freaking thing after another. Why can't my baby just get what she needs and get better? My sweet, innocent, little girl should not have to go through this. This is bullshit!" Carl stood and walked away from the table.

Anna stood to follow him, and Shirley stopped her, "Let him go dear. He needs a few minutes. Trust me." Anna sat back down but worried because of what Carl had asked her earlier in the day about giving Zoey his heart. She felt like she should tell his parents what he said, but also didn't want to betray his trust.

Carl walked down the hallway until he saw what he needed: the chapel. Carl walked in. Thankfully no one was in there. He really needed to be alone. As he sat down, he looked up at the old wooden altar. It was clear the altar had seen a lot of praying knees over the years. The finish was worn and tear-stained. Carl began to cry and cry out to God. The only words he could manage to say aloud were "God, please, save my baby."

While Carl sat crying out in the small empty chapel of the hospital in Memphis, the storm in Chicago wasn't letting up, the driver of the ambulance got even more impatient and grabbed his phone and called his friend Mike who he knew had four-wheel drive that could plow through the snow. "Mike! Hey bud, I need your help. I'm about six miles from your house stuck in this traffic because of all the snow. I have a little girls heart that I have to get to the airport and get to Memphis can you come and pick us up and get us there?"

Mike replied, "Of course man! I'll be there in fifteen

minutes." Mike showed up in eleven minutes. The transport team loaded up and started their way to the airport. Once they arrived, Jacob's phone buzzed; it was a text from the transplant team.

Jacob read the text. Jacob looked over at Owen, "Man, it is about damn time. Fire it up and let's get out of here." As soon as the transplant team stepped onto the plane Owen shut the doors and Jacob started moving the airplane towards the runway.

"Dad, hey this is Owen, we are taking off now." Owen called to pass along the update as he walked back towards the cockpit.

"Copy that. Thanks guys! Have a safe flight. I'll see you guys at the airport. I'm heading to the helipad now." Ryan hung up from talking to Owen and called Dr. Conrad. "Dr. Conrad, this is Ryan Sullins. The flight crew just called. They are taking off now."

"Thank you, we are getting her prepped now." Dr. Conrad hung up the phone and turned to Danielle. "Okay we need to get started, the flight is leaving from Chicago now we have about an hour and a half before the heart should be here. I want to be ready and waiting when it gets here."

Danielle texted Anna to let her know that the flight had left and the heart was on the way from Chicago. "The heart has left Chicago. I've got to go find Carl." Anna turned and looked at Shirley, "Do you know where he would be?"

"I'll check outside. Carl, you go look up in Zoey's room. Anna, is there a chapel or something? Maybe go check there?" Shirley stood and started walking out of the cafeteria.

Anna walked down the hallway to the chapel. As she stepped in, she could hear Carl weeping. Her heart broke for him knowing the worry and the pain he was feeling. She approached him slowly and gently touched his shoulder, "Carl sweetheart."

Carl didn't bother trying to wipe his face before turning to Anna. "Anna, I don't know what I'll do without her. I just, I just don't think I can do this."

"Carl, the flight crew called. They are on their way here. They made it through the storm and should be here soon. Her heart is on the way here." Anna pulled a tissue from the pack in her scrub pocket.

"Wait, what?" Carl took the tissue and looked up at Anna confused. Anna explained again that the storm cleared enough for the transplant team to maneuver through traffic. "Oh my God, Anna that is incredible. Zoey actually has a chance? I might not lose my baby girl!" Carl jumped to his feet and hugged Anna. He held onto her tight crying and thanking her for coming to find him. It didn't take long for Carl and Anna to find Carl's parents. The four decided to wait in the surgical waiting area for any word on Zoey's condition.

The Journey Back

Shortly after takeoff, Jacob turns to Owen, "Looks like we can make up a little time. Here's hoping they can save that little girl after all of this." The remainder of the flight was silent with the exception of light radio chatter.

All of a sudden, the Wing Anti-Ice Alert sounded. Jacob calls out to Owen, "We have an issue here. We are forty minutes out, we have to drop down to warmer temperatures to get rid of the ice on the wings."

Owen called Memphis International and requested to descend to ten thousand above ground level. "We are clear to ten thousand Jacob".

Jacob repeated, "Clear to ten thousand."

After about five minutes, the alert went away and Owen called out "Memphis International in sight, clear on three, six left."

Jacob repeated, "Clear on three, six left." As soon as they landed in Memphis, they were directed by Air Traffic Control to taxi to the small corporate jet hangar where Ryan was waiting with the helicopter. "We are pulling over to the helicopter, be ready to go when we stop. They will airlift you over to the hospital." Jacob called out to the transplant team.

As the plane slowly taxied to the hangar, the transplant team readied their things including the small white cooler holding Zoey's heart. When the plane stopped, they quickly yet carefully exited the plane and rushed over to where Ryan was standing. "Get in, they are waiting for you at the hospital." Ryan called out over the sound of the helicopter blades whirling through the air. The team climbed into the helicopter and Ryan slammed the door signaling to the pilots to take off.

Less than ten minutes after leaving the airport, the helicopter was preparing to land at the hospital. "When we land, make sure you stay low until you clear the blades." The co-pilot turned and called out to Madison and the team in the back of the helicopter. All team members gave a thumbs up that they understood the directives.

Word traveled quickly to the surgical team that the helicopter was landing on the roof with the transplant team and Zoey's heart in tow. In the operating room, Dr. Conrad and his team had already removed Zoey's damaged heart and had found even more damage than they initially projected. "There's no way she would have made it with this heart. Look at the damage. It is a miracle this poor girl has made it this long," Dr. Conrad commented as he handed Zoey's heart to a surgical intern assisting in the surgery.

As the replacement heart arrived in the operating room, the team worked quickly to prepare the heart for the transplant. Throughout the surgery everything went smoothly and exactly according to plan. It was now time to remove Zoey from the bypass and see if her new heart would support her little body. The initial shocks from the internal paddles yielded no rhythm. Dr. Conrad for the first time had his doubts that the transplant would save her. Was he too late? Had her little body just given up? He took a deep breath and gave her one more shock with the internal paddles and the whole operating room fell silent. Then, the miraculous. The monitors started to beep: she had a heartbeat. The entire room erupted with cheers.

In total the surgery lasted five hours. Exhausted, Dr. Conrad turned to his team after finishing the final closing stitch, "Great job guys. If she has any chance of life, it is because of the work we did in here today. She has a chance because of you. Now, we wait."

Zoey is taken to recovery. Dr. Conrad and Danielle walk to the waiting room to find Anna, Carl, and his parents to fill them in on Zoey's condition. "Mr. Murphy?" Dr. Conrad taps Carl on the shoulder, waking Anna who had fallen asleep on his shoulder.

"Yes, Dr. Conrad, how is she? How is my Zoey?" Carl jumped up almost knocking Anna over.

"Well Mr. Murphy, everything went exactly as we hoped. I did find her heart was a lot more damaged than we initially thought. There's no way she would have made it or even had a chance without this transplant. She's in recovery now resting. We will get her moved back to her room in the CCU within an hour or so. She will still need to stay in the hospital for a while longer, but she should be waking up soon."

Carl couldn't contain his relief as he hugged the doctor and shook his hand thanking him profusely. Carl turned to his parents and hugged them both. As he turned to hug Anna, he noticed she was trying to slip away unnoticed. "Anna, wait where are you going?" Carl ran after her.

"Oh, I just felt like this was a family moment and didn't want to get in the way." Anna smiled with tears of joy in her eyes.

"You're right, this is a family moment, and you belong. You belong right here with our family." Carl smiled and reached his hand out for Anna's hand. She looked at his hand and up at his face. With a smile on her face, she reached out and took his hand. The two returned to Carl's parents holding hands. The next hour felt like an eternity waiting to go see Zoey. When Danielle texted Anna that Zoey was in the room and ready for visitors, the four practically ran to Zoey's room.

As they walked into Zoey's room, Carl nearly collapsed seeing Zoey. She looked so much better than she did when he saw her last. There were no machines breathing for her. No machines pumping blood through her body. She had the monitors and her IVs with medication, but nothing else. Finally, Carl felt like they were making progress. As he walked over to Zoey and brushed his hand beside her face he whispered softly, "Sissy, Daddy's here baby. I love you baby girl." As Carl spoke, Zoey smiled softly. "Mom, Dad, Anna, come here did you see that? She smiled! Sissy, baby, Memaw and Pepaw are here too. So is Anna."

Zoey smiled and tried to open her eyes slightly. "Carl, sweetheart, we need to let her rest a little more. She's been through an awful lot today." Anna touched his hand.

"Sissy, you get some rest. Daddy will be right here. I love you so much." Carl kissed Zoey's head and turned to Anna. "You're right. She needs some rest." Carl, Anna, Shirley, and Carl Sr. walked over by the door to talk without disturbing Zoey.

"We are going to go ahead and head back to your house. If anything changes call us and we will be right back." Shirley hugged Carl and then hugged Anna. As she hugged Anna she whispered in her ear, "Thank you so much for being here for him. We love you." Anna smiled and fought back tears.

"If it is okay, I think I'll stay here with you, Carl. That is, if that's okay with you?" Anna turned to Carl.

"Of course it is okay with me." Carl smiled and the two walked back into the room and sat down on the couch. "Thank you so much for being here for me and Zoey. I honestly don't think I would have made it through this without you Anna." Carl leaned over and put his arm around Anna.

Anna laid her head on Carl's chest, "There's nowhere else I'd rather be than right here with you Carl." Carl and Anna sat on the couch and fell asleep listening to the steady soft beeps of Zoey's heart monitor.

Early the next morning before dawn, Carl awoke when he felt Anna stand up suddenly. As he cleared the sleep from his eyes, he saw Anna and Mallory working feverishly on Zoey. "Anna, call Dr. Conrad. She's crashing!" Anna rushed to the phone and dialed Dr. Conrad's number and tried to remain calm while filling him in on Zoey's condition.

"Anna! Anna? What is going on? Zoey baby? Anna, what is going on?" Carl rushed over to Zoey's side.

"Carl, I'm sorry you need to step out. Carl, come on let them work." Anna pulled Carl back as a team of nurses and doctors rushed into the room. "Carl, come on, we need to step out." Anna pulled on Carl's arm and pulled him into the hallway.

"Anna, what is going on please, tell me what is going on now." Carl pleaded with Anna as he reluctantly followed her out of the room.

"Carl, she's not doing well. Carl, I don't know what is happening, I just know she isn't doing well." Anna hung her head and cried.

Carl called and woke his parents up. "Mom, Mom you guys need to come back to the hospital. Something is wrong with Zoey."

"We are on our way." Shirley and Carl Sr. jumped up and ran to the car without bothering to change out of their pajamas.

As Carl hung up the phone Dr. Conrad stepped out of Zoey's room into the hallway. "Mr. Murphy."

"Dr. Conrad, what is going on with Zoey? How is she? Is she okay? Is it the heart?" Carl was near hysterics by the time Dr. Conrad stepped out of the room.

"I can't lie, it isn't good. I've ordered some tests, but the preliminary diagnosis is that she is rejecting the heart. I've increased the anti-rejection medications and added a few other protocols to try and head this off." Dr. Conrad knew in his mind this was the worst case scenario but wanted to wait until he knew for sure before he broke the news to Carl and his family.

"Do whatever you have to do to save my baby. You hear me? *Save* my baby!" Carl was trying control his temper but was getting angry. His baby had been through so much, he just wanted her to be better.

"Carl! Carl, what's going on? Where's Zoey what happened?"

Shirley heard Carl raising his voice with the doctor and came running down the hallway.

"Mom, we don't know for sure, but they think she is rejecting the heart. We are back to waiting. Waiting to see if she is rejecting the heart, waiting to see if the medicines will help. Waiting to see if my baby will ever wake up again. Mom I'm just so tired of waiting. I want my Sissy back!" Carl broke down crying.

Dr. Conrad disappeared down the hall followed by several interns and nurses. Over the next several hours there was a steady flow of nurses and doctors into and out of Zoey's room. Just around lunch time Dr. Conrad finally returned to talk to Carl and his family. "Mr. Murphy. Can I speak with you in the hallway sir?" Carl, Anna, and Carl's parents followed Dr. Conrad into the hallway. As Dr. Conrad turned to speak to them another alarm sounded in Zoey's room causing Anna and the doctor to rush back into her room. Several nurses came running down the hallway into the room.

A few minutes later Anna and Dr. Conrad walked out of the room with very solemn looks on their faces. Anna was so heartbroken she couldn't bring herself to look Carl in the face. "Mr. Murphy. Zoey is in full rejection. The medications are not helping. Her body is rejecting the heart. There's nothing more we can do for her. I'm so sorry Mr. Murphy. I really am." Dr. Conrad turned to Anna who was crying. "Anna, you really need to talk to him about donating her organs. We need the paperwork signed before we can move forward." Anna nodded her head without ever looking up.

Carl and his parents returned to Zoey's side. As he stood

there looking down at his sweet baby girl, Carl couldn't speak, no words would come out of his mouth. He could only stand there weeping for his baby. Anna approached Carl. Without saying a word Carl turned, looked into her face and took the papers. He signed them without ever looking away from Anna's face. Anna kissed his cheek and took the papers to the doctor who was waiting in the hallway. "They need more time. How long can we give them?" Anna asked Dr. Conrad.

"An hour at most. Once she codes again, we only have a short time to get her into the operating room and harvest her organs. I'll wait as long as I can." Dr. Conrad took the documents and walked away.

Anna returned to the room and stood behind Carl with her hands on his shoulders. Carl's parents stood on the other side of Zoey's bed holding her hand, crying. Two hours passed by as the machines slowed down minute by minute. Finally, the alarm sounded and Zoey was gone. Carl burst out into tears crying out, "No, my baby. Not my baby!"

Upon seeing the alarms on the monitors, the transplant team moved quickly to take Zoey into the operating room. Carl stood without saying another word and walked out to the chairs in the hallway. He sat down and put his head in his hands. A few minutes later Anna walked out and found him sitting in the chairs. As she tried to stir him, she quickly realized something wasn't right. She couldn't stir him. "Carl! Carl! Oh my God, someone help me! I've got a code blue! He's not breathing. Get me the crash cart! Carl! Carl!" Anna struggled and laid Carl to the ground opening his shirt to start CPR.

It took a few seconds for the other nurses to realize what was happening. A large group rushed over to Anna and Carl bringing the crash cart with them. Carl Sr. and Shirley stepped out of the room just in time to see their son lying on the floor lifeless with Anna performing CPR. Finally, a nurse got the defibrillator and put the paddles on Carl's chest. "Clear!" The nurses all stepped back and they shocked Carl. Anna reached down and checked for a pulse. Nothing. "Shock him again! Clear!"

After the third shock Carl's eyes opened. He was lying in a hospital bed surrounded by doctors and nurses. "He's back! We've got a heartbeat." Confused, Carl looked around. He wasn't sure where he was or who these people were around him. As he tried to move his arms, he felt multiple IV's attached to his arms. His head hurt and there was a sharp pain in his chest from the shocks of the defibrillator. As the room started to clear, he looked around and saw his mother and father sitting on the couch with Zoey Grace sitting between them crying.

"Zoey?" Carl managed to squeak out. He wasn't sure what was going on. Was he dead? Was it all a dream? He didn't even fully know where he was.

"Daddy!" Zoey tried to jump up and run to her daddy's bedside but was stopped by her grandparents.

"Woah sweetheart, we have to be gentle with Daddy." Shirley tried to calm Zoey down.

Carl looked around and saw Anna standing near his bed reading the numbers on the monitors. "Anna?"

Anna stopped and turned looking at him confused. "Um, yes?"

"What happened? Where am I?" Carl looked back at his parents and at Zoey.

"Sweetheart, you are in the hospital. You were in an accident." Shirley walked over to Carl's side.

"Accident? Wait what day is it?" Carl was confused and felt lost.

"You and Zoey were on your way home from seeing Clair on Zoey's birthday. There was a drunk driver that crossed over the yellow line on the highway and hit you head on. You have been in a comma for just under two months." Shirley tried to give Carl as many details as she could without upsetting Carl or Zoey. "After the accident, you laid on the highway until someone came by and saw the accident. He helped get Zoey out of the car and called for help. He's been back a few times to check on you."

"Wait, so Zoey is okay?" Carl is still confused.

"Yes Daddy, I'm fine. Memaw can I *please* go hug Daddy now?" Zoey was anxious to get up from the couch and get over to her daddy.

"Okay but be gentle. No rough housing," Shirley responded as she motioned for Carl Sr. to let Zoey come over to the bed.

Zoey gently climbed up the bed and laid beside her daddy. As Zoey hugged her daddy, he hugged her tight. "Daddy, I've missed you so much! I was a good girl for Memaw. I even made a new friend!"

"Baby, I have missed you so much! Tell me about your friend." Carl looked at his mother and smiled. He was finally realizing this had all been just a nightmare. His baby girl really was okay. He was so consumed with the fact that Zoey was okay, he never even bothered to ask what injuries he had actually sustained in the accident.

"Well, Daddy, her name is Anna. She is a nurse. She had a

daughter named Clair like Mommy. She went to Heaven like Mommy too. She has been taking really good care of you Daddy. She even brought me this bear. Pepaw, where is my bear?" Zoey turned to Carl Sr. reaching for the fluffy pink bear sitting behind him on the couch.

"Here she is, Sissy." Carl Sr. smiled and handed the bear to Zoey.

"Look here she is Daddy. Her name is Frankie. Isn't she soft?" Zoey thrust her bear into Carl's arms so he could feel how soft and squishy her bear was.

As Carl sat listening to Zoey tell him all about her time with his parents and everything he missed over the last 2 months his mind wandered. So much of what Zoey was telling him was so familiar, yet he knew it was all a dream, but how? Twenty minutes later, there was a soft knock on the door, it was Anna coming in to check on Carl.

"Hey, sorry, I didn't want to disturb you guys. I just need to come check the monitors. It looks like one of the leads may have fallen off or got disconnected." Anna walked over and saw the problem immediately, Zoey had accidentally unplugged one of the wires.

"Daddy, this is my friend I was telling you about. This is Miss Anna!" Zoey got so excited she unplugged another wire.

Shirley started to make Zoey move out of the bed, but Anna stopped her, "Oh no she's okay. I'll move the wires. She's missed her daddy." Anna smiled at Carl and Zoey and moved the wires so Zoey wouldn't disconnect them again. "It is nice to finally meet you, Mr. Murphy. I've heard a lot about you from your baby girl."

"She's been telling me a lot about you as well. Thank you for keeping her company for me. Please, call me Carl, Mr. Murphy is sitting on that couch over there." Carl smiled and nodded his head over towards his father.

"Please, call me, Anna. I've really enjoyed spending time with Zoey. She is such a beautiful little girl. She reminds me of my baby girl." As hours went on, Anna would come in and check on Carl and Zoey periodically.

Better Than a Dream

After a couple of days, Carl was cleared to go home with a couple months of physical therapy until he gets full mobility back. As Carl and Zoey prepared to leave, Anna stepped into the room to tell Zoey and Carl goodbye. As Anna turned to leave Carl started to speak up but stopped himself. Anna turned to Carl, "Carl was there something else you needed?"

Carl started to blush and tried not to stutter but couldn't find the right words. Finally, just before Anna walked out of the door Zoey spoke up, "Oh Daddy, will you just ask her already?"

Embarrassed, Carl spoke up, "Um, well I was actually wondering if maybe you might want to have dinner sometime? You've done so much for me and my Zoey and I just, well, I guess I just wanted to say 'Thank You' and treat you to dinner? I understand if you—"

Anna stopped him, "I would love to." Anna smiled and winked at Zoey.

Zoey squealed with excitement. Carl was excited and

nervous at the same time. "Sorry, I don't know why this is so hard. I guess since Clair passed, I've really not been out on a date at all."

"Oh, I understand Carl, trust me. I've not been on a date since my husband passed." Anna walked back over to where Carl and Zoey were standing, "There's something about you and especially Zoey. She's really grown on me the last couple months. I'm going to miss you little one." Anna reached down and hugged Zoey. Anna reached into her pocket and pulled out a small pink notepad and pen. She wrote down her number and handed it to Carl. "Carl, call me when you are ready for that dinner. I'm off on Thursdays and Fridays and after seven every day."

Anna walked out of the room and to the elevators with Zoey and Carl. Just before Carl and Zoey stepped into the elevator, Zoey turned and ran over to Anna and gave her a big hug. "I'm going to miss you, Anna!"

"Miss Zoey Grace I am going to miss you to. Hopefully I'll see you soon, okay?" Anna smiled and winked at Carl.

When Carl and Zoey got downstairs, Carl's parents were waiting at the front door with the car. "We ready to go? You got everything?" Carl Sr. asked as he took Zoey's backpack from her.

"Yep, we got everything. Daddy even got Anna's phone number so she can come see us!" Zoey jumped in her car seat and started to get herself all buckled in.

"Really? A phone number, eh?" Carl Sr. smiled and winked at Carl who was red faced from embarrassment.

"Yeah, yeah, yeah. Can we just go now? I'm so ready to be home in my own bed." Carl climbed in the backseat next to Zoey.

Once home, Carl could definitely tell his mother had been staying at his house while he was in the hospital. Everything had been rearranged, probably multiple times. He struggled to find things but was just so happy to be home he didn't say a word about it. He wanted to call Anna but didn't want to seem too desperate. He picked up his phone multiple times to dial the number but sat his phone back down each time. Finally, he dialed the number and chickened out again, only when he sat the phone down he inadvertently hit the call button on his phone. After a few seconds he heard Anna talking on his phone and lifted it to his face, mortified.

"Hello? Hello? Is anyone there?" Anna called out on the other end of the line.

"Um, hello? Anna?" Carl was trying his best not to stutter.

"Yes. Who is this, please?" Anna asked.

"Um this Carl, Carl Murphy, from the hospital." Carl was so nervous he nearly forgot his own name.

"Oh! Hey, Carl! I'm so glad you called!" Anna's voice changed as soon as she heard it was Carl. He could hear in her voice she really was glad he called, and he could feel his nerves calming down.

"I hope this isn't a bad time. I, I had your number here and didn't know if I should wait or go ahead and call you." Carl hadn't called a girl in so long he honestly didn't really know what he should say.

"No, it is a great time. I just got home a little while ago. I'm just sitting on the couch. How are you feeling?" Anna reached up and turned off the television so she could hear Carl better.

"Honestly, I feel great. This is so crazy, it's like I was never gone, well except my mother has rearranged my house while I was gone." Carl and Anna laughed. "So, I was wondering, do you think you might want to go to dinner one night?"

"I'd love to. Carl, I do need to tell you something though." Anna paused. "I haven't been on a date since my husband passed away. I'm not real sure on the whole dating thing. I don't want you to think I don't want to go or that I'm not interested it's just—"

Carl interrupted her, "Oh my gosh that makes me feel so much better. I haven't dated since Clair, and I am so nervous. I feel like I'm screwing this up so bad." Carl felt relieved to be able to say the words out loud.

"No, you aren't screwing up. How about we start small. What are you doing later? We could go get an ice cream. There's this great little place I know of." Anna was hopeful she wasn't moving too fast and was trying to make Carl more comfortable.

"That actually sounds pretty great. Tonight would be great, my parents are staying in town a couple days to help me get back into the swing of things so they would keep Zoey, I'm sure. Do you want me to come pick you up or we can meet there?" As soon as Carl said the words, it dawned on him he hadn't driven since the accident, and he wasn't actually sure he was comfortable driving just yet.

"Actually, how about I come by and pick you up. Since I know where the place is and all." Anna felt like he would probably be nervous driving the first time since the accident.

Relieved, Carl replied, "Okay that sounds great. I'll text you the address."

An hour later there was a knock on the door, it was Anna.

"Oh Carl, your date is here." Carl Sr. called out when he opened the door. Anna blushed.

Shirley walked by and popped Carl Sr. on the back of his head. "Ignore my husband, come on in dear."

"No, no, no, Mom we are going. Thank you for keeping Zoey. We shouldn't be too long." Carl walked by and kissed his mother on this cheek and rolled his eyes at his father on the way out the door. "Sorry about my dad. He lives for embarrassing me."

"That's okay, my dad did the same thing." Anna laughed.

They got into her car and headed to the ice cream parlor. It was an old fifties style ice cream shop. They ordered their ice cream and sat in a corner booth away from everyone else. Carl was nervous and wasn't really sure where to start.

"So, what do you want to talk about Carl?" Anna asked.

"Well, there is something I have been wanting to ask you but wasn't really sure how or when to ask you." Carl was starting to feel nervous again.

"Carl, I've cleaned your bedpans for the last month. I know pretty much everything about you so please, ask me whatever you want." Anna chuckled.

Carl started to talk and stopped when he heard Anna say that, "Wow I didn't think about all of that." They both laughed. "Well, here's the thing; while I was out, I dreamed about you. I dreamed that you had a husband and a little girl that you lost in a car accident. Then today you told me that you hadn't dated since you lost your husband and Zoey said you have a little girl."

"Yes, I did lose my husband and daughter in a car accident three years ago. Maybe you heard me and Zoey talking about it in your room? I did tell her that I had a baby girl named Clair that went to Heaven with her daddy three years ago." Anna stopped and took a bite of her ice cream.

"Anna, I really hope I'm not bringing back any painful memories." Carl was deeply worried he was screwing this date up. He really did have feelings for Anna, and even if the relationship he knew was all a dream, he wanted to at least try for that in real life.

"Oh no sweetheart, you aren't. It is okay. You can ask me anything." Anna scooted closer and put her hand on Carl's. "I feel like I've known you my whole life Carl. Taking care of you and helping Zoey these last couple of months has brought back feelings that I didn't think I would ever feel again. When you called, I was so happy to hear it was you I actually started dancing around the house excited when we hung up," Anna laughed

Carl was laughing, "I did mine and Zoey's happy dance too when I heard we were going for ice cream tonight. Anna in my dream, we had this awesome relationship and got very close. I know it was a dream, but I'd honestly like to try and have that in real life."

Anna smiled, "Well we can give it our best shot. How are we doing so far compared to the dream?"

"Honestly, nothing could compare to being here with you right now. The dream didn't even come close." Carl smiled and scooted just a little closer to Anna.

"Now see you keep talking like that and we will get along just fine." The two laughed and finished their ice cream. They talked about their spouses and their daughters. Carl felt like he had picked up right where he left off in the dream. Anna felt like she might have actually found someone she could actually have feelings for like she had with her husband.

After a couple hours, Anna took Carl home. When she pulled into the driveway, she put the car in park and they both turned to each other. "Carl, I have to say, this has been the best night I have had in a really long time. I have really enjoyed sitting and talking to you. I don't want to make this awkward, but I feel like if I don't say this out loud, I just might burst."

Carl was worried but tried not to show it. "What's up Anna?"

"Carl, I have feelings for you. I know we haven't known each other long but there's just something about you, and Zoey. Man, I love that kid. I never thought I could ever feel this for someone after I lost my family but there's just something about you two that feels right and that feels familiar. Do you know what I mean? Oh man, I don't think I'm saying this right." Anna was definitely nervous. She felt like a teenage girl talking to her high school crush for the first time.

"Anna, I really enjoyed tonight too. And no, you're not crazy. I feel the same way about you. I know it sounds strange, but I feel like I've known you forever. And Zoey, man that kid is smitten with you. She's not shut up talking about you since we got home. She introduced all of her toys to Frankie Bear and I've heard about all the stories you sat and read to her while I was out." Carl reached over and took Anna's hand. "Anna, I never thought I could have feelings for another woman like I had for my Clair, and I knew the moment I laid eyes on her she was the one for me. Anna, I felt the same way when I opened my eyes and saw your face."

As Carl leaned over to kiss Anna on the cheek, the porch

light came on, the front door opened, and Zoey came running out of the house. "Daddy! Memaw, Anna's here too!" As she ran to the car, Anna rolled down her window. "Anna did you come to see me? Did you bring me an ice cream too?" Zoey was so excited she was all but climbing into the window.

While Anna talked to Zoey, Carl quietly exited the car and walked around to the driver's side door where Zoey was. "Anna text me later or call me. This little one should have been in bed a long time ago."

Anna smiled, "Maybe the three of us can do dinner tomorrow, or maybe we can hang out all day? I'm off tomorrow and don't have any plans."

"I don't know, Zoey what do you think? Do you have any plans for tomorrow? You think we should go hang out with Miss Anna tomorrow?" Carl smiled at Anna and looked down at Zoey who was jumping up and down with excitement. "I think that's a yes! I'll give you a call in the morning. Text me when you get home though so I know you made it alright."

Never A Dull Moment

*A*nna smiled and slowly backed out of the driveway as Carl picked Zoey up and twirled her on the way back to the house. Once inside, Zoey couldn't contain her excitement and immediately ran up to her grandmother to tell her the exciting news that she and Daddy had a date with Miss Anna the next day. Shirley couldn't help but smile. Seeing that her son was not only back with them but may also have finally found someone to share his life with again made her heart leap for joy. She had prayed and prayed for God to send someone to Carl and Zoey and had all but given up after the accident.

Not getting the excited response she was looking for from her grandmother, Zoey ran over to her grandfather and started jumping up and down to tell him about the exciting plans for the next day. While Carl Sr. listened to her talk, he couldn't help but smile. He hadn't seen her that excited in months. Finally, after a few minutes of Zoey rambling incoherently, Carl Sr. stopped her, "Zoey, sweetheart, you are going to have to slow down. I can't understand a word you are saying baby."

Annoyed, Zoey stopped talking, took a deep breath and

climbed up into her grandfather's lap. She put her hands on his cheeks and got as close to his face as she could, "Okay Pepaw, I'm going to talk *real* slow since you can't hear fast." As slowly as she could, Zoey said, "Pepaw, Daddy and I are going to go to the zoo tomorrow. We are going with Miss Anna. You know, the lady from the hospital. Daddy, and me, and Miss Anna are going to go see alllllll of the animals. If you need us, we will be at the zoo, okay? Was that slow enough Pepaw?"

While Zoey tried her best to speak slowly for her grandfather, Shirley and Carl stood in the door way laughing. "I tell you one thing, that girl is about the funniest thing I've ever seen. Where's the camera when you need it?" Shirley and Carl laughed until suddenly Shirley realized something seemed off about her husband. "Zoey baby, come here, get out of Pepaw's lap. Carl, honey, are you okay? You don't look so great."

"Dad, hey Dad, are you okay?" Carl and Shirley walked over to Carl Sr. who was looking pale and out of breath.

Zoey jumped down crying, "I'm sorry Pepaw. I'm sorry I didn't mean to hurt you. Please don't be upset."

"I'm fine, I'm fine. I just got out of breath is all. My arm feels a little funny. Maybe it was just how Zoey was sitting. It's nothing you two get out of my face damn. Zoey baby it's okay, Pepaw is fine. Your daddy and Memaw are just being silly." Carl Sr. was annoyed at his wife and son for treating him like he was some delicate flower.

"No Dad, you are *not* fine. Mom, we need to take him to the hospital. He may be having another heart attack." Carl started grabbing his keys and Zoey's jacket.

"Oh, hell no we don't. I'm not having another heart attack.

It's just some gas from that chili I ate earlier. You two act like I'm dying every time I fart, I swear." Carl Sr. rolled his eyes and refused to get out of the recliner he was sitting in.

"Wait, where did you get chili from?" Shirley stopped what she was doing and turned to her husband with a highly annoyed look on her face.

"Woman, if you must know, when you were at the store, I found a can of chili up in the cabinet and made myself a chili pie with the corn chips I brought home from the hospital." Carl Sr. rolled his eyes at his wife.

"Um, Dad? I haven't bought a can of chili in a really long time. That can was probably over a year passed the expiration date." Carl looked at his father with a look of confusion.

"Boy, why in the hell would you keep a can of chili passed the expiration date? That doesn't make a lick of sense. Hell, I may need to get my stomach pumped."

"Hey, I didn't tell you to go through my cabinets. Seriously though, you don't look good Dad. We need to get you to the hospital. Please, after all we have been through, can you please not fight us on this?" Carl zipped up Zoey's jacket while Shirley stood in front of her husband insistent that he get out of the chair.

"Look, how about instead you call that cute nurse to come over. What's her name Zoey?" Carl Sr. turned to Zoey.

"Carl Anthony Murphy, if you don't get your ass out of that chair right now and get in the car so help me." Shirley was getting angry and everyone in the room knew it. Seeing the anger in his wife, Carl Sr. rolls his eyes and gets out of the chair to go with Shirley, Carl and Zoey to the hospital.

Within a few minutes of arriving at the Emergency Room, Carl Sr. is already getting annoyed. "Look, I told you I am fine, why are we wasting time sitting around here? It makes no sense for us to just be sitting here waiting for nothing. I am fine, let's go home." Carl Sr. starts to walk towards the door and stops fast when he sees the look on his wife's face.

Carl, trying to speed things along, walks to the Admissions desk, "Excuse me, I'm sorry to be a bother but my dad is a gotten to be a little impatient in his old age, do you know about how much longer it will be?"

The nurse behind the desk types some information into the computer and responds, "I do apologize, we've got an incoming trauma from a car accident and we have had several other traumas come in since you guys checked in. It could be an hour or so unless your father is currently having chest pains, or pain or numbness in his left arm or jaw."

"Oh wow, yeah let me go check with him. He was having pain in his arm earlier, but I'm honestly not sure right now." Carl turned and walked back over to where his parents and Zoey were sitting. "Dad, are you having any pain in your chest or pain in your arm? Or trouble breathing?"

"What you spend a couple months asleep in the hospital and now you are an MD?" Carl Sr. was annoyed and ready to go home. "I'm fine, my chest is fine. I told you already I got trapped gas, I shouldn't have eaten that old ass chili that *someone* didn't throw away. Can we go home now?"

As Carl and his father stood talking near the admissions desk, another nurse came to the desk and told the admissions nurse that the incoming trauma was one of the nurses from the fourth floor, Anna. "Wait, did you say Anna was coming in? Is she okay?"

"Excuse me sir, you need to go have a seat we will get you back as soon as possible." The admissions nurse was trying to remain polite but was getting annoyed at Carl's questions.

"I heard you say Anna from the fourth floor is coming in. Look, I need to know if that is Anna Beard and how she is. That is my girlfriend. I've been trying to call her and let her know what was going on with my father but couldn't get in touch with her." Carl was getting upset and his father could see there was something going on.

"Sir we cannot give you any information about other patients due to privacy laws. Please, Mr. Murphy, take a seat and wait for your name to be called." The nurse was now getting angry that Carl would not leave the desk and continued to ask questions about another patient.

The other nurse standing at the desk talking to the admissions nurse started to walk away but heard Carl's name and stopped. "Wait, are you Carl Murphy? You were the one that was in a coma for a while from an accident, right?"

"Yes, yes that is me."

"I've heard Anna talk about you. Step over here." The nurse nodded her head over to the side of the desk where she could talk to Carl without being overheard. When they were alone, she answered him, "Anna was in an accident. She was involved in a hit and run. She has a head injury. They were taking her up to get a CT scan when I came down. If I can get any information to you I will but I'm honestly not supposed to tell you any of this without her consent."

"Oh my God, thank you. Can I go see her?" Carl felt like his heart was sinking in his chest.

"I can't do that I'm so sorry. I could already get in trouble for even telling you she was here. If I can get you more information later, I'll come find you." The nurse walked away from the desk.

"Carl, son what is going on?" Carl Sr. saw Carl standing at the end of the desk fighting back tears.

"Dad, Anna was in a wreck and was hurt. They said she has a head injury but won't tell me anything else and won't let me go see her because of some damn privacy bullshit. They even knew my name and know we are dating but won't let me see her." Carl was getting very upset.

As Carl turns to wipe his face and compose himself so Zoey doesn't see how upset he is, Carl Sr. walks over to the admissions desk and tells the admitting nurse that he is having shortness of breath, chest pains and pain in his left arm. Immediately another nurse comes from behind the desk. "Mr. Murphy, please come with us we will get you back into a room right away and get the cardiac work up started." Carl Sr. grabs Carl and takes him back to the room with him.

As Carl and his father got settled into the room, Carl Sr. leaned over to his son, "Look, I'm fine, go find Anna."

"What Dad? What did you do? They aren't going to let me just wander around back here." Carl started to look around to see if any of the nurses could hear them talking.

"Boy, go find your woman." Carl Sr. pushed his son out of the curtained area they were sitting in.

Carl peeked his head out of the curtain and saw no one was watching so slowly, one by one he peeked into each curtain until he finally found Anna. As he slid into the curtain, seeing her lay there lifeless with cuts on her face and a bandage on her head the feelings of seeing Clair in the bed lifeless, and Zoey from his dream overwhelmed him. He rushed to her side. He took her hand, kissed her cheek and whispered softly in her ear, "Anna, it's me Carl. Sweetheart please be okay. I can't lose you. I've finally found my love again and I can't bear to lose you."

Anna slowly opened her eyes and looked up at Carl. She tried her best to smile when she saw his face, "Carl? What happened? Where am I?"

"Hey sweetheart, you were in a wreck. You are in the Emergency Room." Carl looked around to make sure he wasn't going to get in trouble for being in the room with her.

"But h-how did you know I was here?" Anna was confused and out of it.

"Honestly, I think it was God. My dad started having chest pains, so we brought him in. While he was being impatient at the desk, I heard them say you were in an accident and being brought in. Dad faked chest pains to get me back here to find you. Oh, Anna I was so scared I had lost you. I know this sounds crazy but Anna... Anna I love you. I know it hasn't been long, but I knew when I saw you that I loved you and that I would always love you." Carl couldn't keep the tears from streaming down his face as he spoke the words to Anna that he was afraid would push her away.

"Carl, I love you too. It is crazy, especially because most of the time we've known each other you were asleep. I just knew the first time I saw you in that bed that there was something about you. And then when I saw Zoey, I mean come on, who couldn't fall in love with that angel face?" Anna squeezed Carl's hand. "I'm so glad you are here. I don't know how but I know God put us together for a reason and even brought you to the ER tonight for me."

Carl leaned down and kissed Anna's forehead, "Sweetheart I will always be here for you." As Carl stood up Anna pulled him closer to her and kissed him for the first time.

"Um excuse me, but what are you doing in here?" An older nurse walked into Anna's room and over to Carl and started to escort him out.

"No wait Miss Sarah, he's my boyfriend. I want him here. Please, don't take him out." Anna spoke up. Hearing Anna call him her boyfriend made Carl's heart leap for joy inside of his chest.

"Oh okay, sorry, I didn't know." Sarah let go of Carl's arm and walked over to Anna's side to check her IVs. "We should be getting the report back from the CT scan soon." Sarah left the curtain and left Carl and Anna in the room.

"Hey, how is your dad doing?" Anna asked Carl who had totally forgotten that was the reason he was at the Emergency Room in the first place.

"Oh God, I need to go check on him. I'll be right back. Will you be okay for a few minutes?" Carl didn't want to leave Anna's side, but he knew he needed to check on his father.

"Yes sweetheart, I will be just fine. I'm not going anywhere." Anna smiled and squeezed his hand. Carl leaned over and kissed Anna again before walking out to go back and check on his father. "I can get used to kisses like that," Anna smiled.

Carl walked back down the little hallway and over to the

curtained room where his father was. As he opened the curtain, he immediately saw his father sitting on the bed eating an ice cream cone. "Dad! Seriously man, what the hell? You are here for a heart attack and you are sitting here eating an ice cream?"

"Boy, I told you I had gas. Just keep your voice down. I don't want to hear your mother's mouth." Carl Sr. took another bite of his ice cream.

"Seriously though Dad, how do you come in for a heart attack and end up with an ice cream? Have they come in and checked on you?" Carl shook his head as he walked over to the bed where his father was sitting.

"Yes, they said it wasn't a heart attack it was gas. They are waiting on one more test. Give me a few minutes to finish my ice cream before you go get your mother." As Carl Sr. finished his sentence Shirley and Zoey walked through the curtain.

"Wait for a few minutes for you to finish what sir? Seriously ice cream? Where in the hell did you get ice cream? We are sitting out there worrying that you are back here dying, and you are sitting up in this bed eating ice cream!" Shirley was both angry and relieved.

"He is fine mom. They are waiting on a couple more tests. Anna is here. She was in a hit-and-run. She is a couple curtains down." Carl tried to calm his mother's nerves about his father's condition.

"Daddy, can I go see Anna? PLEEEEEASE?" Zoey pleaded with her daddy.

"Yes baby, we will go see her. Mom, are you going to stay back here with Dad?" Carl asked his mother.

"Yes, I'll stay here, you guys go see Anna. If we hear anything

I'll come get you." Shirley hugged her son and walked over and sat on the bed next to her husband taking his ice cream and taking a bite of it herself.

Carl and Zoey walked down to Anna's room. As soon as they walked in the room Zoey took off running to Anna's bed climbing up into bed with her giving her a big hug as she climbed up. "Oh, my goodness, sweet girl! That is the best hug I think I've ever had." Anna smiled as she hugged Zoey back.

"Anna are you sick? Daddy said you bumped your head." Zoey asked.

"I don't feel sick anymore now that I've gotten a hug from a princess!" Anna smiled and winked at Zoey.

"Zoey sweetheart come down out of Anna's bed, you don't want to accidentally hurt her." Carl reached for Zoey, but Anna stopped him.

Scooting over in the bed to give Zoey some room, "No, no, she's fine. If she wants to lay right here with me that would be just fine with me." Zoey smiled and snuggled in close to Anna as Anna put her arm around Zoey. Carl pulled the chair up to the side of the bed and held Anna's hand as she dozed off to sleep with Zoey snuggled close under her other arm.

Carl sat in the chair watching both Zoey and Anna sleeping in the bed. As he sat there watching them, he couldn't help but think about how lucky he was to have found a woman that loved him and his baby girl the way Clair would have loved them. He felt lucky to have found a woman he could love the way he loved Clair.

A little while later Carl could hear his mother trying to whisper searching for him. He opened the curtain and whispered out, "Mom, hey over here." Shirley turned and walked over to where Carl was. "Hey, come look at this and tell me if this ain't the sweetest thing you've ever seen." Carl whispered and walked his mother over so she could see Anna and Zoey snuggled up asleep in the bed.

"Oh, my goodness! Please tell me you took a picture of that with your phone." Shirley whispered as she smiled from ear to ear.

"Oh, of course. I'll text it to you later. I don't have any reception down here. How's dad?" Carl pulled out his phone and showed his mother the picture of Anna and Zoey.

"They are going to run a couple tests to verify it isn't his heart and rule out his gallbladder. I said that stubborn man to stay on his diet and stay away from spicy foods but you know I think it would kill him to listen to me. I love him to death, but that man drives me crazy some days." Shirley rolled her eyes. "I keep telling him I can't handle all this stress and worry about him and his health. We already lost Clair, then not knowing if you were going to wake up. It's all just too much on this old lady."

Carl hugged his mother, "Mom, I'm not going anywhere, and neither is Dad."

"Well, you better not that's all I have to say." Shirley walked over and kissed Zoey and Anna on their heads. "Well, I better get back down there. He's liable to be trying to talk the nurses into getting him a cheeseburger and fries." Shirley and Carl walked out of Anna's room as Carl Sr. was being wheeled by to go to his tests.

"Woah, wait a second." Carl Sr. put his hand up to stop

the nurse that was pushing him in the wheel chair. "Hey, how's Anna?"

"She's doing good, they are waiting on the results from her CT scan but they said it looks like a mild concussion and she will be sore from the seatbelt." Carl walked over to his father. "What about you? How are you feeling?"

"I'm fine, I'm fine. Hey, take me in there so I can talk to my future daughter-in-law." Carl Sr. motioned towards Anna's room.

Before the nurse could tell him no, Carl spoke up, "Dad, she's asleep right now. And 'future daughter-in-law?' Really man? We've been on one date."

"Hey, you never know. A man can wish, can't he? I mean you're single, she's cute and single. Zoey loves her, she loves Zoey. You *clearly* are in love with her. What else do you need?" Carl Sr. laughed as the nurse pushed him down the hallway.

"I'm sorry Mr. Murphy, but we have to go. We've got to make sure there aren't any blockages and if we take too long the line for the CT Scanner will be longer and you still have an MRI yet to go." The nurse was trying not to be rude but knew she had limited time.

"Oh whatever, there's no blockages. Hell, I've been waiting all damn day around here what's a little longer? Can you just take me back and let me peek in and see my granddaughter? Are we seriously in *that* much of a hurry? Please dear?" Carl Sr. turned on his charm and used his sweetest voice.

"You are trying to get me in trouble. Okay, I'll take you back through but you have to be quick. Just a peek in, then we have to go and you won't fight me on these tests anymore? Deal?" The nurse stopped and leaned over so she could see Carl Sr.'s face.

"Done! Throw in an ice cream after and I'll be your best patient ever." Carl Sr. smiled and winked at the nurse as she turned him around and took him to look in on Anna and Zoey. As they turned the corner and Carl Sr saw Zoey and Anna asleep in the bed he commented to the nurse, "Is that not the sweetest damn thing you've ever seen? Have you ever seen anyone so smitten with a little girl? That lady, she sure loves that baby."

The nurse smiled, "Yeah, I know Anna, she's a good person. I've heard her talking about a little girl over the last couple of months. It looks to me like that baby loves Anna as much as Anna loves her." The nurse leaned down, "Can we go now before I get in trouble?"

"Yeah, yeah, yeah. Let's go. You aren't going to be poking me with any more needles, right? I'm already feeling like a pin cushion today." Carl Sr. motioned for the nurse to go ahead and push the wheelchair down the hall.

While Carl Sr. rides down the hallway for his tests, Carl and Shirley stepped out into the hallway to talk without disturbing Anna and Zoey. "Son what's going on? You seem like you want to talk to me. Now's the perfect time." Shirley leans in and checks on Zoey and Anna.

"Well Mom, it's just, I think— no, no, no, I *know* I love her. Zoey clearly loves her. She loves Zoey. What if that's all, what if she loves Zoey and not me? *Is* that enough?"

"Oh son, how can you not see it? Anna is smitten with you baby. When you walk in the room her face lights up. She's in pain from a car wreck and she is resting better with your baby in her arms than she was laying in that bed alone. While you were out of it, she was in the room every day, even on her off days playing with Zoey. You should hear how much better Zoey reads now because she sat and read with Zoey every day." Shirley put her hand on Carl's shoulder, "You need to tell her how you feel son. Let her tell you how she feels about you hon."

About that time, they heard Anna and Zoey start to wake up. "Good morning, beautiful." Carl smiled

"He's talking to you Anna, he calls me Sissy." Zoey smiled.

"Actually, I was talking to both of my beautiful ladies. How are you feeling Anna?" Carl walked over and kissed Anna on her forehead.

"Um excuse me? Where is Sissy's kiss Daddy?" Zoey had a sassy tone and silly grin on her face until Carl walked over and kissed her forehead as well.

"Excuse me, I need to talk to Anna alone." Dr. Emma Ryan walked into the room. Carl helped Zoey off the bed. Carl, Zoey and Shirley started to walk out of the room.

"No Carl, wait." Anna called out. "Dr. Emma Ryan, he can stay. That's my boyfriend. I'd like it if you would stay Carl."

Hearing Anna call him her boyfriend made Carl's heart nearly jump out of his chest. "Sissy, go with Memaw, I'll be right here with Anna, okay?" Zoey smiled and took her grandmother's hand and skipped along beside her.

"Okay, here's what we've got. You have a mild concussion, whiplash, and a bruised sternum from the seatbelt. You are going to be sore for a few days at least. With the concussion, we prefer you not be alone for twenty-four hours. If you don't have someone at home, we can admit you for observation." Dr. Emma Ryan paused for Anna's response.

"Oh, she won't be alone. I will be there to take care of her. Whatever she needs." Carl reached down and took Anna's hand.

"There you go, I have someone to take care of me. Does that mean we can go home now?" Anna squeezed Carl's hand.

"Absolutely. I'll get your discharge papers ready to go. It shouldn't take too long. It's good to see you again Anna. Next time, just come to visit, okay?" Dr. Emma Ryan laughed and left the room.

"Anna, I hope I didn't come across as too pushy just then. I guess I should have asked you if it was okay if I took care of you and not just assumed." Carl was genuinely worried he had overstepped.

"Oh no sweetheart, I was actually worried about asking you to help me. I'm not really good at asking people for help. Thank you so much for being here for me." Anna looked up at Carl with tears in her eyes.

"My parents are actually staying in my extra room. I can sleep on the couch and you can have my bed." Carl reached over and wiped the tear from Anna's face.

"Or, you and Zoey could come stay at my house tonight?" As Anna finished her sentence Zoey and Shirley came back into the room.

"Yes, Daddy let's do that! Let's have a sleep over at Anna's!" Zoey came running over and jumped up into the bed with Anna again.

"Easy baby, be easy with Anna." Carl was worried Zoey was going to hurt Anna.

"She's okay! For our sleepover, are we going to make popcorn and watch movies? I'm sure we can find something on the TV to watch tonight. Maybe read some books?" Anna smiled and put her arm up for Zoey to snuggle back up next to her.

As Zoey snuggled back up with Anna in the bed she turned and looked at her daddy and said, "Um Daddy, we are going to need to go home and get my sleeping bag, my pillow, some movies, and my books. Okay?"

Carl, Anna, and Shirley all laughed. "Yes ma'am," Carl replied.

As the nurse returned to the return with Anna's discharge paperwork Shirley heard Carl Sr. being returned to his room. "Ah I hear your father. I'm going to head back over to sit with him. You guys be careful. If I don't see you again tonight, we will definitely see you tomorrow." Shirley walked over and kissed Zoey's forehead and gave Carl a hug. "Anna, if you need anything dear you let me know, okay?" Anna smiled

"Mom, call me and let me know what they say about the old man when you find out okay?" Carl replied to his mother as she hugged him.

"Hey, who the hell are you calling an old man? You know I can hear through these curtains boy. I'm not too old to whoop your ass still." Carl Sr. yelled through the curtains as he was wheeled passed Anna's room.

Shirley rolled her eyes and laughed. "I can't take him anywhere. You guys be careful. Love you"

"I'm going to go pull the car around to the front. Sissy, are you going to stay with Anna, or do you want to walk with me?" Carl asked Zoey as he dug through his pockets for the car keys.

"I am going to stay with Anna. You heard the doctor Daddy,

he said she can't be alone." Zoey hugged Anna tighter. Anna smiled and hugged Zoey back.

As Carl walked out to go to the car, Shirley walked with him. "Sweetheart, are you okay?"

"Mom, I'm scared. I really like Anna, I mean I *really* like her. I think I'm in love with her." Carl was hesitant.

"Okay, I'm not seeing a problem here." Shirley stopped and looked at Carl with a look of confusion. "Look, I know it is none of my business, but I want you to listen to me, and not like your father, I mean *really* listen to me." Carl started to interrupt her. "No, don't interrupt just listen. Son, your father and I won't be here forever. We aren't getting any younger. As Zoey gets older, she is going to need a woman in her life to help her with things that a daddy just can't help her with. She needs that woman to love her and guide her. For the few months I've been around Anna, I can tell she has a heart of gold and she loves Zoey. She loves you. Whether you see it or not, your father and I see it. Don't let her slip through your fingers. Tell her how you feel."

"Thank you, Mom. That was what I needed to hear, well everything except how you and Dad aren't going to be around much longer. You can't be talking like that." Carl hugged his mother and they started walking towards the door.

"Oh, one more thing Carl, don't break her heart. She's been through so much just like you have, and I don't think she can take another heartbreak." Carl smiled at his mother and assured her he wouldn't. Shirley turned and walked back to Carl Sr.'s room and Carl went to the parking lot.

Once he got to the parking lot, he had trouble finding his truck. He had only bought it the day before and wasn't used to looking for it in the parking lot yet. The only way he could find it was to push the panic button to make the horn honk and the lights flash. "Hell, I really have turned into my father, walking around the parking lot lost." Carl mumbled to himself.

Carl found his truck and pulled up to the front door just as Anna was being wheeled out of the front door with Zoey sitting in her lap. "Daddy, Daddy! I got to ride in the wheelchair with Anna" Zoey jumped up and went running to her daddy.

Carl smiled at Anna as he reached down and picked Zoey up. "Okay Sissy, in you go. Get buckled up while I help Anna in the truck, okay baby?" Zoey climbed over into her seat and buckled her seatbelt.

"I can walk. They just made me ride in the chair because it is hospital policy." Anna smiled as she stood up and walked towards the truck. Carl rushed over and helped Anna into the truck. "It is just a bump on my head. I'm fine really."

"Bump on the head or not, I— I mean we are going to help you and take care of you while you get better. Isn't that right Sissy?" Carl winked at Zoey in the back seat.

"Damn skippy!" Zoey responded.

"Hey now, where did you hear that! Remember those bad words we don't say... that's one of them" Carl frowned at Zoey while he and Anna both tried not to laugh.

"Wait, which word? Damn or skippy? Pepaw says that all the time Daddy." By now Carl and Anna couldn't contain their laughter.

"How about let's just not repeat anything Pepaw says okay?" Carl laughed as he made sure Anna was cleared from the door and closed her door. Carl walked around the truck shaking his head laughing at Zoey.

Carl climbs into the driver's seat and leans over to help Anna put on her seatbelt taking the time to sneak a quick kiss while he was helping her. "Ew gross Dad," Zoey called out from the back seat. Carl and Anna laughed.

"Okay, everyone buckled up?" Carl asked as he turned around and checked with Anna and Zoey. "So, we are going to swing by and grab some clothes from our house. Do we need to go pick up any of your medicines or anything else at the store on our way to your house?"

"Dad, we have to get my toys and my sleeping bag too not just clothes!" Zoey called out.

Laughing Carl responded, "Yes Sissy, we will get your toys and sleeping bag."

Anna laughed at the two of them. "I do have some prescriptions and I don't think I have a lot of food at home so we may need to grab something for dinner and of course some popcorn for mine and Sissy's movie night." Anna looked backed at Zoey and winked at her. As she turned back toward the front Carl could tell Anna was in pain.

"Sweetheart, are you okay? You don't look so great" Carl leaned over and put his hand on Anna's.

"Yes honey, I'm just sore. We do need to pick up an ice pack when we got to the pharmacy." Anna smiled through the pain and squeezed Carl's hand. "So, what are we going to eat for lunch Sissy?"

"Oh, Daddy? Can we go get fast food for lunch? Cheeseburgers and fries from the clown place?" Zoey got excited.

"Now Sissy, you know we don't eat at those places. Maybe we can make an exception just for today if that is where Anna wants to go. What do you say Miss Anna?" Carl leaned over to Anna.

"How about we go to that place with the games and rides? We can have pizza and Sissy can play, and maybe we can talk?" Anna suggested.

"I don't know Anna, those places are always really loud. Are you sure you feel up to going somewhere like that?" Carl asked.

"I'm game if that's what Sissy wants to do. What do you think baby girl?" Anna looked up at Zoey in the mirror instead of turned around again.

Zoey was so excited she could barely sit still in her seat. "Yes, yes, oh yes Daddy, please can we do that?'

"Okay, if you are sure we'll go grab our clothes and toys and head over to the game place. Maybe if we get there early it won't be insane." Carl smiled. In his heart he felt the love Anna had for Zoey. To sacrifice and go to a place like that knowing Anna was in pain and not feeling well was more than just a friendship, she truly loved Zoey.

While at Carl's house, Zoey immediately ran to her room to start packing her backpack and grab her toys and sleeping bag. While Zoey worked on packing her stuff, Carl gave Anna a quick tour of the house. As they reached his room for him to pack a few items to take with him to Anna's, Anna sat down on the bed. Seeing her sitting on the bed, Carl couldn't help but admire her beauty. He stopped what he was doing and walked over to her, placed his hands gently on her face and kissed her softly. As he pulled away Anna pulled him back closer and kissed him again. Shirley was right, Anna did feel the same way about Carl.

They finished packing the things they needed for the night. Before going to the game place, they dropped Anna's prescriptions off at the pharmacy and picked up an ice bag. Once they reached the game place it was all Carl and Anna could do to get Zoey to sit down and eat before running off to play games. Now alone, Carl moved over into the booth next to Anna.

"Now that we actually have some time alone, Carl, I really think we need to talk. I feel like there are things on both of our hearts that we need to tell each other. If you want, I can start." Anna took Carl's hand and turned to look him in the face.

"You are right. I know I have something I feel like I need to tell you, or I am going to explode. I'll let you go first, ladies first." Carl smiled.

"Okay, here I go," Anna smiled. "When I lost Clair and James, I thought my life was over. I felt like I lost my heart. I never thought I could find love again and honestly, I wasn't sure if I even wanted to find love again. But then, I met Zoey Grace and eventually you when you decided to wake up and join us in the real world." Anna smiled. "I knew, I knew immediately that there was something different about you both. There was something drawing me to you both. Carl, I'm just going to say this, please don't take it wrong and I hope I'm not being too forward or moving too fast: Carl, I love you. I am completely in love with you and Zoey, I can't forget Zoey. She has my heart, Carl."

Hearing what Anna said made Carl's heart leap for joy in his chest. "Oh Anna, you just don't know how happy it makes me to hear you say that. I have wanted to tell you that I love you since the moment I opened my eyes and saw your face. I never in a million years thought I would find another woman that I could love, that would love me, and that would love my baby girl the way we loved Clair and the way I know Clair would have loved Zoey. The moment I laid eyes on you, I knew God had sent me an angel. Anna, I love you. I can't imagine not having you in my life and in Zoey's life."

"Oh, I can't imagine not having that baby girl in my life. Oh, and you too Carl." Anna laughed. The two leaned in close and kissed again this time more deeply.

"Oh, that is so gross!" Zoey walked over for another drink of her drink. "Do you *have* to slobber on each other like that?" Carl and Anna laughed.

Zoey played for a little longer. She looked over at Carl and Anna and could tell that Anna wasn't feeling well. "Daddy, it is time for us to go now. We need to take Anna home she doesn't feel good."

"You know Sissy, I think you are right," Carl replied before Anna could insist on staying to let Zoey play longer.

On the way home, Carl stopped at the pharmacy to get Anna's medicines. "Here you stay in the car with Sissy, and I'll run in and get everything." Carl put the truck in park and started to get out.

"Wait you need some money for the prescriptions. I'm not sure how much it will be so here just take my card." Anna started looking for her purse.

"Um, no I got this. Anything else I need to get while I'm in here?" Carl smiled.

"Don't forget the popcorn for the movies!" Zoey shouted from the back seat.

"Oh Lord, how could I ever forget the popcorn. Anna, you

need anything while I'm in here? Something to drink? Snacks? Anything at all?" Anna just smiled and shook her head no.

While they were sitting in the truck alone, Zoey unbuckled her seatbelt and climbed on to the center console between the front seats. "Anna, are you in love with my daddy?"

Anna smiled, "You know what Zoey, I am. Is that okay with you? Does that upset you?"

"Naw, I think he loves you too. Are you going to marry my daddy and be my new mommy?" Zoey asked.

"Well sweetheart, he has to ask me first and that's probably a good ways away from where we are now. But between us girls, I would probably say yes if he asked me. Why do you ask sweetie?" Anna put her hand on Zoey's.

"Well, the other night I heard Daddy praying and I heard him tell God he was thankful for bringing you into his life and for bringing someone into his life that loved me so much. Is that true? You love me too?" Zoey was smiling from ear to ear.

Anna, fighting back tears and to take a second to answer so she wouldn't start crying and upset Zoey, "Zoey Grace, I love you just like you are my own little girl. When I prayed last night, I thanked God for sending you and your daddy to me too." Zoey leaned over and hugged Anna as tight as she could. Even though Anna was sore from the accident, she didn't feel any pain while Zoey was hugging her, only happiness and joy. "Here comes your daddy, you better climb back in your seat and buckle up." Anna smiled as Zoey climbed back into her seat and scrambled to buckle up her seatbelt.

"Hey now, what are you two girls talking about in here."

Carl smiled as he opened the door and saw Zoey putting her seatbelt back on.

"Just girl talk Daddy, you wouldn't understand." Zoey tried to wink at Anna but still didn't quite have the hang of winking with one eye, so she actually blinked both eyes really big. Carl and Anna laughed.

Just before they pulled into Anna's driveway Carl received a call from his mother, he took the call on speakerphone in the truck. "Hey Mom, how's Dad?"

Carl Sr. and Shirley were also on speakerphone in their own car leaving the hospital. "Son it's bad, it's really bad. Carl, you're going to be a brother, I'm pregnant." Carl Sr. joked on the phone.

"Carl seriously shut up, you are not funny. I'm sorry, son, they said it was gas buildup but that he needed to follow up with his cardiologist in St. Louis this week. There was something on the Echo that they didn't really like. We are going to stay tonight at your house and then tomorrow we will head home. How's Anna doing?"

"I'm doing well Mrs. Murphy," Anna responded.

"Oh sweetie, I didn't know we were on speaker, I'm sorry you had to listen to my husband's failed attempt at being funny. Please, call me Shirley. Honey you are family!"

"Yes ma'am." Anna smiled at Carl.

"How about you guys come over to the house in the morning and I'll cook breakfast for everyone, and we can see you before we head back up to St. Louis?" Shirley insisted.

"That sounds like a plan. We will see you guys in the morning. We just picked up Anna's medicines and are pulling up in her driveway. If you need anything let us know." Carl and Zoey both told Memaw and Pepaw they loved them before they hung up the phone.

Carl parked the truck and promptly ran around to Anna's side of the truck and opened her door helping her out of the truck. Once he had Anna out, he opened Zoey's door and helped her gather the four bags of toys and books she brought with them, along with her sleeping bag and pillow. Zoey hopped out of the truck and ran over to hold Anna's hand leaving Carl carrying everything.

"Excuse me little girl, do I look like your pack mule? You can carry some of your junk ma'am." Carl lifted up some of the bags towards Zoey.

"Daddy, Anna needs my help. I can't carry that stuff and help Anna." Zoey turned around to her daddy and continued walking with Anna.

"Sweetheart I am fine, go help your daddy so he will let you stay up late and watch movies with me tonight." Anna stopped and turned back towards Carl and smiled.

"Okay you stand *right* here. Don't move until I get back, okay?" Zoey ran to her daddy to get her backpack and another bag. As soon as she grabbed her bags she turned and ran back to hold Anna's hand. "Okay, I'm back." Anna and Carl couldn't help but laugh. While Anna laughed, deep down it touched her how much Zoey cared about her and how much Zoey wanted to help.

As Anna slowly stepped up to the door, it dawned on her she didn't have her purse or even know where her house keys were. "Oh no, I don't have my keys, or my purse. How are we going to get in?" Anna turned to Carl with a panicked look on her face.

"It's okay, I have your stuff. They handed me the bag with

all your things at the hospital, remember?" Carl smiled as he opened the white bag with Anna's purse and other belongings that she had on her when the ambulance brought her into the Emergency Room.

"Oh, thank God. I don't even remember them handing you that. Thank you so much. What would I do without you?" Anna smiled at Carl as she reached into the bag and took out her purse.

"Here, I'll hold your purse while you find your keys." Zoey was so excited to help she dropped her bag of stuffed animals as she reached up to hold Anna's purse for her.

As Anna found her keys, she looked at Zoey and said, "Thank you sweetheart, what would I do without *you*?"

Zoey turned to her daddy and said, "See I told you Anna needed me." Carl and Anna laughed.

Anna unlocked the door and was escorted inside by Zoey. "I guess I'll just grab this bag you left here on the porch since you have your hands full helping Anna." Carl laughed and picked up the bag Zoey dropped.

As they settled in, Anna gave Carl and Zoey a tour of her house. When they walked down the hallway there was a room at the end of the hallway where the door was closed. Anna passed by and showed Carl and Zoey the bathroom. "Anna, what's in there?" Zoey asked pointing at the closed door.

"Oh, that room? Well, that was Clair's room. I don't usually go in there." Anna tried to smile and hoped Zoey would just move on so she didn't have to talk about it anymore.

"I'm sorry Anna, I didn't mean to make you sad." Zoey walked over and hugged her.

"Sweetie, you didn't make me sad. Do you want to see Clair's room? I wouldn't let just anyone go in there but if you want to, I'll take you in there." Zoey's sweet little face just melted all of the sadness away.

"Maybe we should wait until Anna's feeling better. I think she needs to go sit down for a little while and rest. Don't you think she needs to rest, nurse Sissy?" Carl winked at Zoey.

"I agree Daddy. But Daddy, I'm not the nurse. I'm the doctor." Carl and Anna couldn't help but laugh. The three of them walked into the living room. "Okay, what do we want to watch first?"

Anna smiled, "Your pick Dr. Zoey." Zoey smiled and picked out her favorite movie and handed it to her daddy to turn on. "Carl, while you are up, would you mind getting me something to drink so I can take my medicine. I think everything they gave me in the hospital is wearing off."

"Absolutely what do you want to drink?" Carl asked as he put the movie in.

"I should have some sweet tea in the fridge. The cups are to the left of the fridge." Anna replied.

"Anna, can I have some tea too please?" Zoey asked.

"Of course sweetheart, you can have anything you want, that is if your daddy is okay with it." Anna smiled at Carl.

"Okay, so that's two sweet teas. I'll go ahead and pop your popcorn while I'm in there too. Anything else I can get for my two favorite girls?" Carl turned and smiled as he saw Zoey snuggled up to Anna on the couch.

"Nah, that should be good." Zoey replied. Carl shook his head and went into the kitchen. As Carl walked back into the living room with the teas and popcorn, he handed Anna her tea first and then made Zoey sit in the floor at the coffee table so she didn't make a mess. A few minutes later Zoey turned to her daddy and said, "Daddy, I have a deal for you."

Carl smiled, looked at Anna and then back at Zoey, "Um okay what's your proposal?"

"Well I don't know what a proposal is, but how about this; instead of you sleeping on the couch, I will sleep on the couch and watch TV if you will sleep in Anna's room so you can keep an eye on her? Now Daddy, you have to keep an eye on her, you can't be keeping her up all night snoring okay?" Zoey took another bite of popcorn.

"Well, I think we should let Anna decide that. What do you mean *me* keep her up all night snoring, I don't snore, *you* snore." Carl laughed.

"Oh no Daddy, you sound like a bear growling when you snore. I don't snore." Zoey started laughing.

"Zoey, does he really snore *that* bad? I don't know, maybe I don't want him to be the one to stay with me tonight if he snores like a bear." Anna laughed.

"Hey now, I don't snore that bad. Y'all quit picking on me." Carl laughed and pretended to pout.

"If your daddy is okay swapping with you and sleeping in my room, I guess I can deal with his snoring." Anna winked at Zoey.

"I guess I can make that swap." Carl smiles at Anna.

"Yay!" Zoey jumped up and hugged her daddy and quickly stepped back, "I mean, good. Make sure you watch her close. You heard the doctor. He said I am in charge of making sure she is okay tonight."

"Yes ma'am, I promise I will watch her close and make sure

she is okay all night." Carl sat up straight on the couch and tried his best not to laugh.

"Well since it seems like that has been decided, I'm actually really tired. Zoey would you be upset if I went to bed early and didn't stay up late with you tonight sweetie?" Anna was visibly tired and in pain.

Zoey walked over and put her hand on Anna's head like she was checking her temperature, "Hmmm you are right. You feel warm you need to go to bed. Nurse Daddy, our patient needs to be taken to her bed." Zoey looked at her daddy who was trying not to laugh.

"Yes doctor, I'll take care of her." Carl stood up and helped Anna off the couch and helped Anna to he bedroom. Once in the bedroom, Carl helped Anna to the bed and tucked a couple pillows behind her to make sure she was comfortable.

"Carl, can I ask you something?" Anna reaches out and grabs Carl's arm.

Carl turns and sits on the bed beside Anna, "Yes, you can ask me anything."

"Are you okay sleeping in here with me? I don't want to push you too far too fast. I know we haven't been seeing each other very long but..."

Carl interrupted her, "Anna, I love you with all my heart. I know it sounds crazy, but I can't see myself without you in my life. Zoey is absolutely smitten with you and has talked non-stop about how happy her mommy would be that she's got a new mommy to take care of us." Anna started to cry. Carl reached out and wiped her tears and said, "Oh Anna please don't cry,

I didn't mean to upset you. Maybe I should sleep on the couch with Zoey."

As Carl stood to walk away Anna pulled him back towards her, "No Carl, these are happy tears. I am so in love with you. I never thought I would or could feel this way about another man ever. I always thought I was lucky to find my first love, but now I know I've found my last love. I never thought I could love another little girl like I loved my baby girl and I love Zoey Grace like she is my own. When she looks up at me with those big blue eyes my heart absolutely melts. Hearing you say that you feel the same way, well Carl it feels my heart with so much happiness and joy." Slowly, Anna reaches up, puts her hands on Carl's face, pulls him towards her and kisses him.

After a few minutes, Carl stands up, still holding Anna's hand and smiling from ear to ear. "I am going to check on Zoey one more time before I come to bed. Do you need me to bring you anything on my way back?"

"I am going to need a bottle of water. I'm sure I will be needing my medication first thing in the morning." Anna smiles and squeezes Carl's hand.

Carl leans back over and gives Anna another kiss. "I'll be right back."

Anna smiles and says, "Ya know, a girl could get used to this."

Carl laughs as he walks into the living room to check on Zoey and get Anna a bottle of water from the kitchen. When he walks into the living room, Zoey was already fast asleep on the couch surrounded by all of her stuffed animals and toys. Carl turned the TV off and quietly walked into the kitchen to get the bottled water. As he walked back around the corner her heard

Zoey talking. He thought she was talking to him, but before he could answer her, he listened and realized she wasn't talking to him, she was talking to the picture of her mother she had brought with her. Carl stepped back around the corner so Zoey wouldn't see him so he could hear what she was saying.

"Mommy, we are at Miss Anna's house. She is so nice. She is really pretty just like you. Her favorite books are the same ones you and Daddy used to read. Mommy, she loves me and Daddy. She told me so. I hope you don't get sad that we love Miss Anna. She told me that you will always be my mommy and she will never replace you. Mommy I love you so much and I'll never stop talking to you ever no matter what. So please don't be sad when you see us with Anna. Daddy still gets really sad that you aren't here. When he is with Anna, he laughs more and is happier. Memaw says he is going to need someone to help him take care of me too. I think I would like Miss Anna to help him with me, even though I don't think he needs help. He's a good Daddy. He taught me to ride my bike and tie my shoes. None of the other kids in day care can tie their shoes. Oh, and Mommy, one more thing because I'm really sleepy now; Anna's baby Clair is up there in Heaven too, if you see her, will you tell her I am taking real good care of her mommy and she doesn't need to be sad either. Night night Mommy, I love you."

As Carl stood there listening to his baby girl, his eyes filled with tears. He quietly snuck back into Anna's room, wiping his face so Anna wouldn't see he had been crying.

"Is Zoey okay out there on the couch?" Anna smiled as Carl came back into the room.

"Yeah, she's all snuggled up with the bazillion stuffed animals she brought with her." Carl walked over to the other side of the bed and started to tell Anna everything he had overheard Zoey saying to her mother.

"Oh, my goodness that is the sweetest thing I have ever heard. She is such a tender hearted child. You should be proud of the baby girl you've raised. I am sure Clair would be proud of both of you," Anna said with tears in her eyes.

Carl and Anna talk for a few more minutes then turn out the lights and drift off to sleep. A few hours later, Carl woke up to find himself hanging off of the edge of the bed with no blankets. He tried to roll over but found something in his way, he reached over and picked up his cell phone to see what was pushing him off the bed. Zoey had come into the room in the middle of the night with her Frankie Bear and was snuggled up with Anna and had moved him over to the edge of the bed. He couldn't help but smile. Carl reached down and gently moved Frankie Bear out of the bed and moved Zoey over just enough so he could get back into bed and snuggle up with her and Anna.

The Dawning of a New Day

The next morning, Carl and Anna woke up early before Zoey did. Anna rolled over and realized that Zoey had crawled into bed with them and was hugged up to her. She smiled as Carl helped her to gently get out of bed without waking Zoey. Carl helped Anna to the kitchen to sit down at the table.

"How did you sleep?" Carl asked Anna as he grabbed the coffee out of the refrigerator and started towards the coffee maker on the counter.

"I slept really well. I had the sweetest little snuggler all night apparently." Anna laughed as she pointed to the cabinet where the coffee filters were kept. "How about you? How'd you sleep?"

"Well, once I made a little room for myself, I slept great. The edge of your bed is really comfy." The two laughed. "Zoey hasn't crawled into bed with me in years. She usually can't stand the sound of my snoring."

"I guess I did sleep hard, I didn't feel her get into bed and I didn't hear any snoring all night." Anna laughed as she tried to stand up to go help Carl.

"No, no sit down I got this. My mom wants us to come have

breakfast with them before they leave and go back to St. Louis. If you don't feel up to it, I completely understand. My dad can be a lot to take sometimes, and you have been through a lot in the last couple days." Carl finished starting the coffee and walked over to Anna rubbing her shoulders while he waited for the coffee.

"You just do not know how good that feels on my neck. I expected to be sore but not this sore. Breakfast with your parents sounds awesome. For the record, I love your dad, he is hilarious." Anna laughed.

"Please don't tell him that, he will only get worse." Carl laughed and walked over to pour the coffee. "Cream? Sugar? Milk? How do you like your coffee?"

"I've got some flavored creamer in the fridge. Should be in the door on the second shelf." Anna pointed to the refrigerator.

"I'll let you pour until I see how you like your coffee." Carl handed Anna the creamer and set the coffee mug down in front of her.

"Pretty much, make it look like weak hot chocolate. I love coffee but hate the taste." Anna laughed as she poured the coffee. About that time Zoey came stumbling into the kitchen half-awake with her hair in a mess all over her head. "Well, good morning sunshine. It looks like you slept well." Anna laughed as Zoey walked over and put her head on Anna's shoulder.

"I woke up and you were all gone." Zoey was pouty this morning.

"Aw, baby girl I'm sorry. You were just sleeping so well we didn't want to wake you up and your daddy said he would take care of me while you slept. Being a doctor is tiring work you needed your rest." Anna smiled and winked at Carl.

"When are we going to have breakfast with Pepaw and Memaw? I'm starving." Zoey looked up at her daddy.

"Well, how about I call and make sure they are awake while you go tame your hair and brush your teeth? I can smell your morning breath all the way over here." Carl laughed as he pulled his phone out of his pocket to call his mother.

"Deal! Tell Memaw I want bacon not sausage, and real bacon not the fake stuff she makes Pepaw eat." Zoey yelled back as she ran to the bathroom to brush her teeth.

Carl helps Anna to her room and leaves the room while she gets dressed. A few minutes later Zoey comes running down the hall with one shoe on and the hairbrush stuck in her hair calling for her daddy to help her. Carl laughs and helps Zoey get the brush out of her hair. About that time Anna came walking out of the room fully dressed and ready to go. "Here, why don't I help Zoey with her hair while you go get dressed." Anna smiles.

"Oh, my goodness, that would be awesome thank you so much." Carl kisses Anna on the cheek and walks down the hallway to the bathroom to get dressed and brush his teeth.

"You know, it's okay if you and Daddy want to be boyfriend and girlfriend. I talked to my mommy about it last night. We decided y'all can even hold hands if you want to." Zoey looked up at Anna.

Anna smiled back at Zoey and said, "Are you sure it won't bother you? You know I don't want to upset you."

"No it is okay. Me and Mommy talked about it, and I told her not to be sad. We still love her, and she will always be my mommy, we just love you too. I also told her to let little Clair know that I am taking good care of her mommy down here. I like how you brush my hair. My daddy is so rough, he just doesn't know how to do hair good like a mommy does." Zoey smiled, "He tries though."

Anna had to fight back her laughter. "Well, in his defense, he doesn't really have a lot of hair on his head, so he hasn't had much to practice with has he?" The two were still laughing when Carl walked back down the hallway to Anna's room.

"Why do I feel like you two are laughing at me?" Carl asked as he gave Zoey a silly look.

"Because we are Daddy!" Zoey laughed.

Carl walked over and started tickling Zoey until she squirmed away. He leaned over and kissed Anna. "Thank you for helping me with her. I struggle with all that hair."

Anna smiled and laughed a little, "So I've heard."

Carl helped Anna to the door and into the truck. Once everyone was all buckled in, they headed back to Carl and Zoey's house for breakfast with Memaw and Pepaw.

As soon as they walked into the door, Zoey ran over to her Pepaw and hugged him tight. "Pepaw, did you get all that gas out that made you so sick yesterday?"

"Lord, yes, he was letting out that gas all night!" Shirley yelled from the kitchen.

Carl helped Anna to the couch and then joined his mother in the kitchen. "Good morning, Mom. Need me to help with anything?"

"Actually, we need to run to the store. That will give us some time to talk." Shirley grabbed her purse and the two of them walked into the living room. "Zoey, your daddy is going to drive me to the store. I forgot to get stuff for breakfast. Can you sit here and watch these two while we are gone?"

"Yes ma'am. Um, Memaw?" Zoey stopped Shirley.

"Yes, dear? What is it baby?" Shirley knelt down to hear Zoey better.

"Can you get me the *real* bacon and not the fake stuff you make Pepaw eat?" Zoey asked.

Carl Sr. spoke up, "Yeah Memaw, we want the *real* stuff not that cardboard crap you make me eat!"

Shirley laughed and said, "Okay, this *one* time I'll get the real stuff. But you let your Pepaw know as soon as we get home he is going back on his diet. Deal?"

"Deal! Pepaw! Memaw is going to get us the real stuff, but she said you got to go back to eating that junk when you get home!" Zoey yelled as she ran over to her Pepaw and climbed up into his lap.

"Anna are you okay here with my dad and Zoey while I run my mom to the store?" Carl walked over to Anna.

"Of course I am." Anna looked up at him and smiled.

Carl leaned over and kissed her. "Do you want anything special for breakfast or do you need me to pick up anything?" Anna smiled and shook her head no.

Once they were in the truck, Shirley wasted no time at all, "Okay, spill it. How did it go last night?"

"It went well. We all slept in Anna's bed. We had a nice long talk before Zoey crawled into bed and you were right. She feels the same way about me and Zoey as we feel about her." Carl smiled as he pulled out of the driveway.

"She told you she loves you? I noticed there was some kissing going on. How does Zoey feel about that?" Shirley asked.

Carl told Shirley what he overheard Zoey saying to Clair and that he had heard Zoey tell Anna that morning that they could be boyfriend and girlfriend if they wanted to, it was okay with her and her mommy.

Shirley smiled and said, "If that ain't the sweetest little girl. You've done good with her son. I'm glad you have someone that will help you with her and that loves her like Clair did."

It didn't take Shirley and Carl long to get everything they needed to cook breakfast. Once they got back to the house, Carl walked into the kitchen to help his mother cook breakfast. "Son, I don't need help, go sit in there with Anna and keep her company. Who knows what all stories your father has been telling her while we were gone?"

Carl poured Anna a cup of coffee with the creamer he knew she liked and took it to her in the living room. "I picked up some creamer while we were at the store. Let's see if I got it right."

Anna took the cup and took a sip, "Perfect. Quick, while your dad and Zoey are in the other room, can I have another kiss?" Carl smiled and leaned down and kissed Anna.

"Okay, that's enough of that mushy shit. I haven't even had my coffee yet." Carl Sr. laughs as he walks in the room and sees the two kissing.

"What is 'mushy shit?'" Zoey walks in and asks. Everyone starts laughing and Zoey looks embarrassed.

"Remember what we said about not repeating what we hear Pepaw say?" Carl looks at his dad and rolls his eyes. "Why don't you come show Anna how to work this dang TV, I can never figure it out." Zoey smiles and runs over to sit on the couch with Anna.

"Daddy isn't so good with the TV, I'll show you where my channels are." Zoey smiles and takes the controller from her father.

Not wanting to watch cartoons, Carl Sr. decides to go see what Shirley is up to in the kitchen laughing, he says, "Woman, you got my breakfast ready yet? If not, I'm just going to have to eat some left over chili."

Not amused by his attempt at humor Shirley responds, "I'm making the biscuits now. There's coffee over there ready if you want a *small* cup. I'll let you know when it is time to eat. Until then, get out of my kitchen."

Walking over to the coffee pot Carl Sr. jokes with his wife saying, "Alright now, don't get lippy with me woman. You know who the boss is in this here household. You know what I say goes."

"Yeah, yeah, yeah, I know. I know you're the 'general' blah blah blah. Now, get your butt out of my kitchen. You're being a general pain in the butt." Shirley laughs and throws a hand towel at him as he walks out of the room.

A few minutes later Shirley yells that breakfast is ready. Carl Sr. and Zoey pretend to race to the table to be the first ones sitting at the table while Carl helps Anna off the couch and to the table. Once Carl has helped Anna to the table, he goes into the kitchen to help his mother bring the food out to set on the table for everyone.

As Shirley walks to the table and sees Zoey and Carl Sr. playing at the table she asks them, "Excuse me you two, did you wash your hands before you sat down?" The two of them got up and went into the kitchen to wash their hands. "Those two, I swear I can't tell which one is the five year old sometimes." Shirley laughed as she handed Anna the plate of bacon to start making her plate.

"Thank you, Mrs. Murphy." Anna smiled as she took the bacon. "Everything looks so good. I can't tell you the last time I had homemade biscuits."

"Aw thank you sweetheart. Please, call me Shirley, or Memaw, or Mom. Anything but Mrs. Murphy." Anna smiled and nodded. "How are you feeling today? Carl said you took quite a hit."

"I'm sore, I'm real sore. I haven't seen my car yet. They told me it would be this afternoon before I could go see it and get my things out of it. I don't really know what happened. One minute I was sitting at the red light and the next minute I was at the hospital waking up and Carl was standing beside my bed." Anna held her plate out of Shirley to place a scoop of scrambled eggs on her plate.

Zoey and Carl Sr. returned from washing their hands. Both of their shirts were wet from them playing in the water. "Really you two? Did you make a mess in the kitchen? I just finished cleaning in there."

"Who us? We would *never* make a mess, just maybe wait a little for the floor to dry before you go in there." Carl Sr. laughed and nudged Zoey.

"Can I say grace?" Zoey asked as she scooted her chair to the table. Shirley smiled and nodded. "Good, Pepaw bow your head I'm going to say grace that way we can eat, okay?"

Carl Sr. smiled, "Well get on with it, then. I'm starving little girl."

Zoey bowed her head and held her hands together up by her face, "God is great, God is good, thank you God for our food. And God I want to say one more thing, God thank you for bringing Miss Anna to me and daddy. Thank you for Pepaw and Memaw. Thank you for this delicious meals we are about to eat. Thank you for Frankie Bear, Tinker Bell, Charlie, Cuddles, Puddles, and Peanut. Thank you for the electricity. Thank you for the TV and all my stuff. Oh and God please tell Mommy and little Clair that we love them and miss them very much." Carl clears his throat to tell Zoey that was enough. "Daddy just one more! And God, thank you for looking after Miss Anna and Pepaw last night. We would be lost without them. Amen!"

"Good Lord child. I told you I was starving and I didn't think you were ever going to stop praying." Carl Sr. laughed as he bumped Zoey.

The five ate breakfast and talked about their plans for the day. Carl and Zoey were going to take Anna to look at her car and take her to talk to her insurance agent about getting her a rental car or find out what she needed to do about her car. Carl Sr. and Shirley were planning to leave right after breakfast to head back home. Shirley had already made the phone call to the cardiologist and had Carl Sr. an appointment for early the next morning.

As they finished breakfast Carl helped his mother clear the table and took the dishes into the kitchen. Anna stood and slowly walked into the kitchen and over to the sink to help Shirley wash dishes. Carl insisted she didn't need to help but

Anna and Shirley both were looking for an opportunity to talk just the two of them.

Once alone, Shirley turned to Anna, "Anna, sweetie I need you to do me a favor."

"Yes ma'am?" Anna wasn't exactly sure what was coming next.

"Please, be gentle with Carl and Zoey. They have been through a lot and I don't know if they can take being hurt again. Please don't break their hearts."

"Mrs. Shirley, I can promise you I would never do anything to hurt either of them. I know it is hard to believe, but I love them. I really do. I can't imagine not having them in my life. Both of them. I never thought there could ever be another man in my life after I lost my husband, but I know Carl is who I was always destined to be with. And Zoey, oh my goodness. I love that little girl so much. It is like she was always supposed to be mine. I know it sounds crazy and I don't fully understand it myself." Anna was fighting back tears and so was Shirley.

"I am going to trust you with my babies. I know you love them. I can see it in your eyes when you look at them, especially Carl." Shirley hugged Anna tight then remembered Anna was sore from the wreck and let her go. "I'm so sorry I forgot about you being sore."

"No, you are okay. It's been a while since I had a mom hug me too. I lost my parents when I was really young. It's been nice being around you and Mr. Carl." Anna smiled and hugged Shirley.

Carl walked into the kitchen and saw the two hugging. "Is everything okay in here?"

"Yes, why don't you help Anna to the couch? I can finish

these few dishes myself sweetheart. You go sit down and rest."
Anna reluctantly agrees and Carl helps her to the couch.

After getting her settled on the couch, "I'm going to go make
sure Mom doesn't need any help. Dad, be nice." Carl leans down
and kisses Anna on the forehead.

"Well, ain't that sweet. There's nothing better than waking
up to a kiss on the forehead; unless you're in prison, then it is
just creepy." Carl Sr. laughed. Anna started laughing so hard
she was crying.

"Really, Dad? Really? I swear there's something wrong with
you." Carl walked into the kitchen, "Your husband, I swear."

"Oh Lord. Do I even want to know what he's doing now?"
Shirley looked over her shoulder at Carl as she was washing
dishes.

"He's making jokes about being in prison and getting kissed
on the head." Carl just rolls his eyes and shakes his head as he
pulls a towel out of the drawer to start drying and putting away
the dishes his mother is washing.

"Yep, that sounds about like him." Shirley laughed. "Carl,
stop harassing Anna and get your crap packed up, I want to
be on the road before eight!" Shirley yells into the living room.

"Woman, you are not the boss of me. We had this discussion
earlier, remember?" Carl Sr. yells back as he gets off the couch
and starts walking to the guest bedroom to pack his things.
Anna shakes her head and laughs at the two of them.

"Mom, I wish you guys could stay a little longer. I really
appreciate all you've done to help take care of Sissy while I was
out after the wreck." Carl leans over against his mother. "At least
you could stay until we know for sure Dad is okay."

"If he is in there running his pie hole, he is fine. If he would just listen to me, he wouldn't have ended up in the ER to begin with. Lord knows that man is as stubborn as the day is long. I got him an appointment for first thing tomorrow morning with his cardiologist. Dr. Katie knows how to set him straight. Plus, I think he has a crush on her and that red hair, so he behaves when he's around her." Shirley and Carl laughed. "Besides, you need to be focused on taking care of Anna right now. You two don't need a couple old folks hanging around you while you are trying to start a relationship. Especially with your father's mouth!"

Carl laughed, "Yeah if she can handle him, she can handle anything."

"In all seriousness son, we really do like her. I have a feeling things are going to work out really well with you all. You just better treat her right or I'll bring your father back here to stay with you and eat up all your expired chili again." Shirley nudged Carl with her shoulder and the two of them laughed.

Shirley and Carl finished the last of the dishes as Carl Sr. finished loading the car. "Did you get my bag out of the bathroom?"

"Of course I did," Carl Sr. shouted as he walked back to the bathroom to get the bag he forgot.

Shirley shook her head, "That's your father. Call us if you need anything. I'll call you when we get to St. Louis to let you know we made it home safely." Shirley hugs Carl and kisses him on the cheek. She then walks into the living room where Zoey and Anna were sitting on the couch watching cartoons. She walks over and kisses Anna on the cheek. "Bye sweetheart. You let us know if you need anything too, okay? Zoey Grace, get up here and give Memaw some lovin'! We have to get out of here. Be careful when you squeeze Pepaw, you know he's full of gas today." Zoey jumps up and gives her grandmother a big hug and a kiss then runs over to her grandpa and does the same.

Carl Sr. walks over and kisses Anna on the forehead, "You call us if you need us, okay? If he doesn't act right, you let me know and I'll come back. He's not too old for an ass whoopin'. And this one, you got to watch her. She will steal the covers and hide the remote from you." Carl Sr. laughed as he pointed over at Zoey who was crawling under the blanket she and Anna had been sharing on the couch.

"Thanks for the tip. I'll keep an eye on them." Anna smiled.

After seeing his parents out and making sure they had everything, Carl returned to the living room and crawled under the blanket with Zoey and Anna. Anna leaned up for Carl to get his arm behind her and laid her head over on his shoulder. It didn't take long before Zoey and Anna heard snoring. She looked up and Carl was fast asleep. Zoey started to giggle and crawled over Anna and started to pinch Carl's nose.

"Shhhh, Sissy, let's let him sleep. He was up and down all night checking on me and Pepaw. I bet he's really tired." Anna whispers to Zoey. Zoey sighs and scoots back over on the other side of Anna and lets her daddy sleep. A short while later Carl wakes up to Anna asleep on his shoulder with Zoey sitting up watching her shows.

Carl moved slightly and Anna woke up. "Oh, I'm sorry, I wasn't trying to wake you up. I just had to move my shoulder a little, my hand was starting to go to sleep."

Anna looked up at Carl and smiled. She really liked the feeling of waking up next to him, even if it was just waking up from a nap on the couch. Looking down at Anna's sweet smile Carl looked over at Zoey, seeing she was engrossed in the television he decided to sneak another kiss from Anna while Zoey wasn't looking.

"Now that everyone is awake, what do my two favorite ladies want to do today?" Carl asked.

"Well, I need to try and go make sure I have everything out of my car and go by the insurance office to see what they are going to do. I'm hoping they will get me a rental car so I don't have to keep bumming a ride from you guys. I should probably call and see about getting a copy of the accident report. I don't know how long those things take. Do you?" Anna looked up at Carl.

"Honestly, I don't know. I probably should get a copy of my accident report. I haven't even thought about it." Carl made a face like he was trying to remember something. "I honestly don't even know who I would call about my accident report. I don't know exactly where we were. I guess they would have a copy in Nashville at the Highway Patrol Headquarters. Oh, and it is our pleasure to drive you around as long as you need and or want us to. We love having you around, don't we Sissy?" Zoey was so engrossed in her show she never even heard the conversation.

"While you call Nashville about your police report, I'll call Shelby County about mine. Hopefully they can tell me where my car is. I don't have any idea where it was towed to even. I just heard the paramedics say they thought it would be totaled." Anna leaned up to get her phone off of the coffee table while Carl walked into the kitchen to get his phone to start making calls.

A few minutes later Carl and Anna have made their phone

calls. They both know where they need to go. "They towed my car to the police impound and said we could come this morning and get my things. The report won't be ready for seven to ten business days. What did you find out?" Anna asked Carl.

"My police report is ready, I have to go to Nashville to get it though. They wouldn't release it over the phone to be mailed and apparently they can't email it." Carl rolled his eyes in frustration.

"Sounds like a road trip then." Anna smiled.

"Oh, road trip! I love road trips! Can we go see Mommy while we are there?" Zoey has now joined the conversation and is excited at the thought of going to the cemetery to see her mother's grave.

"Sissy, I don't know that might be kind of weird for Anna." Carl wasn't really sure how Anna would react to going to see his wife's grave.

"No that's fine. We can pack a picnic." Anna smiled.

"Are you sure? We can go by and get your things from your car and go get my report later. I'm not in a hurry." Carl walked over and put his arm around Anna. "Besides after your accident being in a car all day probably isn't going to make you feel so great."

"There's nothing in that car that I need today. Let's go have a picnic with Zoey. I can't think of anything else I would rather do today." Anna smiled and put her head over on Carl's shoulder.

"Yay! Road trip! I'll go get my toys! Daddy, you get the food. Anna, you sit down, Daddy will handle everything. He packs the best picnics just you wait and see!" Zoey took off running to her room to pack her toys.

Carl laughed, "Anna she's right you know, you should sit

down and let me take care of everything. I do pack the best picnics if I do say so myself." Carl helped Anna over to the couch.

"You know, you two are going to spoil me. A girl could get used to being treated like this." Anna laughed as she sat down on the couch.

Carl went into the kitchen and packed the picnic basket. As he placed the snacks in the basket, he couldn't help but think about the day he packed the picnic for himself and Clair the day he proposed. Packing the picnic to go with Anna, he felt that same nervousness he felt that day. While he stood there remembering that day, he wandered off in his mind until Zoey came into the kitchen.

"Daddy are you ready to go yet?" Zoey pulled on Carl's sleeve snapping him out of his day dream.

"Almost sweetie. I've just got to get some juice boxes. Can you get those for me?" Carl turned away from Zoey and wiped the single tear that rolled down his cheek as he thought about Clair.

Within a few minutes they had the truck packed up and ready to go for the day. Carl helped Anna into the truck while Zoey climbed into her seat and buckled up her seatbelt. Within twenty minutes on the road, Zoey was fast asleep giving Carl and Anna lots of time to talk. Anna leaned over and put her hand in Carl's.

"Are you okay making this drive today, Carl? I know this isn't exactly easy for you. If it is too much, we can just stop at another park somewhere else and tell Zoey I wasn't feeling well. I don't want this to be harder on you than it really has to be. I just want to spend a nice day with you and Zoey, my two favorite people. I don't care where we go or what we do as long as I am with you." Anna looked over at Carl and back at Zoey and smiled.

"Oh no, I am fine with us going. I'm going to swing through and pick up my police report. They assured me it would be ready. Then we can head over to the cemetery and have a picnic while Zoey plays. If that is okay with you?" Carl leaned over closer to Anna and squeezed her hand.

Anna leaned over slowly and kissed Carl on the cheek. "I love you Carl Murphy Junior. I can't imagine what life would be like if you hadn't come into my hospital those months ago.

Carl smiled, "I love you too Anna. I can't imagine what our lives would be like if you hadn't been there taking care of both me and Sissy."

Anna looked back over her shoulder and saw sweet Zoey sleeping. "She's an absolute angel."

"Yeah, that's about the only time she stops talking." Carl laughed. "She really is my angel though. I don't think I would have made it without her after Clair passed. She kept me going every day for a long time. She was my purpose for getting up every morning."

"I completely understand what you mean. It was so hard feeling like I had no one and no reason to keep going." Anna dropped her head and was clearly hurting.

"Hey, Anna." Carl reached over and touched her chin. "You've got me and Zoey. We definitely need you."

"Honestly Carl, I do feel like I have a reason to get up every morning. I don't feel like I'm walking through life alone anymore since I met you. I never thought I would find someone that I felt this way about and I have thanked God every day since I met you." Anna looked up and smiled with a tear in her eye.

"Don't forget about me, you love me too right?" Zoey was awake and chimed in.

"Oh, of course! Don't tell your daddy, but I love you the mostest Zoey." Anna and Zoey laughed.

"Why do I feel like I'm getting ganged up on here?" Carl laughed.

A few minutes later Carl pulled into the Highway Patrol Office in Nashville. He turned to Zoey and Anna, "Would you ladies like to sit here while I run in and get my accident report? It shouldn't take long."

"Can I stay here with Anna?" Zoey pleaded.

"We can stay in the truck. Don't take too long, we may have to break into these snacks," Anna and Zoey laughed.

Carl ran into the office to get the report while Anna and Zoey stayed in the truck. He returned to the truck with a large envelope a few minutes later. "Are there any snacks left?" Carl laughed. "We ready to go? Where we headed?"

"Daddy, we're going to see Mommy! I want Mommy to see Anna and all my new toys." Zoey was so excited. Carl knew he had to take Zoey to the cemetery.

"Oh, that's right. I almost forgot." Carl smiled at Anna.

The three drove over to the cemetery and Zoey was so excited she couldn't wait to get out of her seat and started scrambling to unbuckle her seatbelt. As soon as Carl opened her door, she grabbed her toys and took off running to her mother's grave. Carl walked around and helped Anna out of the truck and grabbed all of the picnic supplies. While Carl spread out the blanket and setup the picnic, Anna slowly walked over to another area of the cemetery close by. Carl finished with getting the food ready and looked up to call out to Zoey and Anna when he noticed Anna was kneeled down beside two small graves clearing the leaves and debris from the headstones. Zoey walked over, sat down beside her, and put her arm around Anna.

Carl slowly walked over to them and he could hear them talking. "Anna don't cry. Clair is playing in Heaven with my mommy. My mommy says you can be my new mommy, and she will be Clair's mommy in Heaven until you get there." Zoey hugged Anna.

Carl walked over to the two of them and knelt down beside them. He read the headstones and quickly realized it was Anna's husband and baby girl's graves. He immediately regretting bringing her there and causing her more pain. He stood and turned to walk back and started to pack up the picnic when Anna joined him.

"Are we not eating lunch?" Anna reached over and touched his shoulder.

"I'm so sorry Anna. I didn't know they were in the same cemetery as Clair. I never would have agreed to come if I had known. I never would have come knowing it was going to cause you pain." Carl stopped what he was doing and turned to face Anna.

"Carl, I knew when you described where Clair was. If it was a problem, I would have told you I didn't want to come. Thank you for bringing me Carl." Anna put her arms around Carl and kissed him. "Thank you for being worried about me." She kissed him again. "Thank you for being you." After one more kiss they decided to go ahead and stay for lunch.

After lunch Carl, Anna, and Zoey walked over to Clair's grave one last time so Zoey could say goodbye before they got back on the road. Zoey ran ahead to her mother's grave. With Zoey out of earshot Carl stopped and turned to Anna, "Anna, I know I've told you this already, but I just feel like I need to say it again."

"What is it, Carl?" Anna looked worried.

"Look, I don't want you to think that I don't love you or that I can't love you because I still love and miss Clair. I never thought it would be possible, but I love you too just like I love her. I just don't want you to feel like you don't have my heart, because you do." Carl looked over his shoulder towards Zoey and back to Anna. "I know that Zoey feels the same way. She's never taken to anyone the way she has taken to you. I know we can't replace what you've lost, and we would never try."

Before Carl can say anything else, Anna interrupts him. "Carl, I understand what you are saying completely. I feel the same way. I'll always love my husband and I'll always miss my baby girl. I hope you know that I would never try to replace Clair. Even though I love and miss my family, I do feel like I have a new start and a new family with you and Zoey. I love you two more than I ever could have imagined. To be honest, I've tried not to love you both. I felt guilty, like I was replacing what I lost with someone else, but I feel like it isn't that you two are replacing what I've lost. You two are additions to my life, not replacements."

Carl and Anna start walking again towards Zoey hand in

hand. As they walk over to Clair's headstone, Anna leans down and starts to clear the leaves away from the base of the headstone. "Oh Anna, you don't have to do that, I'll take care of that." Carl leans down and starts to help her.

"Oh, I don't mind. I feel like I have a connection to Clair. After all, she did give me a beautiful little girl to love." Anna smiled and winked at Zoey.

Zoey took a few more minutes to tell her mommy goodbye and then reached up and took Anna's hand and then reached out her other hand for Carl's hand. The three returned to the truck hand in hand. Zoey climbed in the backseat and strapped herself into her seat while Carl helped Anna into the truck.

As soon as they were all in the truck Zoey spoke up. "Daddy, I have a question."

Slightly worried about what Zoey was going to ask, Carl looked over at Anna and then back at Zoey, "Um okay Sissy. What's the question?"

"Daddy, if you and Anna get married, can I have a baby sister? I really want someone to play with." Zoey looked up and smiled her sweetest smile and her daddy.

There was an awkward silence as Carl and Anna both looked at each other not knowing exactly how to answer that question. "Sissy, I'm not real sure about that. Me and Anna aren't there yet. We will talk about that when we get there." Carl looks at Anna who was trying her best not to laugh. "Oh sure, laugh it up." As Carl started the truck, Carl and Anna both burst out in laughter.

"Hey, what's so funny?" Zoey tried to lean up to see what she had missed.

"Nothing sweetheart. What do you want to listen to?" Carl shook his head as they pulled out of the cemetery.

Within a few minutes, Zoey was passed out asleep in the backseat of the truck. Seeing that she was asleep, Carl turned down the radio so he and Anna could talk. "It just dawned on me I really haven't ever asked you about your family other than your husband and daughter. Sorry, I guess I have been a little self-centered. You know everything about me and my crazy family."

Anna smiled, "Oh no, you have been anything but self-centered. There's really not a lot to know about my family. My parents were both killed in a car wreck when I was little. We were on our way home from vacation and my father fell asleep behind the wheel. Both parents and my little brother were both killed. My grandparents raised me until they passed away when I was in nursing school. Now, I just have an aunt and uncle that live somewhere out West, in California, I think. I've never met them, so pretty much it is just me."

Carl immediately felt bad. "I'm so sorry Anna. You really have dealt with a lot of loss in your lifetime. And you know it isn't just you anymore, right? You have me and Sissy." Carl reached over and took Anna's hand.

"You know, for the first time in a long time, I actually don't feel like it is just me anymore." Anna smiled and kissed Carl's hand. "Now are we going to talk about Sissy's request?" Anna laughed.

"You know, we haven't really talked about anything like that either. Do you want more children someday?" Stopped at a red light, Carl looked over at Anna to try to see her facial expression when he asked the question.

"You know, honestly, I had never even considered having any more children after I lost my baby girl. For one I've not been with anyone since I lost her, and I was probably a little afraid I couldn't love another child like I loved my Clair-bear. But since I met you... I can honestly see my future with you and Zoey and maybe even a baby or a puppy at least." Anna smiled.

"You don't know how big of a relief it is to hear you say that. I haven't been able to see myself getting re-married or having any more kids until I met you. Since I met you, I find myself planning for a future that I didn't really think existed anymore after I lost Clair." Carl smiled.

"Well, I guess we will just have to see what the future holds for us then won't we?" Anna smiled and squeezed Carl's hand.

"Okay, so now onto the next important items of discussion. Where do you want to eat for dinner, and would you want to stay at our house tonight or do you want us to stay with you again?" Carl smiled.

"We can stay at your house, we just need to go by my place and grab a few things." Anna was secretly relieved that Carl wanted her to stay with him again. She still wasn't feeling one hundred percent better from the wreck and didn't want to stay alone just yet.

"And dinner?"

"Well, what's the princess's favorite place to eat? I promise after I get to feeling better, I am a good cook and will cook for you guys. For tonight, though, I really don't feel up to cooking." Anna replied.

"Oh, that girl, man she would be ecstatic if I told her we were hitting a drive thru. She never gets fast-food unless my mom and dad are in town and then it is only because she and my dad sneak off to get it." Carl laughed.

"Well, since it has been a long day, maybe we should hit her favorite drive thru and just head home?" Anna asked.

"Works for me." Carl smiled.

A few minutes later Zoey wakes up. "Oh my gosh, I am starving. Are we ever going to be home?"

Anna laughs, "Sweet girl you just ate an hour ago and you are already starving? What do you do with all that food?"

"I have a high met, um meta, metab... Daddy what is that thing that lets me eat all that food and run around like a crazy woman?" Zoey leaned forward to get her daddy's attention.

Laughing Carl answered, "Metabolism, baby. You have a high metabolism, and yes, you run around like a crazy woman."

"Yeah, that thing." Zoey laughed.

"Well, we are going to stop and pick up food right after we go get some stuff from Anna's house. Is it okay with you if she spends the night at our house tonight since we stayed at her house last night?" Carl looked up at Zoey in the rearview mirror.

"Yes! That would be good. Hey guys, I have an idea!" Zoey was so excited she was nearly jumping up and down in her car seat.

Worried, Carl looked at Anna and then back at Zoey in the mirror, "I'm almost afraid to ask what your idea is with the ideas you've been coming up with today. But okay, I'll play along, what's your idea?"

"Anna should just move in with us! Then she wouldn't have to stay alone, and she could be there to play with me whenever she wanted to and we wouldn't have to go pick up stuff every day." It was obvious by Zoey's facial expression that she felt like she had hatched a brilliant plan.

"Well, it is a little soon for me to be moving in with you don't you think? I mean what if you decide you don't like how I cook or what if your daddy decides I snore too loud?" Anna smiled and looked back at Zoey.

"Well, you can't be any worse of a cook than my daddy, so that isn't a problem for me really. And, you can't snore louder than Daddy. He sounds like a bear growling for real." Zoey's eyes got really big as she made a growling sound.

Carl and Anna couldn't contain their laughter hearing Zoey's impression of Carl snoring. As they laughed, they told her they would think about her idea and get back to her. Once they picked up Anna's things and dinner, the three headed back to Carl's house. Carl unloaded the car while Zoey helped Anna into the house. A few hours later, it was time for Zoey's bedtime.

Carl went into Zoey's room to tuck her in and read her a story. Before he could start reading Zoey stopped him, "Daddy, would it be okay if Anna read me my story? I don't want you to be sad, but I really want her to read me my story tonight. You can read me my story tomorrow night Daddy."

"Of course it would Sissy. Do you want to go get her and ask her, or do you want me to?" Carl smiled knowing his baby girl loved Anna as much as he did.

"Oh, I'll go!" Zoey jumped out of bed and ran into the living room.

"Of course you will, any excuse to get out of bed." Carl laughed.

A few minutes later Zoey came walking back to her room

holding Anna's hand. "Carl, are you sure it is okay for me to read her story to her? I don't want to overstep."

"Oh, it is fine. I really needed to go take a shower, so it is pretty perfect actually." Carl smiled and kissed Anna on the cheek and then kissed Zoey on her forehead. "Just don't let her trick you into reading more than one. She only gets one and then it is lights out."

As Carl walked out of the room, he stopped in the door one more time to see Anna and Zoey snuggled up reading Zoey's favorite book.

It didn't take long for Zoey to fall asleep once Anna started reading the book. She slowly slipped out of Zoey's room and gently closed the door. She felt like her heart was going to jump out of her chest. She made up her mind that tonight was the night. She quietly crept down the hallway and into Carl's room and in to the bathroom where Carl was in the shower. She undressed and slipped into the shower with Carl.

Several minutes later Carl quietly whispers in Anna's ear, "Why don't we move this into the bedroom?"

Anna smiles and kisses him, "That sounds like a brilliant idea."

Carl grabs some towels and softly kisses Anna while he helps her dry off. He takes her hand and leads her to the bedroom. A little while later, Zoey hears some noises coming from her daddy's room and walks in to check on Anna. "Daddy? Is Anna okay? Does she need some water?"

Embarrassed and mortified, Carl answers, "No baby, she is okay now. You can go back to bed baby."

"Can I sleep in here with you guys?" Zoey asked as she started to walk from the door towards the bed.

"Baby, don't you want to sleep in your bed with Frankie Bear and all your toys?" Carl asked.

"I brought him with me. So can I sleep in here?" Zoey walked closer.

"I have an idea, how about I come lay down with you and Frankie for a little while in your room?" Anna was fighting back laughter.

"Okay!" Zoey got excited.

"I'll meet you in your room, so go get tucked in and I'll be there in just a second." Anna and Carl both breathed a sigh of relief.

When Zoey left the room Anna leaned over and kissed Carl and told him, "Hold that thought, I'll be right back."

After reading another story or two, Zoey fell back asleep, and Anna was able to sneak out of Zoey's room and back into Carl's room to resume where they left off.

"Man, what took so long? How many stories did you have to read?" Carl laughed as he lifted the covers for Anna to crawl back into bed and back into his arms.

"Only two. Now, where were we? Oh, that's right, I remember now." Anna smiled and picked up where they left off.

The next morning, Anna was the first one awake. She was careful not to wake Carl and Zoey as she got dressed and went into the kitchen to make some coffee. Within a few minutes Carl walked up behind her, moved her hair and gently kissed her neck.

"Good morning beautiful. How are you this morning?"

Anna turned around and kissed him, "Oh I am incredible. I haven't felt this good in a long time. Words fail me. I was really scared and worried but then you just put me at ease, and well, let's just say it was definitely your night Mr. Murphy." Anna kissed Carl.

"Well, I am glad to hear that. I'm here whenever you need me to put you at ease." Carl laughed and then kissed Anna again.

"Well, you know, Zoey *is* still asleep. How about this time we lock the door?" Anna winks at Carl.

"Uh yeah, let's definitely make sure the door is locked. Let me grab a cup of coffee and I'll be good to go." Carl kissed Anna's neck as she turned to start fixing his cup of coffee. As he reached his hand into her shirt, he heard the little pitter-patter of Zoey's feet running down the hall and pulled his hands back.

"Good morning, Anna!" Zoey yelled as she came prancing into the kitchen.

"Hey what am I? Chopped liver? No good morning for me?" Carl laughed.

Zoey sighed, "Good morning, Daddy." Carl grabbed her and picked her up spinning her around kissing her cheeks. "Daddy stop your whiskers are scratching my face."

"Well, I guess I need to go shave then huh. Can't have my whiskers scratching your face." Carl laughed. "I'll go shave and then I'll come back and fix breakfast how does that sound to my two lovely ladies?"

"How about while you go shave, Zoey and I will make breakfast?" Anna smiled and winked at Zoey. "Since I heard you weren't that great of a cook and all." Zoey burst out laughing.

"Hey, that works for me. I'll be back in a few, you two

behave." Carl kissed Zoey's cheek again and then kissed Anna's cheek.

"Anna, why did you get out of my bed last night? I thought you were going to stay with me?" Zoey asked as she climbed up on the barstool so she could see what Anna was doing.

"Well, you know, I heard your daddy snoring and thought he was coughing so I went to check on him and I guess I just fell asleep in his room. I'm sorry baby girl." Anna was looking through the cabinets for the ingredients to make biscuits.

"That's okay. Were you sick last night? I saw Daddy trying to help you feel better." Zoey had a look of concern on her face.

"Um, well yes, I was choked on something. Your daddy was helping me." Anna wasn't really sure how to answer Zoey or what exactly she had seen.

"He was helping you by patting you on your bottom? He usually hits my back when I am choked," The look on Zoey's face went from concerned to confused.

"Hey Zoey, do you know if your daddy has any flour? I think I am going to make biscuits and gravy to go with sausage and eggs." Anna was trying her best to change the subject quickly.

"Oh yeah! I love biscuits and gravy! That's my favorite. Can you make scrambled eggs? Daddy always burns the eggs." Zoey pushed the stool over to the cabinet and started to climb up so she could get the flour for Anna.

"Here baby girl, I'll get it. What's all this talk about me burning eggs?" Carl walked in and grabbed the flour out of the cabinet. Zoey giggled and ran out of the room.

Anna walked over and leaned in close to Carl and whispered, "Oh my *God*. She definitely saw more than we thought she did last night. She just asked me why you were patting me on my bottom to help me clear my throat." Anna was mortified. Carl laughed and Anna elbowed him, "That's not funny. We have to make *sure* we lock the door from now on."

"Yes, we have to be more careful, can you imagine if she had walked in earlier when we first went to bed. I don't know how we would explain *that.*" Carl laughed and Anna rolled her eyes as she started laughing.

The Start of a New Life

A few days later, both Carl and Anna returned to their normal work schedules and Zoey started back to school. Rather than going back and forth between the two houses, Anna stayed every night she wasn't working with Carl and Zoey. When she did work, she usually ended up having breakfast with Carl and Zoey before they left for the day and then slept at Carl's house until she had to be back at work. After four months, Carl decided it was time to propose but wasn't really sure how he should do it. With Clair, he was so nervous he nearly ruined the night and was afraid he would make the same mistake with Anna. He decided to call his mother for a little advice.

"Hey Ma, how are you and Dad doing?" Carl asked as soon as his mother answered the phone.

"Oh hey, son! We are doing good! Carl, turn down that dang TV, your son is on the phone." Shirley turned to Carl Sr. and threw the magazine she had in her hand at him. "How are Zoey and Anna doing?"

225

"They still shackin' up? That's my boy!" Carl Sr. laughed in the background.

"Oh my God, Carl, shut that crap up. You both know how I feel about that. It ain't right, I tell you, it just ain't right." Shirley commented as she shook her head.

"Mom, I know how you feel, that's why I am calling you I need your help." Carl was trying not to get frustrated at his mother's lectures.

"Help? Is everything okay with you and Anna?" Shirley stopped lecturing and started to become concerned.

"See, I told you he waited around too long that girl done gone and found her someone else." Carl Sr. chimed in.

"Mom, everything is fine! We are fine! I want to ask her to marry me for God's sake." Carl was really getting frustrated and regretting calling to ask his parents for advice on this one.

"Oh, thank God! I was really worried something had happened. Wait, you are going to ask her to marry you? Oh, Carl that is the best news!" Shirley was so excited. "See, Carl, I told you she wasn't leaving that boy she loves him too much, you old codger." Shirley threw another magazine at her husband.

"Woman, you got one more time calling me that and throwing them damn magazines at me and I'm going to put you out in the yard." Carl Sr. sat up and threw the magazine back at her.

"Do you have a ring yet?" Shirley asked Carl.

"No, honestly, I don't really know what to buy or if she wants a ring or how and when to ask her. I was so nervous when I asked Clair that I damn near messed up the whole night. Hell, I thought I was going to crap my pants by the time I got the words out to ask her. I just don't want to do that again." Just thinking back to the night he proposed to Clair had his stomach churning from his nerves.

"Son, I have an idea. Why don't you let Zoey ask her? You can give Zoey my mother's engagement ring and have her ask Anna. That way Zoey will be included and when she sees the ring, she will know it was from you." Shirley stood up and started to walk to her bedroom to make sure she could find her mother's ring easily.

"Oh Mom, that actually is a brilliant idea. She and Zoey love to go on picnics and Granny's ring is awesome. Are you sure you would be okay with me giving it to Anna?" Carl was loving the idea of Zoey actually asking but he wasn't really sure how he would keep Zoey from spoiling the surprise.

"For Anna, of course I am okay with it. Your father has a doctor's appointment in Memphis next week if you can wait that long we will bring it with us and give it to you then." Shirley found the ring and started to clean it off.

"That would be perfect. Wait, why does dad have an appointment in Memphis? Is everything okay?" Carl was starting to get a little worried.

"Oh yeah, it is just his usual VA visit. Nothing to worry about." Shirley put the ring back in the box. "I even found a beautiful box Zoey can use to give Anna the ring. It will be perfect Carl!" Shirley was getting so excited that Carl was going to propose to Anna.

"Oh, Mom this is going to be perfect. I will just have to wait and tell Sissy *right before* I want her to ask her. She can't keep a secret to save her life." Carl laughed.

"Well baby, she's only six," Shirley replied.

"Well, she's five for two more weeks but yeah, you are right." Carl smiled as he looked down at a picture of Zoey and Anna that he had on his desk at work. "Okay, well, call me when you guys get into town, and I'll come meet you. Do you want to do dinner with the three of us while you are here? You can stay at the house and go home the next day."

"Honestly son, I don't really think there's room for us with everyone living under one roof now. Surely, you aren't planning to sleep in the same room with your girlfriend with me and your father under the same roof." Shirley was clearly not comfortable with the idea.

"Mom, I am grown you know. It isn't like I'm a child and you don't know what's going on anyway. If it bothers you that much, you guys *could* stay at Anna's house." Carl was really trying not to laugh at his mother's naivety when it came to his sex life.

"Oh, that would work as long as Anna is okay with it. We will see you next week. Love you son! Give everyone hugs and kisses for us!" Shirley walked back into the living room with her husband so he could say good-bye to Carl.

The next six days seemed like the longest six days. Carl met with his parents over lunch and got his Granny's ring from his mother. He explained how he planned to propose that night at dinner because he just couldn't wait any longer. He had reservations for the five of them at a nice restaurant in Downtown Memphis. Shirley was beyond happy that she and Carl Sr. would be present to see the proposal.

That night during dinner, Carl leaned over to Zoey and asked her if she wanted to go see the ducks. Excited Zoey jumped out of her seat and was ready to run over to the fountain to see the ducks. Anna offered to come with them but Shirley engaged her in conversation so Carl and Zoey could slip off alone. Once they got to the fountain out of Anna's sight, Carl kneeled down and showed Zoey the ring.

"Baby girl I want to show you something. You see this, this was my Granny's ring. Do you like it?" Carl asked as he opened the ring box.

"Oh Daddy that is pretty. Is it for Anna?" Zoey got excited.

"Yes, baby that is exactly who it is for. I want her to marry me. Is that okay with you?" It dawned on Carl that he hadn't actually asked Zoey if she was really okay with him marrying Anna.

"Yes Daddy, that is perfect. Now Anna can be my mommy and you can get me a baby sister for my birthday next week!" Zoey jumped and hugged her daddy tight.

"Hold on baby girl, we can't get a baby sister for your birthday next week. That takes time. I need you to help me out though. Can you do that?" Carl tried not to laugh.

"I can help. I'd like to help Daddy!" Zoey was so excited she was jumping up and down. Carl had to quiet her down so Anna didn't hear them.

"Okay Sissy this is what I want you to do: when we go back to the table, I want you to walk over to Anna and ask her if she will make your daddy the happiest Daddy in the world and be your mommy. Then hand her this box, okay? You think you can do that? Now you can't drop this box, it would make me very sad and upset Memaw okay?" Carl made sure he was looking Zoey in the eyes so she understood how important the ring was.

Zoey smiled from ear to ear, "You mean I get to ask her to marry us?"

Carl smiled, "Yes baby, I like that very much. We want Anna to marry us." Zoey squeezed Carl's neck tight then pulled him to get him to stand up so they could go back to the table. Carl handed Zoey the ring and she very carefully walked back to the table holding the ring box like she was holding a precious treasure.

As they approached the table, Zoey walked pass her seat and over to Anna. She tapped Anna on the shoulder and held out the ring box. "Anna, will you make me the happiest mommy in the world and marry us?"

Anna smiled with a confused look on her face as she looked at Carl who at this point was shaking his head and laughing. Carl walked over beside Anna and Zoey and got down on one knee. He opened the ring box from Zoey's hand and said, "Anna, I can't imagine my life or Zoey's without you in it. Will you marry us and make our family complete?"

Anna looked at Carl with tears in her eyes and said, "Yes, absolutely YES!"

Carl slipped the ring on Anna's finger and hugged her pulling Zoey into the hug with him. Carl looked over at his parents who were both crying and smiled.

Zoey ran over to her Pepaw and said, "Guess what Pepaw! I'm getting a baby sister for my birthday next week!"

Shirley started to choke on her water as Anna and Carl both tried to explain there was *no* baby coming next week and told the story about Zoey asked for a baby sister when they got married. As everyone laughed, they began discussing the wedding. Anna explained that she honestly did not want a big wedding and that she really just wanted it to be the five of them and a minister if that was okay with Shirley and Carl.

"Well, you know," Carl Sr. spoke up, "I am an ordained minister. I can marry you two. You go get a license and I'll get you two hitched in no time at all. Heck I won't even charge you much." Carl Sr. chuckled as Shirley swatted at him.

"Actually, Mr. Murphy, that would be kind of cool. Can you really marry us?" Anna asked as she looked over at Carl.

"Really? You want my dad to marry us?" Carl wasn't sure if Anna was joking.

"Why not? That would make it a family event for sure!" Anna smiled. "Besides, I *love* your dad. We will for sure get some laughs in."

"Mom, what do you think?" Carl looked at his mom.

"If Anna thinks it would be a good idea, then I'm all for it. You might want to make sure and write out exactly what you want him to say. Let's face it; we all know he still won't stick to that." Shirley laughed.

"It sounds like a plan. Now we just have to figure out the date." Anna reached over and took Carl's hand.

"Well, I could take off tomorrow and we could see about going to get a license. Mom and Dad, you think you could stay a few more days?" Carl turned to his mother.

"We don't have anything going. Ever. Why don't you guys look at your schedules and get married when you can take a week or two off after the wedding and we will take Sissy with us home to St. Louis so you guys can have some grown up time." Carl Sr. smiled and winked at Carl.

"Well, you know I may be able to take the rest of this week and next week off. That would save you guys a trip back down here. Carl, do you think you can get the rest of the week and next week off? That way we could even have Zoey's birthday at Memaw and Pepaw's house next week too." Anna looked over at Zoey. "What do you think Zoey?"

"That would be great! Can we have my birthday at the Zoo?" Zoey was so excited she was jumping up and down. "I'm getting a new mommy, a new sister and my birthday at the zoo Pepaw!" Zoey ran over to her Pepaw and hugged him.

Laughing, Carl tried to calm Zoey down, "Okay Sissy, slow down just a little. We can have your party at the Zoo. I'll call and let Joe at work know I need to work remote the next two weeks." Carl turned to look at Anna, "Are you sure this isn't too fast? I don't want you to feel rushed."

Anna smiled, "Not at all. If we could get married tonight I would!"

The next morning Carl, Anna, and Zoey got up early and headed over to the County Clerk's Office to get everything in order for the wedding.

Once the paperwork was all signed, Carl turned to Zoey and Anna and asked them, "So, are you two ready for your spa day?"

Confused Anna asked, "What do you mean spa day?"

"I had my mom call and schedule you three a spa day. You all deserve to be pampered. After all, you do have to put up with me forever now." Carl laughed. "I'm going to drop you two off with my mom at the spa while Dad and I go run some last minute errands to make sure everything is perfect for this afternoon."

"You sure you don't need me to help with all of that? That's a lot to put on you sweetheart." Anna didn't want to seem like she didn't trust Carl with the details but also didn't want him to get overwhelmed.

"Hey, I already picked the perfect bride, clearly I have good taste." Carl leaned over and kissed Anna as he opened the door for her to get into the truck.

Anna reached back and helped Zoey get buckled in as Carl walked around the truck. When he got into the truck she turned to him, "Babe, we haven't even talked about a place or what we are going to wear. Are you *sure* you don't need my help today? Zoey can go with your mom, and I can stay back and help you guys."

"*Mommy!* He is trying to surprise you, *gosh.* Let's go get spa-ed." Zoey rolled her eyes.

Carl and Anna couldn't help but laugh at Zoey. "Okay, if you insist. I'm just not used to someone taking care of me." Anna smiled at Carl as they headed out of the parking lot and to the spa.

When they arrived at the spa, Carl opened the door for his two ladies and kissed each of them on the cheek. He walked over to his mom and whispered in her ear making sure she had everything lined up. She nodded and the three ladies walked into the spa to enjoy a day of relaxation.

Carl picked up his father and the two headed out to get everything ready for the wedding. A few hours later as they were finishing the final touches on the archway for the wedding, Carl's phone rang. It was Anna. "Carl this is too much!"

"What is too much?" Carl wasn't sure where Anna was in his day of surprises that he had arranged for her.

"All of this. Carl, I don't deserve this all." Anna was almost in tears. "The day at the spa was already over the top. You didn't have to send us shopping too. Sweetheart, I am just happy I am getting to marry you."

"Anna, you deserve more than just a day at the spa and a new dress. You are the love of my life, and you deserve nothing but the best. You, Zoey, and my mom are the most important women in my life." Carl smiled at his dad and gave him the thumbs up.

"Your mom just told me once we get dressed, I have to put on a blindfold. What else do you have planned Mr. Murphy?" Anna asked.

"Just follow her instructions; she gets mean when you don't listen. Just ask my dad." Carl laughed.

Three hours later Shirley, Zoey, and a blindfolded Anna pulled up at the wedding location. It was a quiet piece of property Carl and Clair had purchased shortly after they found out they were expecting Zoey with the intention of building a house. After Clair died, Carl only visited the property to cut the grass and occasionally hunt. Today, Carl and his father had built and decorated a beautiful archway overlooking a small pond partially lined with trees. Carl directed Shirley to pull up so that Anna would step out of the car onto a rose pedal-lined pathway he had created. It was all Zoey could do to contain her excitement when she looked out of the window and saw her daddy and Pepaw dressed in suits and all the pretty flowers.

As soon as the car stopped, Zoey unbuckled herself and jumped out of the car running to her Pepaw. "Oh, Pepaw you look so handsome! Even Memaw said so!"

While Zoey twirled around in her pretty new dress with

Pepaw, Carl walked over to the door to help his bride out of the car. When Anna stepped out of the car, she was so beautiful she took Carl's breath. He leaned over and kissed her on the cheek as he gently removed her blindfold. When she opened her eyes, she was speechless. She couldn't believe Carl and his father had done all of this for her.

"Oh Carl, I feel like I'm dreaming. I can't believe you did all of this for me." Anna was fighting back tears of joy.

"Well, shall we?" Carl held out his arm for Anna to take his arm and walk down the flower pedal aisle.

"Alright you two, let's get this show on the road before it gets dark and the skeeters carry us away." Carl Sr. smiled as Carl and Anna walked up. "Alright, you two ready?" Anna and Carl both look at each other, smiled and nodded. As Carl Sr. starts to talk Carl cleared his throat and motioned towards his father's pocket. "Oh yeah sorry, I forgot we wrote all this down. Seems like someone doesn't trust me to just wing it." Carl Sr. reaches in his pocket and pulls out a folded sheet of paper and starts to read over it. "Okay, yada, yada, don't need that. Y'all know why we are here don't need to say that. Um, let's see, how about we just go to the vows. Y'all wrote your own vows, right?"

Shirley rolled her eyes as Anna and Carl both pulled out the vows they had written for each other. "Sissy, you got your vows too?" Carl Sr. looked down at Zoey who was smiling from ear to ear. "Carl, you go first son."

Carl reached out and held Anna's hand, "Man, I hope this makes sense. Anna," Carl stopped and took a deep breath. "My beautiful Anna. From the moment I dreamt of you until this moment, I knew that you and I were meant to be. I always knew there was a piece of me missing, and I knew when I saw your face that you were that missing piece. You have healed me in ways I never thought possible and loved me like no one else could. You've loved my daughter like no other. I love you. I give you my hand in marriage and my heart for all of eternity." As Carl finished, he folded his paper and put it in his pocket looking up at Anna who had tears streaming down her face.

"Good job son. Alright Anna, your turn." Carl Sr. reached in his pocket, pulled out a handkerchief and handed it to Anna to wipe her face.

"Carl, my love." Anna looked up at Carl and smiled. "You have taught me what it is to love again. How it feels to care for someone and how it feels to be cared for in a way no one else has ever made me feel. When I look into your eyes, I see a man with a heart for God and a love like no other. It is easy for me to get lost in love knowing that you are there with me and will never leave my side. Not only did you give me yourself, you gave me a daughter; a family. I love you, Carl Murphy. I feel like I always have and I *know* I always will." As Anna finished and folded her paper, she looked up at Carl who also had tears streaming down his cheeks. She handed him the handkerchief his father had loaned her.

"Aw, ain't that sweet. Okay lil' one, you're up. Make these two crybabies cry some more." Carl Sr. motioned for Zoey.

Zoey didn't have a paper, she had memorized what she wanted to say. She reached up and took Carl and Anna's hands. "Anna, thank you for loving me and wanting to be my mommy. You have made my daddy so happy that he smiles a lot. I mean *a lot*. I promise I will be a good girl and be the best daughter ever. Daddy, thank you for letting Anna be my new Mommy. I promise I will be the best big sister to the new baby sister you are getting me." Everyone erupts with laughter.

"Okay. Do you two have the rings?" Carl Sr. asked as he tried to contain his laughter at Zoey's vows.

"Oh no, I didn't get you a ring Carl." Anna looked mortified.

"No, we will get rings later. I didn't get your wedding band yet either." Carl squeezed her hands.

"Oh no, we have your rings for you." Shirley stepped closer and pulled a small antique box out of her purse. "This was my daddy's wedding band." She handed Anna a simple gold band. "And this was my momma's wedding band." She handed Carl a small gold band. "They were married for seventy-two years. They would have wanted you two to have these. May they bring you as much happiness and love as they brought my parents."

Carl turned to his mother and hugged her with tears running down his cheeks again. Anna smiled and said, "Shirley, this means more to me than you will ever know. Thank you."

The two exchanged rings just as the sun faded. Carl Sr. pronounced them husband and wife and they kissed. As they kissed the last bit of sunlight faded from the sky.

Out of the silence in the darkness Zoey spoke up, "So when do I get my baby sister?"

J. Kenkade School of Publishing
Bring Your Story.
We'll Help you Write it!

For School inquiries or to hire a writing
coach: www.jkenkadepublishing.com
(501) 482-1000

Also Available from
J. Kenkade Publishing

ISBN 978-1-944486-87-7

Purchase at www.amazon.com or www.barnesandnoble.com

All who hear tales of Madam MaRooska's world-renowned yet ex-clusive specialty resort at Bellingfast Estates clamor to be granted attendance every year. One of the most compelling events in this two-week excursion is an elaborate masquerade ball in which guests can disappear into the personas of any historical figures they wish. However, Constance Stallings knows firsthand just how quickly this game of illusions can turn nefarious. Born into wealth and privilege but determined to make a name for herself as an au-thor, she embarks on a second trip to Bellingfast with her family in the hopes of finishing her novel, The Angel Doll, and perhaps even uncovering the tragic mystery that looms over her last encounter with the seemingly cursed estate.

Also Available from
J. Kenkade Publishing

ISBN: 978-1-955186-20-9
Purchase at www.amazon.com

The goddess of water, Reina rules her country with an iron fist, enforcing her view of peace with great ruthlessness. She was not always so cruel; however, at one point, she ruled her people justly, with her friend Clara by her side. When a nation of humans decided to not heed to the authority of the gods, a war broke out. It was man vs god, a true David vs Goliath situation. In the heat of battle, Reina bore witness to her friend's last moments, sending her into a dark spiral. This twisted version of herself that we see today is what came of her after the war, a reclusive leader that rarely shows herself to her people. What do the threads of fate hold for Reina? Will she reopen her country and spare her people from their agony? Or will her nation stay in a state of limbo forever?

Also Available from
J. Kenkade Publishing

ISBN: 978-1-955186-23-0

Purchase at www.amazon.com

Winters is a captivating and passionate Christian suspense novel about a powerful, spiritual family who is anointed and ordained by God Almighty. You will feel love, pain, heartaches, compassion, grace, mercy, suffering, and God's spirit, all in one story. Find out why Winters is about the coldest season of the year in more ways than one. Come and live in the minds and hearts of Stella, Abe, Mr. Perkins, The Langley family, Hattie, Benjamin, and Minnie. So much more awaits you in this powerful Christian suspense novel. Both fiction and nonfiction, Winters will give you a chill like never before.

Also Available from
J. Kenkade Publishing

J. KENKADE PUBLISHING PRESENTS

TRUSTING
Hands

A SELECTION OF POEMS

JIMMY VEATCH

ISBN: 978-1-955186-18-6

Purchase at www.amazon.com

A collection of poems inspired by one man's story of love, pain, loss, and newfound hope and joy.